OLD SOULS

BOOK ONE

C.G. GARCIA

The characters and events portrayed in this book are fictitious. Any similarity to real persons, living or dead, is coincidental and not intended by the author.

http://www.cggarciaauthor.com

ISBN-10: 0615966691
ISBN-13: 978-0615966694 (Paperback)

This one's dedicated to my mother, Erlinda,
who has achieved her own immortality
within the hearts of her family

PROLOGUE

The child moved slowly down the empty road, unaware of the eyes that watched the small figure approach from within the shadows of an alley. Rahzon smirked. It seemed Chance had decided to be his comrade tonight after all. Only moments earlier, he had stopped beneath the eaves of a bakery for a smoke, irritated that his hunt had yet again been unsuccessful, when he had caught movement in his periphery. Had it not been for the soft footfalls, he might have thought the kid an apparition. It was almost too good to be true after the frustration of the past three days.

Squinting a bit against the darkness, practiced eyes carefully analyzed what little they could see in the moonlight as the child neared. Short hair. A boy, he decided, around six or seven years old. His clothes were well-fitted with no immediate visible holes or tears, his feet booted. Though his head was down as if he were worried of his footing across the cobblestones, the little of his face Rahzon could see was in all initial appearances clean and unmarked.

His smirk widened. He was too clean, too well dressed to be a street kid. The boy's hands swung open at his sides, empty of the rocks or long sticks that were currently popular with the local riffraff, not to mention walking around so openly without even attempting to move unnoticed. Perhaps he had been separated from a caravan somewhere along the road or from his family in the marketplace. Not quite the noble stock he had been aiming for, but definitely better than the street trash he'd had to make do with lately. Yes, this potentially could be the prize that had eluded his group for so long.

Rahzon quickly emptied the still burning leaves from his pipe onto the ground and placed it back into his belt pouch. He then casually strolled out of the alley before the boy could walk past. He did a double-take in feigned surprise and stopped directly in the child's path.

"Out a bit late aren't you?" he called in what he hoped was a friendly tone. Sometimes kids spooked as easily as deer.

However, the boy didn't stop, didn't even slow down. He might as well *have* been an apparition for all he reacted.

Forcing a smile, Rahzon tried again, "Not a good time to be wandering around, kid. You lost?"

His head still down, the child steadily approached and without a glance, calmly stepped around Rahzon as if he were merely a stump in the road.

"No."

The reply was so soft that it had already been swallowed by the night air before Rahzon could fully register it.

Feeling a bit peeved, he turned and firmly caught the boy's left arm before he could walk out of reach. The boy paused but still did not look at him, a slight tensing of his arm his only reaction. Rahzon frowned. What was wrong with the kid? Usually, at this point, they either struggled or screamed.

He tugged the kid's arm irritably. "Hey, don't ignore me!"

For the space of three breaths, the boy maddeningly did just that before slowly turning his head to finally look at him. His eyes were almost completely hidden behind dark, messy bangs the color of the surrounding night.

"Let go," the boy said firmly, a commanding in his voice that was grossly out of place coming from such a young child.

Rahzon tightened his grip. He didn't know why, but something in that voice, in the whole situation was beginning to make him uneasy. It was time to move things along.

"It's too late for that."

He roughly jerked the kid towards him and grabbed him around the waist with both arms, drawing the small back up tightly against his chest. He braced himself for the inevitable kicking and biting as he moved back towards the concealing shadows of the alleyway. However, though the boy stiffened, he otherwise gave no reaction, no cry, as he was borne farther from any hope of rescue.

Rather than feel relieved at his seemingly good fortune, Rahzon's apprehension only doubled. This was unprecedented. Was the kid really so frightened that even his voice had frozen? Where had his earlier bravado gone?

At any rate, he had a prize to present.

Turning the corner, Rahzon stumbled and nearly fell to his knees as his right side suddenly erupted in fire. Crying out more from surprise than pain, he dropped the boy and staggered back, frantically grabbing his side. He brought his hand up to his eyes; it was wet, stained dark. Blood—his blood. His eyes widened. The brat had—impossible!

The kid stood calmly before him, expression still obscured by too-long bangs, a knife dripping a dark liquid gripped in his right hand. He was still there; he hadn't tried to run. What in the three hells was going on?

"Walk away," the boy said, drawing his would-be abductor's attention from the knife back to his face as effectively as an unexpected clap of thunder, "and count yourself lucky that I don't have the time to play with y—"

The kid whipped around mid-word, a second knife suddenly appearing in his empty hand as if birthed by the very night. In the far darkness, Rahzon could barely make out three outlines quietly advancing towards them.

The boy crouched into a guarded position, the knives held threateningly before him. "I see," he said in that maddeningly calm, non-child voice. "Here I thought you were just some random pervert out for easy prey. Turns out you're part of *them*. Maybe I do have time to play with you after all."

The brat's back was turned to him, his attention focused mainly on the other three. The bleeding man ground his teeth in rising fury. So he was a street kid after all. How *dare* the little bastard turn his back to him as if he meant nothing! The others would never let him hear the end of it, marked by a six-year-old ankle-biter, no matter that said ankle-biter was vicious and *armed*.

Still, here was his chance to save face. He didn't care who the newcomers were, but he'd be damned before he let them get to the kid first. Ignoring the burning in his side, Rahzon lunged forward, intent on grinding that infuriating little face into the dirt until he choked. At the same time, the three unknowns charged the boy from the front.

Rahzon felt the slight rush of air coming at him before he saw the knife, years of fighting instincts allowing him to jump back just as the kid's left arm swung in a wide arc towards his midsection. So fast! His feet tangled up, and he fell back, landing painfully on his backside.

For half a beat, everything went dark as a fresh gush of warmth and fire slid down his injured side as the wound was torn wider, but the scream of one of the new arrivals distracted him from this new pain. Clutching his side tightly, Rahzon lifted his eyes in enough time to see both knives slice in a crisscross motion up to the hilts in the belly of one man. The body of another lay writhing, eerily silent but for the scraping of his body against the stones, in a rapidly spreading pool of blood at the boy's feet.

The boy lifted a small foot and kicked the impaled body back into the third man behind him with more force than his tiny frame seemed capable of wielding, freeing both blades. The resulting wet sound brought into mind a butcher slicing into a slab of meat.

As the two bodies went down, the boy turned to him, both knives dripping. A smile that was wrong on many levels stretched across his face.

The tensing of the kid's body was the only warning as he lunged, striking Rahzon in the chest with his knee with enough force to knock the breath from him, knocking him flat. Two knives at his throat silenced him in mid-gasp, the hands rising instinctively in defense falling limp with sudden terror to his sides.

"You little—" he rasped, then choked on the remaining words when the two blades pressed more deeply into his throat. A stream of warmth began to trickle down both sides of his neck, scalding against skin suddenly turned cold. He didn't want to know whether the blood was his.

Eyes of an indeterminate lighter shade of darkness, now only partially obscured by bangs, filled his watery vision even in the gloom. The sounds of his erratic heartbeat and gasping seemed preternaturally loud, almost deafening.

"Take a good look behind me," the boy said softly, his hands clenching his knives so tightly that they shook, biting into Rahzon's neck with every quiver. His eyes narrowed to black slits. "That will be you if we ever meet again."

Before Rahzon could blink, the stinging pressure disappeared from his neck along with the weight on his chest. The boy crouched over him, wiped both blades clean on his jerkin, and almost nonchalantly moved away to sprint off into the night.

For a while, all Rahzon could do was lie there and

stare after the kid until he darted out of sight around the corner, shivering in a warm night that had suddenly turned cold. Slowly, he sat up, grimacing as the fire in his side was reawakened. His eyes fell to his jerkin, intent on assessing the damage, then widened.

Beside the rapidly spreading stain from his side was a thin slash in the leather across his belly running completely from one end of his side to the other. He had thought the brat had missed and he had, but not by very much. He inspected the damage with his fingers. Yes, his undershirt had even been sliced.

He looked over at the fallen men, watching as one struggled out from beneath the still body that had been practically gutted. The man retched as one of his flailing hands became entangled in the other's spilled intestines. A third man lay unmoving in a pool of blood where he had fallen, probably dead.

Unbidden, the words of his father whispered hauntingly across his thoughts.

"You couldn't see him. It's like the wind had taken the shape of a boy, wafting in and out between the men that had him surrounded before they could even so much as blink, leaving death and injury to any man it touched. But that wasn't the eeriest part. Ten men lay dead, but not a drop of blood was spilled, not a mark on 'em. Could only be one of them."

It was a legend of sorts among slavers. A child around four or five had supposedly single-handedly taken out a band of ten slavers during his great-grandfather's time.

Old Soul—a child that was not a child.

He had never really believed the story. Once again his eyes fell to the slice in his clothes. He swallowed hard.

Slowly, Rahzon climbed to his feet, nearly pitching forward as the darkness around him began to swirl. Damn, he had lost more blood than he'd thought.

He staggered over to the only other survivor and said, "Was that what I think it was?"

The man started violently, hands raised instinctively in defense before his eyes narrowed in suspicion. "What's it to you?"

The slaver raised an eyebrow. "I don't believe I've ever seen you around, stranger," Rahzon commented, struggling to keep a level of cockiness to his voice that he just didn't feel at the moment. "You do realize that the Mahze clan owns this territory and that no hunting without permission is allowed? That brat was mine, and your interference has cost me a great deal tonight. However, I did find something the kid said very interesting, as I did the kid. Tell me everything you know about the boy, and I'll let you walk out of this city alive."

The fallen man sneered. "Not very threatening coming from a lone, injured man."

Good point, but Rahzon wasn't about to admit it. If it came down to a fight, he wouldn't be worth much with his injury. The stranger did not appear to be hurt. He had hoped that the mere mention of his clan was enough to intimidate him, but the man hadn't seemed too impressed. Either his lord was a powerful one, or he had traveled a great distance in pursuit of the boy and did not know the machinations of the area. He knew next to nothing about the mythical Old Souls, so what about them could possibly make these men risk their lives in an attempt to capture one?

He mentally swore. The haze permeating his vision was becoming increasingly worse, and if the stickiness of the hand pressing against the stab wound at his side was any indication, he couldn't afford to waste any more time here—nor could he allow that man to leave.

A flicker of movement behind the sitting man caught his eye, and lifting his gaze briefly, Rahzon almost sighed in relief as familiar figures began emerging from the darkness. Some of his comrades had arrived, likely attracted by the screams.

"Perhaps they will be more convincing," he said with a grin, gesturing with a flick of his chin—which he instantly regretted when his neck began to burn.

At least the interloper had enough brains to know when he had lost, though he never said a word. The slump of tensed shoulders said it all as he was quickly surrounded by eight men, two more moving to stand on either side of the slaver.

"What in the three hells happened here?" the man

on his right demanded, staring down at the gutted body at his feet with disgust then looking pointedly at Rahzon's blood-soaked side.

"Later. Now this stranger has something I think we'd all be interested to hear."

Rahzon looked down at the fallen man. "I'll ask again," he said calmly. "Was that boy an Old Soul?"

He could feel the jerk of momentary shock of those surrounding him, but he ignored them. Explanations could wait; for him, time was running out along a steady stream of scalding red.

"A demon, more like," the stranger muttered resentfully.

Rahzon nodded, remembering the image of the boy smiling while another man's life dripped from his hands. He resisted the impulsive urge to finger the wound on his neck. "Why try to capture one?"

It was a long moment before the answer came, but when it did, Rahzon was not disappointed.

1

———

He could feel them watching again, the weight of a hundred eyes pressing into every corner of his body. Always assessing, always demanding answers. Who was he? Why was he here? No matter the place, the city, the air was always heavy with those two questions. Innocent questions, really, but with him, nothing was ever that simple.

Grinding his teeth in frustration, Issai put his spoon down, portion uneaten. This scenario was really getting old. Absently, he mashed long, pitch-colored bangs farther down over his eyes. Was it really too much to ask for one night's peace?

Without raising his head, he peered through the slight tangles at the chaos of the common room. The tavern was crowded tonight. Though he had only been living in this town for a couple of tendays, even Issai could tell this was unusual, considering that this was not a rest day. Not one stool or corner of bench lay unclaimed, the chatter and laughter of the patrons almost deafening. He, like many others, sat on the stone floor against the wall, a bowl of stew balanced in his lap. Below the normal line-of-sight of everyone, one disheveled teenager should have gone unnoticed in all the poor lighting and bustle.

"Should" being the key word, Issai thought darkly, pushing his dishes aside.

At first glance, no one appeared to be watching him, a typical nightly scene of a hundred different scenarios being played out before him. However, none of the faces around him were familiar, none of the regulars present tonight. Word earlier on the streets said the local lord's garrison was due to pass through town on its once-a-moon inspection before heading up to the capital, and many of the seated men wore the uniform of soldiers. Yet this sudden influx of strangers was more like the arrival of a small army than your typical, everyday garrison.

More importantly, within the space of a dozen breaths, every single man in sight had at one point turned to stare briefly at him, which meant one thing.

Time to go.

Issai stood and casually made his way through the throng. Not only was this scenario getting old, but his mild irritation was rapidly turning into fury. He had really liked the energy of this town, smoothly flowing, almost innocent in its mediocrity. It was a place one could really settle into and become lost in its faceless, everyday functions. It had been exactly the place he had been searching for.

Located several days in every direction from any other farm or town, totally self-supporting, one visited Daisha for only two reasons—family or government inspection. Any trade was outgoing and only if a dire need for a commodity due to shortage arose.

Keeping his head low, Issai fought his way through the wandering bodies, feet, and elbows, half-expecting an attack and completely ready for it if it came. It certainly wouldn't be the first time. In a room where no one was looking at you but everybody was watching, you really couldn't be too careful.

The stairway to the rental rooms was almost preternaturally silent compared to the roaring human mass he had just left. He paused at the foot, wondering if it would be better to just turn around and leave town without his pack. After all, it held only a couple changes of clothing, a bit of food, cooking gear, and some odds and ends. It was nothing that couldn't be replaced at the next town. His money pouch and personal effects of value were always strapped to his belt. He never went anywhere without his weapons.

Issai's lip curled slightly. He was so tired of this, of always having to run, of always leaving parts of his life behind, no matter that it was just a couple of frayed shirts. He started up the stairs. Just this once, even if he found more trouble than it was worth, he would leave nothing behind.

Still, being defiant didn't also mean stupid. He moved up the steps as quietly as possible.

Down the hall, Issai stopped short before rounding the final corner to his room's wing, flattening himself against the wall. The distinct sound of metal on metal rang through the air, faint but no less alarming. Carefully, he peered around the corner and immediately pulled back with an inward curse.

Great.

A man stood hunched over his door, fast at work trying to pick his lock. Well, at least that explained the clicking metal.

Every instinct within him screamed for him to get out. His pursuers had never been so obvious and had *never* sent only one to do the job. Either an undeterminable amount of *Shi* lurked in his room, or an extremely unfortunate thief had picked his last room to rob. Trouble, at last, had found him, and he promptly ignored the dry voice inside that told him to "get the hell out, and your pack be damned!"

With a flick of both wrists, two small knives glided into his hands. Shi *or thief, no sense in asking which one from a man a breath away from death*, Issai thought wryly as he charged, jabbing both blades to the hilt into the man's lungs and heart before he could even look up.

Jerking his knives up then free, Issai kicked him away. He then turned and kicked in his own door, allowing the momentum to tumble him headfirst into his room. He rolled over swiftly across the rug back onto his feet. His knives sprayed drops of blood as he whirled his outstretched arms into a complete circle, slashing at any possible attackers.

Three dark forms fell screaming to the ground as he pulled out of his swing and jumped back to avoid the thick staff aiming for his head. He staggered a bit as something grazed his back, then slashed out at the figure he saw coming in for another hit. He barely registered a splash of warmth on his hand before he was on to the next target.

Just how many are there? he thought irritably as two more men joined his current opponent, coming at him with staffs from both sides.

He dropped to his knees just as all three men took a swing at him so synchronized that it looked planned in advance and slashed deeply into the upper thighs of all three *Shi* with one outward swing of both arms. Issai flung himself to the side as they toppled into a shrieking mass of limbs and wood.

There was no time to finish them off. Issai had to find his pack then obey his mind's earlier advice to get the hell out. Luckily, those three had been the last of his room's surprises, and they wouldn't be getting up any time soon. He had left his pack at the foot of his bed. Hopefully, in all the confusion, it had not been kicked around—there!

Just as he bent to retrieve the troublesome pack, he heard footsteps pounding down the hall. The reinforcements had arrived.

Not looking forward to another exhaustive fight, Issai shouldered his pack, flipped his knives around to hilt first, and broke for the sole window in the room just as the first two *Shi* appeared in the splintered doorway.

"Don't let him—!"

"Should've left it open," Issai muttered before he crossed his arms over his face and crashed through the glass.

In the midst of shattered glass, he flipped once through the air and landed rather awkwardly and painfully on several bodies below, a wayward elbow striking under his jaw while a knee dug into his back.

The unexpected obstacle disoriented him long enough for a hand to grab his wrist. His free hand automatically flipped around the knife he still held like a vise and sliced his captor's arm from elbow to wrist. The resulting cry barely registered as he continued to slash out randomly, but air was all the blade found.

Using the back of a fallen man for leverage, Issai pushed himself to his feet. He spared a moment to glance around and swore loudly. Perhaps twenty men had surrounded him, standing just beyond his arm's reach. It seemed an unusual amount of planning went into this latest assault; this was more *Shi* than he had ever had sent out for him. However, large numbers or not, they would soon find out how dangerous it was to corner an animal like him.

"Don't be stingy, little boy," someone sneered behind him. "Share some of your good fortune."

The smile that formed on Issai's face made the two *Shi* nearest him take a step back.

"If you insist," was all he said before he pressed his weight back on his left foot and launched himself into the men before him, knives slashing without mercy.

Most of the men in his path didn't even have the time to scream as Issai broke through them, elbowing and slashing at anyone who foolishly stood in his way. Then there were no more bodies and only the night air stood before him as he ran.

Merchant shops and inns blurred together as he concentrated on putting as much distance between the *Shi* and himself as his stamina would allow. No one yet could match him in speed, a quirk of his so-called "good fortune," but that quirk unfortunately did not last indefinitely.

A good-sized forest surrounded Daisha and continued on for several spans. If he made it inside, then he could easily lose these latest bloodhounds.

Soon, the merchant shops began to give way to

homes and eventually the farms that circled the outskirts of the town. Another span and he would reach the forest. Had it been daytime he would have already been able to see the dark outline of trees across the horizon.

How did they find me? Was I betrayed by a townsperson, or did they stumble upon me accidentally?

Unfortunately, he would probably never know. He had no intentions of ever being near enough to them again to ask, and it would be decades before he could even set foot in Daisha again.

As he neared the forest, Issai realized that he was closely pursued. He had been so focused on the rapidly nearing shadow of trees that he didn't notice it right away. Only when the pounding of hooves on the earth had become almost deafening did he realize that they were nearly upon him. Damn animals. Although no human could match his speed and stamina, he was no match for a horse at full gallop. Would he make it?

Issai slowed just long enough to glance over his shoulder, and what he saw made his blood run cold. It was a small army. That was the only way the mass of horse riders bearing down on him could be described. One glance had not been enough to assess exact numbers, but if Issai had to guess, he was being pursued by no less than a hundred *Shi*. All previous *Shi* had only been comprised of groups of five, ten, or at the most twenty men. Everyone tended to want the prize all to his or herself. Just who was the power capable of assembling such a well-equipped army? The local lord?

Needless to say, there were better ways of gathering information than getting caught, and Issai increased his speed with renewed determination. If he could just reach the forest, then the speed of the horses would become a moot point.

Moments later, the first few trees began to fly by just as something rammed him hard in the back. Issai tumbled forward, landing painfully on his right shoulder. The world twisted around him as he continued his uncontrolled roll, dark shapes appearing in and out of his blurry vision. He managed to stop himself just as two horses were almost atop him, jerking to the side right as a pair of hooves came crashing down over his head.

Issai swore harshly as he rolled into the path of several more horses. Adrenaline surged through his body as he dodged their hooves and struggled to his feet amidst that chaotic sea of horse flesh, narrowly missing being trampled again.

A second blow to his back nearly sent him pitching to the ground again had it not quite met its intended mark. He whirled around and slashed with both knives, meeting nothing but air. That brief respite allowed him to quickly glance around as he pulled out of the turn. Several of the riders that had ridden past him had already dismounted and were approaching with long-staffs while a second surge of riders were breaths away from running him into the ground from behind.

Only one option left.

He surged forward into the frontal assault, barreling through them with knives slashing much as he had done in his flight from the inn. As long as they were on the ground, his speed and agility made little work of those that stood in his way. Knives met flesh while forearms crashed through what remained. He gave no one the time to even bring down their staff, barreling into them until he was free of the suffocating mass.

Although his heart was beating so fast that it almost choked him, Issai forced himself to pick up his speed. He had finally reached the outskirts of the forest. Already he had left his pursuers far behind. He had reached an area where their horses were completely useless.

Still, he didn't slow down, focusing all his concentration on the area before him, mindful of any roots, debris, or low branches that could hinder him. As long as he kept his grueling pace for as long as his stamina held up, he could gain at least a day on them. It was also becoming increasingly harder to see the deeper he went into the forest, branches obscuring what little moonlight the night afforded.

A few moments later, Issai skidded to a halt and jumped back with a shout as a dark figure abruptly landed before him. His chest heaving, he crouched into a defensive position. In the blanketed darkness of canopied tree limbs, this newest challenger was nearly invisible, dressed in black from head to toe, face and head almost completely obscured by a black hood. It was as if a shadow had suddenly come to life to challenge him. Issai hesitated long enough to assess that the figure held no weapon before he attacked. Only the soon-to-be-dead bothered to ask questions first.

He was almost surprised when he crashed into soft flesh instead of passing through the dark apparition. As they tumbled to the ground, Issai thrust a knife forward, intent on slashing the exposed throat. Instead, his blade sliced across the arm thrown up for protection. A sound like a blade being drawn across a whetstone rang in the night air, startling him enough that he did not see the fist coming at his face until it slammed into the side of his head, knocking him to the side.

His arms were immediately immobilized, and a heavy weight settled onto his stomach. Issai shook his head firmly in an attempt to recover his wits then bucked his body to try to dislodge his captor. Shit! He had been careless. This was obviously no amateur he was dealing with. He had grown accustomed to the endless parade of brainless weaklings that he no longer looked for the unexpected.

"Would you stop this!" his captor growled.

Once again Issai was startled. The voice was a baritone still somewhere between a boy's and man's—much like his own. His attacker was only a boy.

He shook his head again. That wasn't important.

"Like hell!" Issai shot back, pulling his knees up and under the body kneeling on his stomach. Focusing all his strength up and in the direction of his head, he managed to throw the boy off him. Then he was immediately on the fallen body, both knives aiming for his throat this time.

Once again, the boy's arms came up, blocking his attack effectively.

"Damn it! Stop!" he grounded out with effort. "I'm not—with—those bastards!"

"And that just solves everything, doesn't it?" Issai sneered, pressing the knives more deeply into the arms protecting his intended target.

Yet, they still did not draw blood. Issai flicked his gaze briefly to the other's arms and cursed under his breath. He had ripped one of the boy's sleeves enough to show not skin but metal the color of a newly forged sword. His eyes followed the tear to the wrist where the metal ended.

I see...

"Would you listen to me! I've been looking for you..." the boy wheezed.

"You and everybody else. Real unfortunate for you that you found me."

Issai thrust a knife forward and tried to slice at the boy's face.

"Shit!" the boy gasped, jerking his face to the side and barely managing to avoid the blade.

He grabbed Issai's arm, just as Issai tried to attack again.

"Stubborn bastard," he ground out, and then he abruptly released Issai's wrist, causing the violet-eyed boy to fall forward unexpectedly, leaving him wide open to the hard punch to his jaw, the momentum shoving Issai off his captive.

Issai once again found himself flat on his back, both wrists pinned on either side of his head, though he still gripped both knives tightly. Even in the darkness, a pair of pale eyes flashed brightly with anger, preternatural in their intensity.

"The Violet-eyed Old Soul," his captor said sardonically. "Will you listen to me now?"

Inwardly, Issai winced. It was the name the *Shi* had branded him with long ago, the damning feature that was the source of all his grief.

"Screw you!" With all his strength, Issai managed to flip them both over, freeing his arms to finally drive both knives up against the boy's neck.

Issai expected him to fight, at the very least to beg, but all the boy did was smile and say wearily, "You know, I really hate infancy."

The declaration was so odd that it gave Issai pause,

and in that brief moment, his eyes met his captive's. He inhaled sharply. The look that stared back at him was as ancient as the dust of the earth, of a time before rivers had formed, mountains had grown, and the surrounding forest had not even taken root.

Suddenly, Issai couldn't breathe as a cold wave washed over his body and froze the air in his lungs. He was falling and couldn't ever remember jumping. His veins were on fire, though he could no longer feel his body, and something torn in his being abruptly began to close.

He *understood*, so acutely that the shock of it was akin to being stabbed through the heart by an enemy with no weapon. In that eternal moment, Issai finally learned the true meaning of terror. Knives fell from fingers that no longer obeyed him.

Eyes now wide and a bit wild, the boy below him opened his mouth as if to speak, but before he could utter a sound, Issai drove his fist hard into his face. As the body went limp, he scrambled back and away, wide-eyed himself and gasping for breath.

Thoughts of slitting the boy's throat no longer existed. The only thing he could do, the only thing that made sense, was to gather his knives and pack and run.

2

I *should have killed him! I should have killed him! I should have...*

Like a mantra, it ran through his head as Issai raced through the forest like a rabbit with three packs of wolves snapping at its feet. Branches slapped his face, scratched at his hands as he flung them aside, but he didn't feel them. He ran with no clear direction or destination in mind except *away*, intent on putting as much distance between him and the boy he had left behind.

Issai ran until he literally collapsed facedown into the brush, too exhausted to even turn over. After all the time, the endless years searching for the unknown purpose behind the urge that drove him, the urge for *something* that encompassed his every moment, he had inadvertently stumbled upon the next piece to the mystery in the very life he had decided not to look anymore.

No matter. He would run, for years if he had to, but he would be a pawn no longer. He'd had enough.

The irony of the whole thing was enough to make him laugh, were he still capable of it. In all likelihood, the gods sure were getting a good one at his expense as usual.

He felt as if something inside was ripping open, deep within in a place he had never known existed. The more he ran, the more it had torn, and the more he was beginning to realize that it was a wound that had always been hurting.

Worse, that inexplicable urge to *do* something had tripled in intensity to the point it was almost unbearable. He had always been able to resist its pull and still function, but that would no longer be an option. Issai wanted—no *needed* to go back to the boy and only his anger prevented him from following this newest, most insistent tug from the ever-present puppet strings.

Slowly, Issai raised his head and scanned his surroundings. He had no idea where he was; nothing looked even remotely familiar. In his desperate flight, he didn't even remember which direction he had taken. He could have just as easily run right back into the waiting staffs of the *Shi* as straight off a ravine.

Issai stiffly pulled himself off the ground and rested his back against a nearby tree trunk. For a while, all he did was close his eyes and rest until his irregular breathing evened out into something a little less noisy. An almost absolute darkness still surrounded him, but in this particular forest, that was no reliable judge of time. Very little light filtered through the densely packed branches even during the day.

He fumbled blindly through the various items attached to his belt until his fingers found the round object they sought, the small compass that was one of his most guarded possessions. Issai brought it closer to his eyes, then pushed his bangs back from his face in order to see more clearly. At least here in the darkness, there was no need to hide his eyes.

The needle currently pointed north. Finally, a little luck had found him. Panicked flight or not, he had unconsciously run in the direction he had intended to go. Although he was uncertain how long or how far he had run, he was fairly confident that he could reach the throneseat within three days. He had enough travel rations to sustain him, and though he hated the press of the crowds of a big city, it was the best place to get lost. He could resupply himself and lay low in the country-side for a while. Then he could have the leisure to decide where to go from there.

Something like pain crossed his face as he closed his eyes. Only a few hours ago he had been contemplating which job to take in his new town, and now the cold forest ground with its prickly grasses and dried leaves had become his bed. How quickly everything shattered around him.

Issai wondered why, after all this time, he was still bothered that things always seemed to turn out so wrong for him. That last spark of hope that he didn't like to acknowledge was disappointed time and time again but still stubbornly refused to fade into the darkness. Was wanting a normal, quiet life really too much to ask for?

Usually, sleep was not something that came easily to him, his mind a constant buzz of worries and one big question that embraced it all, but his exhaustion seemed to slightly dampen the urgent Calling within his being. Issai found himself drifting —only to jerk awake seemingly beats later, heart racing and breathing in half-strangled gasps as if he had been running for hours. His eyes darted around wildly, instinctually looking for danger on their own accord.

He's near.

The thought startled him into full alertness. It was as if someone had whispered it into his mind, a warning he was not about to question or disregard. Barely pausing to shoulder his pack, Issai launched himself into the darkness.

Almost immediately, his body was engulfed in a despair so powerful that for a moment it drove him to his knees, that inexplicable wound in his being beginning to bleed to the point that it had become a physical pain he could feel just beneath his skin.

"I—am not—a—pawn!" he growled through gritted teeth, the rage of countless years the only thing that allowed him to stumble to his feet and move on.

Every step felt more painful than the last. What was this new madness? It had never been this excruciating before. No matter the grief, the torture he had endured throughout his existence, it paled in comparison to this. It was as though his soul was slowly being stretched until it was tearing into shreds. He had not known that such pain was even possible, but despite it or maybe because of it Issai plowed on. The gods were responsible for this, and he'd rather be damned a thousand times over before he willingly allowed himself to lose to them.

He made it a dozen more steps before something slammed into him from behind with enough force to send him rolling quite a distance until his chest collided with a tree. Gasping for a breath that was no longer there, he didn't even struggle when hands seized him roughly and pulled him against something warm and supple, arms embracing him like a vise.

It *hurt*. It was like feeling the weight of a thousand centuries—a thousand different lives ending in a thousand excruciating ways, every moment of despair and pain he had ever felt only to have it all lifted away as if he had finally found the peace he had desperately sought throughout every incarnation.

He was no longer bleeding.

When his senses cleared, Issai found, to his disgust, that he was hugging the black-clad boy from earlier just as tightly, his face feeling suspiciously wet.

With an oath, Issai violently shoved the boy away and scrambled back to a safer distance.

"Get away from me!" he snarled, his chest heaving. He hastily wiped at his eyes, feeling angrier and angrier, but they were dry. The tears were not his own.

Why did this boy have to follow him? Why hadn't he killed him when he had the chance? *How* could he have allowed himself to lose control so easily?

I won't let this happen! I won't let them shepherd me along. My life is my own!

Issai was running before he had made any conscious decision to move. Screw the pain! He still had his speed. He would leave the bastard behind, lose him for good this time. He would run for days if that's what it took. If he never saw him again, he would be...he would be...

Without warning, the darkness before him blurred and came alive, so close that he was unable to dodge. Issai crashed right into it, and they both went down. It was *him*. How had he...?

Issai fought for his life, punching and kicking like a man possessed for what seemed like an eternity, until he could fight no more, until he lay flat on his back, the other straddling his legs into immobility. He stared up at the other boy in defeat.

His attacker had lost the black hood sometime during the fight and now a mass of hair lighter than the darkness that surrounded them, an undeterminable shade of brown, stuck out in wild, long strands around his face and across his bangs. A small portion still remained bound with twine along the nape of his neck, barely long enough to be bound.

"You think," the boy hissed through gritted teeth, "that after hundreds of lifetimes that I would let you escape me so easily?"

Anything else he might have said was silenced with the sting of the knife now pressing against his throat.

"I could end this, you know," Issai said, his voice breathy, but calm. "Just one beat of your heart and it would be over—for you at least."

Despite the blade, the other boy shrugged and smiled. "Try it," he challenged.

Without hesitation, Issai's hand moved to press the knife's edge deeper when he felt a sharp pain explode from his chest as if the blade was stabbing into himself instead, followed by a wave of the blackest despair he had ever felt that rocked him to the very tips of his toes. The knife fell from his suddenly trembling hand as his face tightened unfamiliarly with the urge to cry, even stronger than before.

He closed his eyes tightly against that inadvertent onslaught, feeling the first echoes of weakness in his resolve.

Issai felt the other's weight lift off him, but it was quite some time before he was able to look at the boy again.

"I've had enough," Issai said dully. "I don't want any part of this. I promised myself that I would end this madness with this lifetime."

"Then don't try to leave me again," the boy said heatedly. "Idiot! Don't you get it? It will never end, no matter how many lifetimes we spend running. It will *never* end until we end it *together*. Not just you and me, but the other two as well. You know what we have to do."

Issai stiffened. *Other two?*

"It figures," he spat bitterly.

"What?"

"I suppose you've known from the moment of your first life why we've been condemned to this endless hell while I have lived every moment in ignorance. How nice of the gods to extend you that courtesy."

Then to his further rage, the boy began to laugh.

Issai grabbed the front of the bastard's shirt and wrenched him closer. "What the hell is so damned funny?" he ground out.

With visible effort, the boy swallowed his remaining laughter, but he couldn't quite get rid of the huge grin that threatened to split his face in two. Despite having known him only a few moments, Issai knew with sudden certainty that it was an expression natural to him. Something about it seemed very familiar, very comfortable. However, this new insight only served to blacken his mood even further.

Making a big show of prying Issai's hands from his shirt, the boy said, "For someone who has lived countless lifetimes, you of all people should know that the gods give us nothing."

He sighed, sitting back on his heels. Suddenly, the smile was gone, replaced by unnervingly somber eyes.

"We are pawns, hard as we try to deny it, that's all we really are to them. We can curse and rage and plead all we want, but why should they care how we feel as long as the 'game' is still being played? In the end, we have no say in anything at all except in the freedom to play the game as we choose."

"Or not to play at all," Issai said as he picked himself off the ground, though he made no move to leave. He glared down at the still-kneeling boy. "Maybe refusing this 'game' is the very thing that will set us free. Have you ever just tried to do nothing, to stop searching?"

"Twice," came the prompt reply, "and both times I didn't make twenty, waking consciously from death in enough time to experience the joys of being born again. I don't know about you, but I really *hate* infancy. All that squalling and such—I got on my own nerves!"

Issai turned from him in disgust. "Talking to you is useless." He trudged over to where he had dropped his pack when the boy had tackled him. He had barely managed to pick up one of the straps before the dark figure was before him again. The gleam in his eyes promised danger.

"What now?" Issai barked, more than irritated with the entire situation.

"We're not through yet."

"I beg to differ."

"Stop being such an ass. It won't kill you to listen to me. It's not like we don't have all the time in eternity anyway. We need to come to some kind of compromise if we're gonna spend any significant time together. I can't just let you leave, but I won't follow you blindly either, no matter how cute you are."

Issai abruptly stepped away from the once again grinning boy, his eyes hardening to black slits in renewed fury. *I'm not some damn brat to be cooed over...!*

His pack fell unnoticed as both knives flicked into his hands. The boy's eyes had widened for an instant before he broke down, laughing so hard that he had trouble breathing.

"Joking, joking," he wheezed out, then jumped back with another laugh as Issai took a swipe at him with one of his knives.

Before Issai could even pull back from the attack, the boy shot forward and grabbed both of his wrists, squeezing with enough force to bruise but not enough to cause him to drop the knives.

"Let go!" Issai growled through clenched teeth, jerking both arms back, but he might as well have been pulling against iron manacles for all the good it did. He settled for glaring murderously at the obvious amusement in the other's eyes.

"Jeez, you need to lighten up!" the boy huffed but surprisingly obliged, taking a cautious step back as if trying not to startle a feral animal.

Not expecting that at all, Issai crossed his arms defensively instead of attacking again, still glaring for all he was worth though now he felt more unsettled than angry. "Suddenly, an excruciating death doesn't seem so bad a prospect," he grumbled.

"Uh-uh. You can't get rid of me so easily. If you die, then I die. We'd probably be born as twins or neighbors or something in the next life."

"Unlikely."

The boy sighed, sounding for all the world like a parent at his wits' end. "You're not an idiot; I can sense that, so stop acting like one. Stop trying to deny your fate for just one moment and listen to the voice within yourself. *Don't* even pretend like you don't know what I'm talking about. It'll tell you all you need to know."

Only when the boy pointed it out did Issai realize that he *had* been feeling something different, a presence, one that he had mistaken earlier for merely an increase in the ever-present Urge that drove him. One he had been trying his hardest to ignore. He frowned, considering.

What he felt...

Then the black-clad boy shifted his weight and with a jolt as he physically felt the other boy's movement within himself, he realized the new presence was the other boy. At that moment, all his remaining anger drained from him, and Issai finally stopped fighting what he now understood was inevitable.

Within that presence was an odd mixture of amusement, playfulness, exasperation, weariness, loneliness, pain, fear—and if he dug deep enough, the faintest tinges of hope. And in that garble of emotions, a name encompassed it all.

"*Hahri*," Issai said quietly, lifting his eyes questionably.

The lighter-haired boy started violently as if Issai had stabbed him. His eyes lost all traces of their previous fire. The eyes that now stared back into his own were those same eyes he had seen before—ancient, inhuman.

"You weren't supposed to find that," he said, the once lively voice now a dull monotone. "They had no right to give that to you."

Issai nodded. He knew exactly what he had found, something so personal that he should have never had access to it. Somehow, he had ventured into the boy's very soul and had inadvertently stolen a huge part of him. He sighed mentally as he returned his knives to their sheaths; only one way to fix this.

"No matter the years, the endless lifetimes, we can

never truly forget can we?" he said quietly, allowing centuries of bitterness to color his words. "'Issai' is the boy I cannot forget."

Once again, he bent to retrieve his pack. "Come on," he said roughly, turning his back to the other. "If I'm not mistaken, there are a few caves a bit farther north. I'll listen, but I won't give any promises."

"I OBVIOUSLY CAN'T CALL you 'Issai' when we're around others," Hahri spoke up suddenly as he stirred the contents cooking over the fire.

It was the first time either one had spoken since they had set off together. Upon finding the aforementioned cave system, they had immediately set about making supper in unspoken agreement. Each had taken up a task as if they communed through their thoughts though neither one had any such ability. It was as though they had known each other all their many lives, were well acquainted with each other's habits and skills. Issai had just *known* that Hahri was the better cook, so had left that up to the smaller boy while he set about gathering all the firewood needed and preparing the fire.

Yet, those familiar feelings once again made Issai all the more determined to resume his rebellion against his fate. These were not feelings he recognized; they were not his own. He felt manipulated, even violated, a puppet very much aware of the strings that made him dance, aware that he lacked the free will to cut them.

He wanted to lash out at the only other person around, make him feel his fury, make him hurt like he was hurting, but he knew he wouldn't. He *couldn't*. Hurting Hahri would be like hurting himself—and he was hurting plenty enough. With this strange new bond between them, it seemed even the gods had taken his last remaining freedom away—his individuality.

That's why Issai hadn't really minded giving the boy his true name. As Hahri had felt it a desecration, he saw it as a form of rebellion against the gods, a reclaiming of a little of that individuality he had lost the moment his eyes had met those ancient eyes. Giving another name would only strengthen that rebellion.

However, he would rather die than let Hahri know this.

"Who says that after today you'll even be around to use it?" Issai growled, his eyes never flickering away from the knife he was currently sharpening.

That smile—he knew it was there even without having to turn around to see it. He could feel it burning across the back of his head. It hurt, and he couldn't really understand why. More alien feelings. The hand moving the whetstone across the blade unconsciously began to move more roughly.

"Well, seeing as how I would have to die for that to

happen," came his cheerful reply, "you might as well just tell me."

A light breeze suddenly flowed past him, and Issai looked up into a pair of cerulean-blue eyes that were a mere finger-length away. He violently jerked back. "Damn it! Would you stop doing that!"

Hahri folded his arms across his chest smugly. "Make me," he taunted. "That knife looks sharp enough."

Rage instantly exploded within him. The little bastard was mocking him *again*! In the next breath, Issai was on his feet, grabbing a fist-full of Hahri's shirt to force him closer while the other hand pressed the newly-sharpened knife into the smaller boy's gut. However, as the cool metal pierced the infuriating boy's skin, that same, inexplicable wave of despair from before washed through him, his own gut feeling as if it had been cut.

He pushed Hahri away and stumbled back. *These are not my feelings!*

With a cry, Issai viciously slashed his own arm in an attempt to rid himself of that alien despair. Perhaps pain of a different kind would distract him enough to take control of himself again. The knife fell from nerveless fingers as he slumped to his knees gasping.

He was totally unprepared for the pained cry of the other boy.

His unwanted companion was clutching his left arm

tightly, blood oozing between the fingers that gripped it and staining shockingly bright through the white of his sleeve. For one bewildered moment, Issai thought he had inadvertently slashed both arms—but no, he had definitely thrust Hahri away, and besides the blood, the other's shirt sleeve had looked completely undamaged.

Issai's vision blurred as he turned to his arm. The wound was worse than he had intended; he had opened his own arm in a curving slice from wrist to elbow, a hint of bone peeking through the dark liquid streaming near the center of the slash. A rapidly deepening puddle of blood lay at his feet, stained his clothes. He was already getting slightly dizzy from the blood loss.

"*You idiot!*" Hahri snarled, reminding Issai of his presence. "Did you eat half your brains for breakfast this morning! Why the hell did you do that for?"

Although Hahri's hand covered a good portion of his own wound, enough of the blood pattern was still visible in the linen for Issai to see that it was completely identical in length to his own, down to the slight curve near the elbow caused by the blade leaving the arm. What in everything unholy was going on here?

"Why are you cut?" Issai demanded harshly, causing his head to swim even worse.

"I *told* you! You die, I die! I wasn't just making that up! Now, do something about yourself before you doom us both to another fourteen years of childhood!"

Still bewildered, Issai turned his attention back to

his own wound. It had been perhaps a dozen lifetimes since he had last done it. Could he do it now? The last time had ultimately cost him his life.

Painfully.

He glanced over at the other boy, at the anger and panic staring nakedly back at him and decided that he could. Issai sat back onto his haunches and closed his eyes. He concentrated on feeling every corner of the wound as well as the depth of damage, gritting his teeth as this seemed to increase the intensity of the pain.

Once he was satisfied that he had traced it all within his mind, his mind formed and released a silent command: *heal*. He stiffened as a rush similar to adrenalin immediately flowed through his body, down from the crown of his head and up from the tips of his toes, sapping all the warmth in its wake until it centered in his arm. The temperature in his abused limb rose to an uncomfortable, but not really painful, level.

Then his arm began to itch and burn horribly, but he resisted the urge to scratch. Another shaky breath and the pain and warmth in his arm disappeared completely; only then could he feel the icy chill that had permeated his entire body.

Shivering in both cold and exhaustion, Issai sagged a bit before he slowly opened his eyes and looked at his arm. If not for the blood that still stained his skin as well as his clothes and the ground, no one would have believed there had been a wound at all. Not even a scar was left behind to show the violence he had done to himself.

His lips curved slightly up as his vision dimmed and he felt himself pitch forward. A pair of hands clumsily grabbed his shoulders before he could completely fall on his face, hitting his forehead against the other's shoulder instead.

"'Senn' is my name in this life," he muttered into the smaller boy's shirt. For some inexplicable reason, it seemed important to tell him this now.

"All of that just for a name," Hahri huffed in exasperation. "Masochistic bastard."

As Issai slipped into darkness, for the first time in a long time, he felt the urge to laugh in genuine amusement.

3

Issai awoke all at once to the feeling of something warm and wet brushing against his mouth. He bolted up, his fists instantly swinging up against any possible threats before he could even open his eyes. A liquid-like *slosh* sounded somewhere above him, and he got a glimpse of a very blurry figure hastily backing out of reach before his body collapsed back onto the ground, too weak to support his weight any longer.

Disoriented, Issai automatically tried to flick his knives into his hands, only to find them gone. A wave of panic washed over him. What the hell? He tried to rise again, but it was all he could do to raise his head.

"What the hell are you doing?"

He blinked. That voice—*him*—Hahri.

Sure enough, the brown-haired boy blurred into vision, glaring down at him, the front of his beige undershirt darkened with a wet stain. A water skin in his hand was tilted as if he intended to empty its contents onto Issai's head.

"Try to help a guy and look what happens," he bristled. "You really need to learn better people skills."

Issai closed his eyes briefly. That's right; he had passed out right after healing his sliced arm.

"You're still here." The tone was almost accusatory.

Hahri rolled his eyes and squatted down. With the flickering fire behind them the only light source, his companion's movement looked almost surreal.

"You noticed. Now be a good boy and drink this. You've been out for almost two days."

Issai pushed the water skin away from his lips. "What!" Come to think of it, Hahri had been wearing a white shirt earlier...

"And that surprises you? Don't tell me that's the first time you've ever done something like that!" The incredulity on his face was almost comical.

"No," Issai said irritably, "it's just the first time I've ever woken up in the same body afterward."

"I see. Care to explain yourself?"

"Where are my knives?" Issai demanded.

Hahri blinked. "What? These?" he asked innocently, dangling them both precariously from the points above his companion. "You fed the ground enough of my blood. I'll just keep these awhile until we've talked a bit. Behave yourself, and I'll give them back to you."

Slowly, Issai brought a hand to his forehead. "What do you want from me?"

Hahri seated himself, cross-legged, at his feet. "Why ask? The same thing you want from me, no matter how much you may deny it."

"You know nothing."

Once again Issai tried to rise, but his body felt unusually heavy. He hadn't been this vulnerable for a long time. Two days. He'd have to be more careful in the future.

He settled for glaring at the boy. "Three hundred seventy-seven lives. That's how long I've walked this earth, and not a day passed without that damned urge to do *something* hounding my every breath. That urge, it's not mine; it never has been."

His eyes narrowed. "Then you appear, and things go from bad to worse. When I look at you, try to hurt you, I feel like the world is ending, my soul is bleeding. I'm hurting *myself*. I feel as if someone has taken over my body and imprisoned my soul. These feelings aren't mine. I didn't *want* to find you. Why would I willingly subject myself to more of that crap?"

The smile that touched Hahri's lips didn't quite reach his eyes. "You'll have to if you want it to end. In a few thousand years time this is the first time we've moved any closer to the truth. Can you honestly pass up this chance? I can no more let you walk away from me than you can walk away. Somebody else, whether a god or just plain fate, may be making us feel this connection between us, but—I can't help but be happy that I'm no longer alone in this." Hahri sighed in mock exasperation. "Even if my companion is an uptight, closed-mouth bastard with a disturbing zeal for knives."

"And *I* thought the gods couldn't be any crueler," Issai spat back.

"Smartass. Oh well, I guess that's better than the silent treatment."

Once again Issai struggled to rise. "Give me my knives back."

"Nope. All in good time, like I said."

Hahri grinned then moved to his knees, grabbing Issai by the shoulders to help him sit up. Issai grudgingly allowed this, mostly because he wanted to be on a more equal footing with Hahri and it saved him the degradation of asking for help.

Hahri sat back on his haunches and reached for the discarded water skin. "First thing's first. You're going to drink this water even if I have to pinch your nose to get it down, have something to eat, and then we can decide what to do from here."

Issai snatched the water skin from him, and while he drank, he carefully watched the other boy spoon whatever kind of stew he had prepared into an unfamiliar bowl. One of his deaths had included poisoning, and he preferred not to repeat the experience. Even though he knew that Hahri and he were the same, he still could not bring himself to completely trust him. Everything within him said to trust him, so in typical Issai response, he rebelled against it. How could he trust anyone when he couldn't even trust his own current feelings?

"By the way, my name's Kye in this life."

The statement was so unexpected that for a moment Issai felt unbalanced—which served to make his earlier anger resurface. He didn't know who he was angrier at, Hahri for complicating his life even more, or himself for his current weakened state.

"You must really not want your knives back," Hahri said cheerfully as he handed the bowl to him. "You've practically got 'kill Hahri' written across your eyes, and although I'll be the first to admit that I can sometimes say things that totally piss people off, I really can't recall saying anything *that* insulting to you. You couldn't possibly still be steamed over me punching you in the face that time? Nothing personal, but you were quite keen on drawing a new smile across my throat. Survival instincts."

"Do you always talk this much?" Issai grumbled, though inexplicably his anger was beginning to cool as fast as it had surfaced.

He mechanically swallowed a spoonful of stew, realizing with no small amount of irritation that his earlier assessment of the boy's skills had been right. Despite the stew's simplicity, the balance of flavors was pleasing.

"I don't like silences. The mind tends to want to fill

them, and more often than not, it's the unpleasant things that find their way to the surface. The weight of centuries isn't high on my list of favorite things to shoulder."

Hahri sat directly across from him, their knees almost touching, and picked up his own bowl. "You know," he said between mouthfuls, "you're the first Old Soul I've heard mention of besides the stories of myself. I figured that you were what my soul was probably pushing me to find, so for the past thousand years I've been searching for you specifically, and let me tell you that you're one hard bastard to track down. By the time I found a town or village that people remembered you, you had been gone for years, sometimes decades. It helped that you seemed to be born violet-eyed every time. Without that little bit of help, I doubt I would've ever found you except by chance, and as you well know, chance is nobody's friend."

"Isn't everyone so appreciative," Issai practically snarled, some little rational part of him resisting the urge to throw his bowl of stew into the other boy's face. "You, *Shi*, every damn person in the world! I'm so glad my curse has given everyone an easier time of it."

"*Sorry.*" Hahri had the decency to look ashamed. "I'm running my mouth off again, aren't I? I should've realized—sorry."

For a while, they continued to eat in silence so thick that Issai was beginning to choke on it. Still, he did nothing to break it, not really wanting to discuss things any further. Many things in his mind needed to be sorted out first.

However, he really couldn't fault Hahri for breaking it a few moments later. Issai was beginning to realize that his was just a personality that couldn't be quieted, and the boy wasn't being noisy just to irritate him. Silence was just too unnatural. It also spoke of a tremendous strength if the implied thousands of years of hardship were not enough to break that unfeigned cheer. It somewhat amazed Issai that Hahri could still find something worth smiling about in a world where he, himself, couldn't even remember what the action felt like.

"You said 'shi' earlier," the smaller boy spoke tentatively. "'Shi' as in the Ancient Common word, *shikahn*? A hunter?"

Issai nodded curtly.

"The way you said it made me think you meant something other than the normal variety."

"I'm the Violet-eyed Old Soul aren't I," Issai replied bitterly. "Like a rare animal they branded me, so why shouldn't they hunt me like one as well?"

"Fools still after immortality, huh," Hahri said with disgust, and once again those ancient eyes stared back at him. So many times he had seen that same look staring back at him in a mirror, so he couldn't understand why he felt a chill every time Hahri did the same. "*Shi*—you couldn't have found a more fitting name for the bastards. If they only knew how exhausting eternity can be. Makes me wonder how the whole myth got started in the first place."

"I've often wondered that myself," Issai admitted. "Ever since my first incarnation, I've had violet eyes, but who was it that realized it? I didn't exactly parade around this fact or that I was an Old Soul. Because of this, violet eyes are now considered an omen of ill-fortune. I'm really surprised that I've never been drowned at birth, but a lot of other children have."

Hahri grimaced. "I wonder why the same isn't true for me," he added thoughtfully. "The only thing I can say that stays the same through every life is my speed. I guess, like your eyes, it's my foremost damning trait. Sometimes, it's just impossible for me to move normally. I might as well be shouting out 'Old Soul here! Immortality on a plate—come and get it!' Still, that speed has also saved my life more often than not, so I really can't complain." He grinned suddenly. "I wouldn't have caught you, otherwise. You must've run like your heels were on fire."

"I wanted no part of this game." Issai caught and held the other boy's eyes. "I still don't. What's the point of any of this? So you found me. What now? The world didn't end; no new power was born or sacred duty assigned. Even that damn urge didn't disappear. If anything, it's gotten worse."

His companion nodded. "I feel that too. Remember,

when I told you that there were two more people we needed to find?" Issai vaguely did, but Hahri didn't wait for an answer. "I didn't feel that until after we sealed our bond—or whatever it was that happened when I tackled you to the ground. It's like wanting to go to two different shops at the same time and knowing that you only have time to go to one. This is far from over."

"So you're perfectly content with spending perhaps another thousand years chasing after rumors and shadows while half the world is out to torture you in hopes that some of your immortality will rub off on them?"

"Better than spending eternity in complete ignorance," Hahri countered. "I don't like being jerked around any more than you do, Issai, but I would like to know if there was ever any meaning in the six thousand plus years that my consciousness has been 'Hahri.' I want to know why I was born this way, why *I* had to be different. Maybe you've long since lost the desire for answers—I can understand that. I can—but for me, everything is pointless without them. I can't do this without you. You are part of my answer, and I'm part of yours."

For a long moment, Issai said nothing, forcing himself to finish his stew though he could no longer taste it. He wanted so much to deny everything Hahri had thrown in his face. Denial was so easy, and he was just so exhausted.

He could just travel farther this time and find some distant land he had never seen, a place where no one had ever heard of an Old Soul. A place where he could forget he had ever met an annoying blue-eyed boy that had mended a tear in his soul he had never known existed.

A place where he would slowly bleed until all he could feel was the cold for the rest of his existence.

That's really what it came down to. He could rant and rave until the end of time about the injustice of it all. He could run until exhaustion killed him or scream to the deaf gods that he was not their puppet. He could do all that because he still possessed the free will to choose. It was the one thing the gods had not taken away. Even so, in the end, all that rebellious effort would change nothing. The urge for something intangible would still be there, and he would still be the lost, ancient soul wandering blindly in a sea of slowly fading light until the darkness was all he remembered.

Issai set the now empty bowl aside. "I'm tired," was all he said, still not looking at the other boy. He all but collapsed to the ground and closed his eyes.

"Hey! You can't go to sleep so soon after you just ate!"

But Issai was through talking for the day. Tomorrow would come soon enough, and if only for just a little while longer, he wanted to pretend that his strings didn't exist.

EVERYTHING WAS ALMOST COMPLETELY black when Issai awoke later, a couple faintly glowing embers on the other side of the cave the only light. He started to stretch then instantly froze when he felt something tug on the sleeve of his shirt. His first reaction was to reach for a knife; his second was to mentally curse when he remembered they had been taken. He carefully turned his head and squinted into the darkness—and felt incredibly annoyed.

Like a child reaching for comfort, Hahri lay curled on his side wrapped in his cloak, one hand gripping his companion's sleeve tightly. Issai didn't know whether to roll his eyes or hit him.

"Let go!" he snarled, wrenching his sleeve from the boy's grasp.

To his further annoyance, Hahri merely muttered something unintelligible and rolled over.

I'd be willing to bet my eternal life that the little bastard has never made it past thirty with bad habits like this, Issai thought cynically as he slowly sat up. Only when he was certain that he wouldn't pitch forward did he move to his knees and crawl over to the dark lump that was his pack. He pulled a water skin from within as well as a few strips of dried meat.

He sat back against the cave wall, and while he gnawed on his breakfast, he began to weigh his options.

Hahri was still asleep, and from his earlier display, it was likely not even an earthquake would rouse him. It would be a simple task to find where the brat had hidden his knives and then slip into the night.

"You think that after hundreds of lifetimes that I would let you escape me so easily?"

Issai closed his eyes wearily. He would have an even more miserable time looking over his shoulder for Hahri than he did the *Shi*. Did he really want the added burden?

You can always kill him—

"You know, I really hate infancy."

He shook his head violently then raked a shaky hand through his hair. This was a new low for him. Hahri had watched over him for two days, and this was how he was going to repay him? Slitting his throat while he slept?

Face it. You're completely and utterly screwed.

On that happy note, Issai returned the water skin to his pack and pulled out a change of clothes. His skin crawled with the need for a bath, but with no streams handy, he'd have to settle for clean clothes. That done, he turned his attention to the search for his knives. No matter what course he decided, he definitely needed his knives.

A quick search of the boy's pack yielded nothing, but he hadn't really expected to find them there. His eyes once again turned to the dark lump across the cave.

Great.

Kneeling beside Hahri, he carefully rolled him over to his back and held his breath. Not so much as an eyelid fluttered. Squinting in the near complete darkness, his eyes scanned the length of the ancient boy's body, seeing nothing even remotely knife-shaped beneath his clothes. Hahri was not wearing a belt, and Issai did not think he would be foolish enough to stuff them unsheathed in the band of his pants while he slept. That left only two probable places—his sleeves or his boots.

Carefully, Issai patted his arms down, coming up empty. Still, the sleeping boy did not stir. Getting the leather pant from beneath the top of the boot took a bit of tugging, but when it came free something clattered to the floor. Finally! He immediately picked it up then scowled. The hilt was too wide, the leather too smooth. He was too familiar with his own to know with touch alone that this blade wasn't his.

For a moment, he considered keeping it, then decided that he would not sink to such a childish level. He slowly inserted it back into the boot, not bothering to re-tuck the pant leg, and then proceeded to inspect the other.

Nothing.

Where the hell did he put them? He glanced down at the boy again. *If he put them in his pants, I'm going to kill him!*

He sat back on his haunches. For a long moment, Issai merely glared down at the boy and then with a growl, finally admitted defeat.

"Wake up!" he hissed, shaking his companion rudely.

"Huh—what—"

"Get up and give me my damn knives!"

"*Now*?" Blue eyes blinked rather stupidly. "What for?"

"So I can slit your throat," Issai snapped. "Why do you think?"

"Whatever," Hahri muttered, rolling over.

"Don't go back to sleep, you idiot!" He grabbed the front of the boy's shirt and brought him up until they were face-to-face. "The knives! Now!"

"Gods! Let a guy sleep, will you," Hahri complained irritably, shoving Issai back until the other boy released his grip and he fell back to the ground. "*You* slept for two days straight. The least you could do is let me get a few hours."

Issai sat back onto his haunches and crossed his arms. "Don't blame me for this. If you hadn't stolen them, then I wouldn't have had to wake you."

Grudgingly, Hahri sat up as well. "Why do you need them now anyway? I haven't sensed anyone near here at all. We lost those *Shi* during that last mad dash of yours. Unless—" His eyes narrowed suspiciously. "You're still trying to run, aren't you?"

Ignoring the accusation completely, Issai said, "Like I could trust your instincts. I just ransacked practically your entire body, and you never even twitched."

Hahri sighed. "That's probably because it was you. Anyone else and they would have been dead as soon as they touched me. Unlike you, I don't need knives to kill."

When it became apparent that Hahri was not going to elaborate further, Issai sighed and closed his eyes wearily. "Just give them to me," he demanded quietly.

His companion raked a hand through his hair and smiled at him in such a condescending way that it instantly pissed him off. "You already have them, Lord Fanatic."

"*What*?"

The smile widened. "If you would've bothered to look in your money pouch, you would've found them ages ago. You could've been halfway to the throneseat by now, and I could've still been blissfully asleep, unaware of all the trouble you were about to cause me."

"Why the hell did you put them in there?" Issai snarled, immediately crawling over to his pack where he had left his belt with money pouch still attached. Sure enough, he could feel them through the leather the moment he picked up the pouch.

"I'm not trying to play games. I thought that was the first place you would look," Hahri replied defensively. "Suspicious bastard that you are, I figured you would check your money pouch every chance you got to see if I had robbed you or not."

"Why not just *give* them to me?" he asked in exasperation.

"Because I wanted to give you a choice."

Issai paused in slipping his knives into the sheaths strapped to his forearms and turned to face the other boy. No trace of the smile remained, not even in his eyes. The ancient Hahri was back.

"A choice," he echoed quietly.

Hahri nodded. "When I tackled you back there, I think that for a few moments, our souls fused. In that short time, I understood everything about you, what drives you, your convictions, your bitterness, everything. Maybe it didn't affect you in the same way. I don't know. You don't talk enough for me to confirm anything, but I know that's just how you are thanks to those moments of enlightenment."

He shrugged. "So it really doesn't matter that fate has brought us together. What does matter is what you choose to do from this point on. If I don't respect that, then I am no better than the gods who have played with our lives for all these long centuries. Kill me, run, or stay to talk. I'm willing to see what happens. After all, you already know my choice."

Issai sat down heavily and laughed. The sound was so alien that it was a long moment before he realized the enormity of what he was doing. However, the moment the ancient boy had finished speaking, it was the only thing he could do, and once started, it was a long while before he could stop.

When he finally looked up at his companion, mirth in his eyes, he nearly lost it again at the look of absolute alarm on Hahri's face. He shook his head. "Idiot. You took any choice from me the moment you opened your mouth. How can I do anything but yield to my fate after all of that?"

"I guess this means that I don't have to worry about you slitting my throat during the night anymore?"

Although said jokingly, a stab of guilt pierced him. How close had he really come to doing just that? Had he had his knives at the time, he probably would have.

"Issai?"

He forced himself to look at the other boy. "Do you really think we can end this?"

"Until I found you, all I really had was a hope," Hahri said. "Let's find the other two first, then maybe I can give you a better answer."

Although not an answer at all, it was more than Issai had ever had, and for that moment in time, it was enough.

4

———

"How did you know that I was going to Nisei?" Issai asked abruptly.

It was the first time either one of them had spoken since they left the cave, and admittedly, the absolute silence coming from his usually loquacious new companion was starting to get under his skin more than the chatter did.

The sun was barely rising, a few stray rays escaping through the now thinning branches above as they neared the forest's edge. The early light reflecting off the smaller boy's head put Issai in mind of a canyon with its many shades of browns, reds, and gold he had seen several lifetimes back.

Hahri looked at him sideways. "I dunno. It makes sense, really. If I wanted to disappear for a while, what better place than a city, right? Besides, I think we're heading in the right direction. It feels right somehow."

"I wondered why you agreed so easily," Issai muttered, then suddenly stopped in his tracks.

Hahri turned and faced him directly. "What?" he asked.

"Why is it that you're having all these feelings of insight, and I'm still being kept in the dark?" Issai snapped.

Hahri shrugged. "Maybe you pissed off the gods more often than I did, and this is their revenge—who knows?"

Issai glared warningly.

The auburn-haired boy threw up his hands in defense. "All right, all right! Serious question, I know. Sorry, it's a bad habit." He fell silent for a moment, his eyes reflective. "I've never felt anything like a directional tug before this life when I finally got pretty close to you. Before, I just felt that I needed to be *somewhere* doing *something*. Just being this close to you seems to have awakened some new type of perception. It's even stronger when I touch you. I can't even begin to guess what any of this means. Just one more clue in the big Old Soul mystery."

"Hn." Issai began walking again, once more finding himself without the proper words to respond and hating it. It had been so long since he'd had a normal conversation with anybody without the usual shadows hanging over him that he was beginning to wonder if he had lost the ability.

With Hahri, he could look him in the eyes and not worry about showing his violet eyes or wonder if he was acting appropriately for the age he appeared. For the first time in centuries, he could just be "Issai."

He just didn't know how to break down the wall he had carefully constructed in order to survive all those years, alone and ignorant of his own fate. Sometimes it was just easier to stay isolated from society and not have to worry about the million ways the people around you could betray or hurt you if you allowed them to get too close.

Perhaps that was why he was so angry; because of Hahri, he *wanted* that human connection—and that scared him.

"Do you really hate me that much?"

Startled, Issai stopped again. He turned to look at the other boy who had paused several paces behind him. Those unsystematic questions again—how could one boy manage to unbalance him every time he opened his mouth?

"Why should it matter?" he asked coolly.

Hahri frowned. "Would it kill you to give me a straight answer for once? It matters, or else I wouldn't have bothered to ask in the first place! You're so tense that it looks like you're ready to attack me at any moment!"

Issai unconsciously shifted into a more battle-ready stance as cerulean eyes fixed on him challengingly. For a few tense moments as they stared each other down, time seemed to stop. Then Hahri blinked and relaxed his body, taut lines of frustration melting into a gentle smile.

"I'd just like to know where we stand," he insisted.

The smile should have been reassuring—he figured that had been Hahri's intention—if not for the eyes that gazed at him without a shimmer of emotion. No anger, no hate, no laughter—not even the gentleness offered by the mask of a smile he wore so readily. Just—nothing. The true eyes of an immortal.

Is that what others see when I look at them? Is that what he sees?

Issai shifted uncomfortably, though the tight expression on his face didn't change. "Listen, I'm just—mad, okay," he admitted grudgingly. "Not particularly at you, but at the same time you are part of it—it's complicated. I don't know you well enough to feel strongly about anything."

He looked away and sighed. "The fact that I didn't kill you should be enough answer for you."

Hahri laughed. "Hmm. So you do have a sense of humor buried in there somewhere."

Startled, Issai turned back to him. His companion's eyes sparkled with life; Hahri looked genuinely delighted, leaving him confused once again. He had thought he had glimpsed a bit of the real Hahri earlier, but now he wasn't so sure. The jokester seemed equally authentic. Could a person really reconcile two such opposing personalities? Or were they just the masks he created to survive the long millennia?

Mentally, he shook his head. Why was he even letting it bother him so much?

It was his companion's turn to look confused as, without a word, Issai turned and resumed walking.

"Hey!" Hahri called as he jogged up to him until they were side-by-side again. "You were totally serious, weren't you?"

"Yes," he replied simply, not looking at the other, not wanting to see what, if anything, those eyes held.

To Issai's relief, they didn't speak much for the rest of the day.

NISEI LAY SPREAD BELOW THEM, dotted with small points of flame like an army encampment settling for the night. The sun was halfway set, giving the two boys standing on the overlooking rise just enough time to reach the city gates before they closed for the night.

Hahri once again donned his cloak and hood after first offering them to Issai, he being the more conspicuous of the two, but Issai had flatly refused. Bad enough that he had to constantly hide his eyes behind long bangs; he didn't want to hide his face as well.

Deep down, he knew he was being unnecessarily childish. Now was not the time to take any kind of risk no matter how small, but his stubbornness had had millennia to develop and was not something that could be easily compromised. Luckily for him, Hahri just shrugged, not pressing the issue. Still feeling somewhat unsettled from the incident that morning, he was in no mood to get into another argument—especially if he knew he was in the wrong in the first place.

Though no one ever paid him much mind before when he first entered a new city, Issai still felt on edge as they walked among several other travelers on foot. He discreetly peered at the people around him as well as the guardsmen that lined the domed passage through the wall, looking for anything out of the ordinary.

"Stop that!" Hahri hissed quietly beside him. "You'll draw attention to us. I know some of those bastards standing at the end—had trouble more than once with them. If they notice me, then we're sunk."

Issai looked at him sharply and whispered, "You never mentioned that you've been to the throneseat before."

"Well, I didn't think we would be here all that long, so I didn't think it was important," he whispered back. "Besides, it was only for a couple days about a year ago. I was just passing through on my way to Ahshi."

Issai glanced at the men in question from the corner of his eye as they passed right under their noses. The general consensus among them appeared to be boredom. Issai doubted that they even bothered to give anyone more than a cursory glance. He relaxed minutely.

"And why is it that those guardsmen have it in for you?" he asked once they were a ways down the crowded main street. He looked at the other boy sharply. "They don't know you're an Old Soul do they?" Great. That was all they needed.

Thankfully, Hahri shook his head. "Nope. I just beat them at dice one night, and they lost big. They thought that they could beat it out of me later as I was leaving the tavern." He laughed. "Obviously they thought wrong. Not only did they lose to a 'thirteen-year-old kid,' but they did it in front of a lot of witnesses. I'm really surprised that they didn't leave the city in shame."

"You said you had trouble with them more than once..."

"Yeah, well, they tried to kick my ass on my way out of the city too." He grinned sheepishly. "I think I may have overdone the punishment a bit that time, but it couldn't be helped. It had been about twenty-to-one. A bit unfair, even for an Old Soul, don't you think?"

Issai ignored him. "Did you kill anyone?"

"Maybe," he admitted after some hesitation. "I high-tailed it out of there at the first opportunity and didn't look back. Sometimes I forget that my speed can add force to my blows, and I don't hold back enough."

This may be a problem, he thought grimly. *Showing such unusual skill and power, someone might have guessed his true identity. Maybe we should go on to Subu instead.* Aloud, he said, "Even though it was a year ago, someone may still recognize you. Which taverns did you go to?"

Hahri sighed then threw his arm companionably over Issai's shoulders. "Don't worry so much. I don't usually go out of my way to find trouble. I'll lay low at whatever inn we stay at tonight, and you can get the supplies for us tomorrow. We can leave right after that if you want."

Issai shook him off. "Whatever. Let's just find an inn before it gets completely dark. I have enough to worry about with the *Shi* without having to worry about all the other nightly predators of a city. I'm in no mood for engaging in petty fights today."

Hahri glanced around. "This is just the Governmental District. If I'm not mistaken, the Traveler District should be down the road a bit then off to the right at the next intersection. I stayed at an inn deeper into the city last year, so it should be okay."

Issai was almost surprised that they reached their destination without any excitement. It seemed almost too good to be true that he had completely eluded that last monstrous batch of *Shi*. He had, after all, given them an additional two days to catch up while he lay unconscious in the cave as a result of his own idiocy. Was coming to the throneseat too obvious?

Well, it was certainly too late for regrets, and perhaps if they did as Hahri suggested and left immediately after gathering supplies tomorrow, then they could stay one step ahead of any possible dangers.

The inn Hahri directed him to was bustling with activity, but not so much that he felt stifled. They followed several people to the main counter.

"Here," the other boy said suddenly, thrusting his pack into Issai's hands and lowering his hood. "You take care of the room, and I'll grab us a table. I'm *starving!*"

Then without waiting for a reply, he slipped into the flood of people coming and going from the common room, leaving Issai to glare after him. The little sneak. Now he was stuck paying for the room.

After stowing their belongings in their room, it took Issai no time to find his irritating companion, who surprisingly was sitting quietly at a small corner table farthest from all activity nursing a mug. He had totally expected the ancient boy to pick a table in the noisiest, rowdiest part of the room.

He was beginning to realize that the reason why Hahri kept throwing him off-balance was because he kept thinking of him as a teenager and not the ancient creature that he was. His earlier observations notwithstanding, there were many things about him that Issai didn't understand. Like it or not, it was a problem that needed to be resolved before either of them could step forward.

"Here, I got you one too," Hahri said as he sat down, thrusting a mug in front of him.

Issai frowned and pushed it away. "I don't drink."

Cerulean eyes sparked with amusement. "No kidding. Do you really think I'd be stupid enough to get drunk now? It's just cider, and before you start sniffing it, I didn't poison it."

Issai scowled defensively. "I wasn't—"

"I hope you don't mind, but I already ordered my dinner," Hahri plowed on, seemingly not even noticing the other boy had spoken. "I didn't want to presume, so I didn't get anything but the cider for you."

"Fine." Issai took a long drink as he discreetly scanned the entire common room in habit. No one appeared to show any interest in them.

"Relax."

Issai turned his attention to the other boy again. "What?"

"You look like a bow ready to loose an arrow," he said with a grin. "It's no wonder you draw attention to yourself. Strung up like that, you look like you've got something to hide—and *stop* that!"

"Stop what?" Issai snapped.

Hahri shook his head and reached a hand across the table, pulling away the hand Issai had been absently using to push his bangs down. "*That,*" he said pointedly.

Issai jerked his hand back. He hadn't even realized what he was doing.

Hahri sat back in his chair. "When you do that, you might as well be shouting for everyone to take a look. Just relax, or better yet, look a little bored. You'll fit into the crowd better."

"And I suppose getting into tavern fights is any better?" Issai countered dryly.

"Hey! That was *so* not my fault. Do you think I enjoy getting attacked? Don't take everything so seriously. I was only trying to give you some advice."

"I don't recall asking for it."

"Doesn't mean you didn't need it."

Luckily, the waiter chose that time to bring Hahri's order, saving Issai from the need to respond, especially when he really didn't know how. Deciding that he'd had enough stew in the last few days, he ordered a couple of meat pies and greens. Who knew when he would have the opportunity to eat well again, especially when they really had no clear idea where they were heading next.

His companion, however, was shoveling in his food as if he hadn't seen a good meal in several tendays. Maybe he hadn't. Although Hahri talked almost nonstop once he got started, he really didn't talk much about himself unless asked directly. All Issai really knew about the boy was the information he unwittingly absorbed in those fleeting moments when their souls seemed to have touched—which really amounted to nothing since it did nothing to ease his current confusion.

"Do you have any idea where we should go from here?" Issai asked when he could no longer stand watching the boy eat.

Hahri swallowed and shook his head. "Not a clue, but don't worry, I think I can fix that."

Issai folded his arms across his chest. "I'm listening."

He shook his head again. "Not here. What I have in mind isn't something I think you'll want to do with an audience."

Issai nodded, but before he could ask something else, his food arrived. They spent the next few moments in silence as they concentrated on their meals. However, even having a mouth full of food could not keep the blue-eyed boy quiet for long.

"Your healing—is that the only special thing you can do?" Hahri asked.

Issai raised his eyes from his plate slowly. Those random questions again. He didn't think he would ever get used to them. Still, he had been wondering the same thing about Hahri, and the boy's question gave him the perfect opening.

He shrugged. "Like you, I'm unusually fast, but since you caught me so quickly, then I'd say you can move faster."

"You have no idea," Hahri said, grinning mischievously. "I'll show you sometime. Anything else?"

"Nothing that I'm aware of—not unless you count knowing little mundane things about you that I couldn't possibly know. My healing ability was something that I accidentally stumbled upon. I never knew it was something I could do until it had been done."

"Really? I was practically born running—my first birth I mean. Until I was reborn for the first time, I always thought that powerful restlessness was the result of my having this unique ability. It took me a couple lives to understand that the urge that drove me to move was because there was something I needed to do and really had nothing to do with my unnatural speed and everything to do with the reason why I was being reborn with all my previous memories intact.

"That aside, everything I can do ties in with my speed. For some reason, no one can ever hear me coming when I'm at full sprint, like I'm really flying, but I can feel my feet touch the ground and everything around me seems to slow down rather than speed up. A time or two, things around me have even stopped completely. Even after all this time, I can't help but feel awe every time I experience it." He looked at Issai curiously. "What's it feel like to heal?"

"Like I'm bleeding to death," Issai replied crossly. "Nothing pleasant about it."

"All right! Don't bite my head off. Jeez."

Issai pushed his chair back impatiently. "If you're finished here, let's go. I want to hear this idea of yours."

HAHRI FLUNG himself onto his bed and slowly stretched. "I haven't slept in one of these in several tendays," he said happily. He flipped over onto his stomach and rested his chin on his folded arms, peering over at his glowering companion. "Your fault, I might add."

Issai's jaw clenched as he leaned back against the wall near the door. "Nobody forced you to start stalking me," he replied darkly. "If anything, I should be the one complaining here, seeing as how you stuck me with the bill."

Undeterred, the boy's grin got wider. "Don't be so stingy. There'll be plenty of opportunities later to pay you back. I'm not so stupid to think that our fate will be resolved anytime soon. It'd be great, but finding you is the first luck I've had in centuries. Still, playing this game is a lot more fun with a partner."

"And while we're on the subject, how exactly are you planning on divining our next destination?"

"Just remember, you did ask," Hahri warned.

Then he abruptly jumped to his feet, leaped onto the bed beside his own, and pulled a startled Issai by the arms up onto the bed as well.

"What the hell are you doing!" Issai shouted angrily, the effect somewhat ruined by a face full of blankets.

"Come on; sit up and give me your hands."

He narrowed his eyes suspiciously. "Why?"

"Just *do* it. Jeez—I'm not gonna do anything weird."

"Says you," Issai muttered irritably, but against his better judgment, he pulled himself to his knees and sat back onto his haunches, allowing the other boy to take his hands.

"What now?"

"Just sit still for a while."

For a long moment, Hahri said nothing, his eyes closed and a frown of concentration on his face. Issai stared at him suspiciously, wondering what he was doing. Already with such close contact, he could feel the ever-present ache within himself ease up into a faint buzzing beneath his skin that was infinitely more tolerable than the constant pain he had been enduring since he had met Hahri. Was this Hahri's doing, or the result of their longer-than-usual direct contact?

That uncomfortable thought instantly made him want to back away to the far wall, pain or no pain. Then the smaller boy's eyes flew open, and he scowled and squeezed Issai's hands hard.

"Why do you always have to make everything so difficult?" he complained.

Issai wrenched his hands free. The phantom ache instantly flared up within him at the loss of contact, but his mind barely registered it. "What the hell does that mean?" he demanded angrily.

Hahri grabbed one of his arms as he started to get up. "Hey, don't get all bent out of shape!"

"I don't have to put up with your constant jabs," he retorted, trying unsuccessfully to shake off the other boy's hold.

"Don't misunderstand. I shouldn't have said it that way. What I meant was that even though you seem to be cooperating with me now, deep down you're really still rebelling; not against me precisely, but—well—against everything."

Issai abruptly stopped trying to reclaim his arm as something unnamable clenched in the pit of his stomach. Hahri was right of course. Down in the darkest depths of his being, he *was* still raging. A part of him resented that it was Hahri and not himself that had pushed him to resume the search. Yet, instead of being angry, he was scared, scared that Hahri could look at him and understand this about him with just a glance. It seemed this ancient boy knew more about him than he knew about himself.

He forced himself to look at the other boy. "Hahri, I—"

"Stop," Hahri interjected. "I'm not saying it's a bad thing. It's just you really need to make up your mind. Whether I like it or not, I can't step any farther without you, and at this rate, nothing is ever going to change."

He sighed and closed his eyes. "I'm just so tired, Issai —and I know you are, too. You're angry; you're bitter. I'm not asking you to let go of that. At this point, I don't even think it's possible. You let me in once. Not willingly, I know, but all I'm asking is for you to let me in one more time."

Finally, Issai understood what Hahri had been trying to accomplish earlier. He sank back down to the bed.

"You were trying to meld our souls again, weren't you? Why didn't you just tell me what you were doing?"

Hahri laughed, though there was no humor in it. "And you would've happily let me do it, right?"

Issai opened his mouth to retort, then immediately shut it. He couldn't really argue with that, and that fact left him once again in the very uncomfortable position of not knowing what to say.

"Listen," Hahri said after a moment of silence. "I don't want to force you. If you need a couple days to—"

"Your sense of 'right or wrong' direction," Issai cut in, finding and holding startled cerulean eyes, "it heightens when you're touching me, doesn't it?"

A ghost of a smile touched the auburn-haired boy's lips. "Not physically. When you're not blocking me out, I just need to feel your presence for the pull to get stronger. Of course, I never felt the pull in any given direction more strongly than when our souls touched that one time. However, the shock of that unexpected experience left us completely bare and defenseless for only a few moments. I thought if we could somehow do it again, only this time consciously and for a longer period of time, then I could get a better understanding other than 'you're moving right.' Touching does help me get centered, though."

"Fine." Issai held out his hands once again.

"You're sure?" Hahri asked cautiously, eying his hands as if they were a pair of vipers ready to strike.

"Just do it, dammit!" he growled.

Hahri rolled his eyes. "Good enough, I guess. You have to help me this time. I know you can sense me too sometimes—when you're not ignoring it, that is. Just focus on that for a moment; I'll do the rest."

Issai nodded and tried not to squirm as Hahri clasped his hands firmly. Following the other boy's example, he closed his eyes. Now that his attention was entirely focused on that point of contact, it seemed as if Hahri was not only touching his hands but also beginning to crawl under his skin.

Bits of alien feelings and thoughts began to flow through him, and his first reaction was to frantically push them away. Then a quick squeeze from the hands that encased his reminded him of what he was supposed to be doing, and Issai grudgingly allowed the small invasive wave to flow freely throughout him until he was no longer certain who was feeling what.

A fog began to enter his mind, easing some of his anxiety away as the foreign feelings awash within him became less foreign, and the sensation of their joined hands, as well as the buzzing beneath his skin, became less pronounced. His mind began to drift as if walking the fine line between sleep and awake, but in contrast, his entire being felt alive with an awareness he had never experienced before—to Hahri, to the patrons downstairs, to even the people outside the inn walls.

"That's it!" Hahri shouted excitedly, causing Issai to nearly jump out of his skin, the fog in his mind instantly clearing.

Out of habit more than anything, Issai snatched his hands back and was already beginning to flick his knives out before he realized what he was doing and dropped his arms slowly to his sides. He sucked in a sharp breath and attempted to calm his racing heart. What the hell just happened to him?

His companion, however, didn't appear to have noticed his disorientation as Hahri leaned forward and grabbed both the violet-eyed boy's arms. "It worked! After you had stopped resisting my presence, it was like I was remembering a memory that had always been hazy more clearly. There were lots of people milling around, and I really didn't recognize anything, but it looked like the marketplace of a large city—stalls as far as the eye can see."

"And the direction?" Best to puzzle out what had happened to him later after he had had some time to settle down.

Some of the ancient boy's excitement seemed to fade. "Actually, I didn't feel anything else on that, just the sense that we are heading pretty much in the right direction. At least I didn't feel the need to go anywhere else when I thought of us going north."

"Do you know how many cities are in the north?" Issai asked as he calmly began to pry the smaller boy's fingers from his arms. Hahri had gripped him so tightly in his excitement that Issai was sure there would be bruises later. However, seeing how genuinely happy the other was at the moment, he couldn't bring himself to spoil the mood by snapping at him.

"Lots I know," Hahri replied promptly, "but at least now we've narrowed it down considerably. Just think of all the centuries we could've wandered around. Think of how long it took for us to finally meet without a starting point. At least this time around we know we're looking for people, and if I see that marketplace, I'll know we're in the right city to look for them. The 'why' of it can wait 'til later."

Hahri slid off the bed and began looking around the room.

Issai frowned. "What are you doing?"

"Where did you put my pack?"

His frown deepened. "On the other side of your bed, why?"

"I'm heading to the bathhouse. It's getting pretty late."

"What! We're not finished yet."

"Like I said, the rest can wait 'til morning. You can find us a map while you're out buying supplies, and we can decide then where to go next. In the meantime, why not enjoy our accommodations while we can. I have a feeling that we'll be roughing it for a good long while."

Not able to find fault with any of that, Issai could only agree and follow his lead. He was itching for a bath anyway.

However, he only made it a step outside the door before he was roughly shoved back into the room. Issai stumbled back against the bed but managed somehow to keep his footing.

"Dammit, Hah—"

"Shit!" Hahri swore as he slammed the door shut and bolted it. He turned to Issai and grinned weakly. "Change of plans. Up for another jump?"

"What?"

The other boy was already moving towards his pack. "Remember those guardsmen I mentioned earlier..."

Issai suddenly had the urge to sink a knife into that retreating back. "Don't tell me..." he growled through clenched teeth.

"Either our bad luck has increased, or the innkeeper has a big mouth. At any rate, unless you want a repeat of what happened in Daisha, I suggest we take a jump."

"I knew I should have slit your throat," Issai muttered as he grabbed his pack and made for the window. "At least open the damn thing first."

A crash sounded behind him, followed by the sound of splintering wood.

"Ah, crap."

"What *now*?" Issai demanded, shoving the other boy aside without waiting for a reply. "We don't have time for your—"

Bars. He had been so preoccupied earlier when he had dropped their packs off that he had failed to inspect the room like always before heading down to the common room. He clenched his right hand into a fist. The one time—after centuries of never failing to do it— the one time he did... The gods must really be laughing themselves sick at the moment.

Five thick bars stretched vertically across the small window behind the dusty pane of glass. So much for that exit. Why did everything always have to be so difficult?

Another crash sounded behind him. Cursing, Issai turned to the door, slipping his knives into his hands. Hahri moved closer to him.

"How many?" Issai asked, his eyes never leaving the quivering door.

He felt rather than saw the other boy shrug. "Who knows? I saw maybe six before I slammed the door shut, but I wouldn't be surprised if those bastards brought their whole garrison for this."

Another sound kick and the door crashed open.

"Follow my lead."

Had Issai not known they were alone, he would have never recognized that low, deadly voice as Hahri's.

However, he didn't have time to think further on it as a flash of black darted forward, and the first two men rushing through the ruined door dropped before he could even take his first step.

When he reached the door, Issai was further hindered by several more fallen bodies and five or six more rushing towards him with swords drawn. Swords —that was different. He had barely an instant to register that Hahri was fighting his own mob near the end of the corridor before he dropped his pack and rushed his enemies at full speed and dove at their legs before they could take their first swing.

He hit the middle two directly at the kneecaps, sending them flying over his back as he slid onto his stomach. He was on his feet and slashing at the backs of the remaining two just as they skidded to a stop and were turning to face him. Both fell screaming to the floor.

Issai turned, intent on helping Hahri, and froze as his eyes met hardened blue eyes across the corridor. At least ten guardsmen lay unmoving in a circle around the teen. In contrast to himself, not a drop of blood stained his companion's clothing, nor were there any visible signs of blood among the fallen.

"Unlike you, I don't need knives to kill."

Without a word, Issai turned away and retrieved his pack. It seemed neither one of them would be getting any sleep that night.

5

———

Somewhere in the distance, a door slowly creaked open. Korin stiffened, his eyes darting from the book in his lap to the entrance of the chamber below. No one was supposed to be awake at this hour, which was why he sat on one of the higher balconies amongst the many statues of the temple as if he were one of them rather than curled up in his bed. He found their quiet presence somehow comforting. It was a small relief to know that these still beings would never ask him questions he feared he would never have the answers for.

Faint footsteps approached, hesitant as if not wanting to be heard or not sure of their destination. Korin closed his book and carefully set it aside. Although the temple did not have much that would attract a thief, one could not be too careful. These days it seemed that more and more people were losing their fear of invoking the wrath of the gods. Crime in Aideya had been on a steady rise for the past five years with no end in sight. The crowds on Temple days even seemed to be thinning. All in all, a disturbing trend.

Peering into the darkness below, Korin nearly fell off his perch when the small form slowly crossed the threshold into the beam of moonlight that stretched across half the marble floor from one of the many high windows in the chamber. Though not really expecting the late night visitor to be a thief, the last thing he had expected was for the person to be a child.

The hidden watcher was too far up to see the child clearly, and in the dim light, could only make out short, dark hair, a boy perhaps no older than nine or ten if his height were any indication. What looked like a long walking stick was belted at his side, but other than that, the child was empty-handed. What was such a young child doing alone in the temple so late at night?

From the shadows, Korin watched the child pause for a moment, head turning to take in the whole of the chamber before approaching the group of statues nearest to him. Korin remained silent, watching curiously as the boy slowly reached a hand to the torso of the statue of the goddess of light, laying it lightly against the marble as if afraid to damage it. Silence filled the chamber as the child stilled for a long moment and then drew his hand away.

"Nothing," the boy murmured.

He moved over to the next assembly of statues and repeated the gesture. This time, he said nothing as he lowered his hand to his side. Then, instead of moving over to the next set, the child just stood staring up at the faces of the earth gods before him.

Once again, Korin wondered what the child was doing and if he should perhaps confront the boy or observe him further. However, before he could decide, the boy abruptly stepped back and pulled the stick from his side. Only when a flash of light glinted from the stick did Korin realize it was not a stick at all.

A sound like a sudden gust of wind rang through the air, and Korin watched in horror as the boy swung a sword at the same statue he had just touched. What had once been a skillfully crafted mid-section was effectively reduced to jagged marble. The sound of chunks of broken marble hitting the ground was deafening in the once silent chamber.

"What do you want from me!" the boy screamed as his sword met a second statue, defacing it as effortlessly as he had the first. "Haven't I paid enough!"

"Stop!" Korin shouted as he jumped down from his perch, landing in a crouch a couple of paces away from the child.

He lifted his head in enough time to see the boy whirl around and raise his sword, bringing it down over his head before Korin could stand. He lurched to the side frantically as the sword slashed down with frightening speed, slicing across his bicep. The momentum of his fall slid him across the floor, and he wasted no time in climbing to his feet to face the boy, not even daring to spare his injured arm a glance. He could feel a small trickle of warmth falling towards his elbow, but not enough to be alarming.

His chest heaving, Korin raised his good arm and offered his hand palm up to the boy. "I did not mean to startle you," he said gently. He took a tentative step forward.

The boy's hands tightened on the sword. "Stay back!" he warned.

Korin nodded and slowly lowered his hand. He offered the child what he hoped was a reassuring smile. "It's all right. I am a monk of this temple."

Rather than calm him, the boy seemed to tense even more, his eyes glittering with malice.

"You are not in any trouble," Korin assured him. "I just want to talk."

"That's how it starts doesn't it?" the boy sneered. "A nice little chat; let's spill our guts together, perhaps even a comforting hug. Such a poor, wayward child..."

Korin blinked, discomfited at the utter sarcasm that dripped from his words. "What are you—"

"*Please*," he said with utter contempt. "Couldn't you at least come up with something more original? You may have been sent for my torment, but I won't submit so easily!"

Once again, the monk found himself at a loss. These were not the words of a child.

"Nor am I so forgiving."

Without warning, the child lunged forward, and it was all Korin could do to twist out of the way to avoid being stabbed. "Stop! I just want to—"

"Shut up!" the boy screamed, bringing the sword down once again with frightening speed.

Korin jumped back and ran for the cover of the nearest statue, his thoughts in disarray. Everything was happening so fast. Soon others would come to investigate the noise. He couldn't have that. With such an unbalanced child, the situation would only get worse if others became involved. He had to regain control fast. Though he loathed using *that* method, it was the only thing he could do considering the circumstances.

Dodging the boy's next attack, he twisted around the statue and uttered a single, quiet word, "*Stop.*"

The air between them seemed to ripple violently as that lone word echoed a thousand times more strongly than the loudest shout, the sound waves generated visible to the naked eye as they shot towards the intended target. The boy teetered backward when the waves hit him, immediately dropping the sword with a shout and raising his hands protectively to his ears. Yet, to Korin's surprise, he did not fall.

Having no time to puzzle over that fact, the monk rushed forward before the kid could regain his senses and retrieved the sword from where it had fallen.

"You—what did you—" the boy gasped, shaking his head violently as if trying to shake water from his ears. He raised his head, and angry eyes widened once they focused on Korin. "Not again!" he raged, and with more strength than any child should have, the boy shot forward, foot kicking at the hand that held the sword before the monk could dodge the attack.

As the sword went flying, a tiny knee in the next instant made contact with his gut. Korin doubled over, only to find himself flying backward as a third blow landed squarely on his forehead. As his back hit the ground, the child was already rushing past, intent on the sword that lay somewhere behind him.

His breath gone, Korin desperately smacked the marble floor with an open palm. He reached for and melded his mind with the weak but resulting sound waves the impact caused until he felt them like they were the tips of his fingers, thrusting them with as much force as his will could safely muster at the child behind him. He knew with a sickening certainty that if he didn't temporarily stop the child before he reached his weapon that instead of running, the boy would not hesitate to kill him in cold blood.

A yell of surprise followed by the clanging of metal, then a more organic impact, let Korin know he had succeeded. Coughing and still gasping for air, Korin pulled himself to his knees and raised watering eyes, focusing on the fallen figure a couple of strides away. Face down, the boy was not moving.

Shivering a bit in the sudden chill that had entered the air, Korin cautiously crawled over to him and slid the sword across the floor beyond immediate reach, his eyes darting in alarm to the still figure as that slight friction echoed preternaturally loud throughout the chamber. Thankfully the boy didn't even twitch.

Still mindful of any movement, Korin sat back on his haunches and carefully grabbed the boy's shoulders. He slowly turned him onto his back. The look on the boy's face was almost angelic in its calm. Only the throb in his head and gut reminded the monk of the violence that lay beyond that calm. The monk released a shaky breath. Everything about the situation was wrong.

Korin placed a hand on the boy's forehead, to comfort the boy or steady himself, he wasn't sure. However, before he could even contemplate what to do next, a force seized his mind, slamming him into what felt like a stone wall though somewhere in the back of his mind he knew that he was still kneeling on the floor.

For one eternal moment, all he knew was the pain of a shattered body until his breath was once again wrenched from his lungs, and something in his very being seemed to tear wide open. It immediately began filling with something akin to lightning, destructive and illuminating. It both soothed and aggravated this new wound further.

Then just as abruptly, it was over, and the monk found himself looking down at the boy whose once passive face was now grimacing as if in agony. Gasping, Korin snatched his hands away from the small body.

For a long moment, he could do nothing but wrap his arms around his own hunched-over body as he trembled violently in reaction, his heart thudding painfully in his chest in belated fear. What had just happened? It was like nothing he had ever experienced, no affliction he had ever heard described.

Korin sucked in a slow breath and struggled to calm the panic that seemed to have permeated his entire being. Although he was only somewhat successful, he forced himself to focus his attention on the child again. The small features had smoothed out a bit, but he was still shifting his body as if he was still feeling some discomfort.

He wrung his hands anxiously in his lap as he stared. Now what? At the very least, he should probably move the boy somewhere more comfortable. The questions could wait until later.

Just as he was struggling to sit the boy up without aggravating the wound on his arm, the first few monks came running into the chamber. Pausing in his struggles, Korin turned to them as several gasped and immediately ran to inspect the damage around the statues.

The nearest monk, however, spotted him immediately and quickly changed course.

"Brother Korin! What has happened here—you're hurt!" he cried, falling to his knees beside the slightly out of breath monk.

Korin waved him off as the young man reached for his arm. "It's just a scratch," he said. "More importantly, this boy requires my immediate attention. Join your Brothers in the clean-up. Please tell them I shall explain everything after I attend to the child."

The young monk clenched and unclenched his hands anxiously. "At least allow me to help you with—"

Korin caught the monk's eyes, and the other froze, eyes widening considerably before he nodded wordlessly. He frowned as he watched the young man practically flee his side to join his Brothers. To this day, he still didn't understand why everyone could only meet his eyes with fear. Like them, he was a servant of the gods; no more, no less. Did it really matter so much that his role was a bit different?

His eyes fell back to the unconscious child and pushed those troubled thoughts away. Now wasn't the time for such contemplation. Shifting one knee, Korin slipped an arm behind both the boy's neck and knees and lifted him into his arms, careful not to jostle him too much as he slowly rose to his feet. His arm throbbed a bit in protest, but the child was so light that he didn't think he would have any problems getting to his chambers.

That is until he took a couple of steps and nearly dropped the boy as a wave of fire rapidly burned its way across every nerve in his body before he could even blink in shock. What in the name of the gods was happening to him?

The child whimpered and began to twist in his arms, his face a perfect picture of pain. Korin forced his feet to move, though every step seemed to push a new wave of pain through him more intense than the last. Even unconscious, the boy cried out and pushed desperately at the monk's chest until Korin could stand it no longer, and he fell to his knees gasping, allowing the sobbing child to slide from his trembling arms to the marble floor.

The relief that immediately followed was enough to bring tears to his own eyes as he sat back onto his haunches, panting as though he had just run several spans. The moment the two were no longer touching, the pain had ceased, leaving only a slight pins-and-needles tingling as if his limbs had started to go to sleep.

The boy had also fallen still, lying splayed across the floor where he had fallen, face slack and expressionless as if in normal sleep. For a long moment, Korin could only stare down at the small body in a sort of helpless confusion. What was going on? All the strange sensations he had experienced thus far seemed to happen only when he touched the child. On a whim, he scooted a bit away from the boy, and even the slight tingling eased away.

It was then that something opened inside—his mind? His soul? He wasn't sure what it was, but it was as if he had walked by a familiar wall and suddenly noticed an open door that he had never known even existed. Was this child the epiphany he had been waiting for all these years, that *something* that he had prayed and prayed to the gods to help him understand?

He reached a hesitant hand towards the boy's face and instantly retracted it at first contact with a cry, feeling as if he had been bitten though there were no physical signs of damage. Rubbing his abused fingers, Korin looked over to the destroyed statues where his Brothers had apparently abandoned any pretense of cleaning up and were, to a man, staring over at him. He sighed wearily. It seemed the others would be getting that promised explanation sooner than he had thought.

He beckoned them over with a wave of his hand, and two of the eldest immediately came over. Although familiar, Korin didn't know them by name.

"Brother Kal said you were hurt," the younger of the two said as he dropped to one knee beside him, the closest Korin knew any of them would come to chiding him. He had long ago given up on any hope that any of his brother-monks would treat him like any other servant to the gods. As far as Korin was concerned, they were all equal, but it seemed his brethren would never learn that lesson.

"We'll take care of the child," the other monk added, already moving to touch the boy at his feet.

"Don't!" Korin cried out more sharply than he had intended, wincing as his cut arm connected with the other man's forearm.

Fear flashed in the man's eyes, making something twist painfully within Korin. Never in all his incarnations had he raised a hand to another for the sole purpose of violence, so why did everyone fear him so deeply? He was not a god with the power of judgment; he was a teacher. Not for the first time did he wonder if they had heard something about him, something untrue, that made them look at him with such alarm.

"Sorry," Korin said contritely. "The child causes me excruciating pain when I touch him, and I am not certain if the same will be true for you."

"Who is he?" the monk on his left asked, eying the boy nervously as if he expected him to suddenly snap at him.

Korin shrugged. "The only thing I am certain of at this point is that he is no ordinary child. He is the one responsible for those broken statues."

"This little boy?" the monk said incredulously.

"Well, he had help. I do not suppose you have found a sword?"

Both glanced at his wound again, and he could see

them put two and two together though neither one said anything out loud.

"He was angry; I am not sure why, but I had to use the Gods' Voice before the situation deteriorated any further. I think it would be best to get him into my quarters before he wakes up. Without his weapon, perhaps he will be more inclined to listen rather than react. I do not believe he came here tonight by coincidence."

"But if we cannot touch him..."

"The antipathy may uniquely be mine." Korin showed them his hand. "I tapped him lightly with my fingers and felt something akin to a bite. As you can see, my flesh remains unmarked. I am not certain it is even a physical pain."

The two monks shared a doubtful look before hesitantly tapping the boy's torso as if testing whether or not he was hot enough to burn them.

"I didn't feel anything. You?"

The other shook his head before emulating Korin's earlier motion and firmly placing his hand onto the boy's forehead. Korin released the breath he hadn't realized he'd been holding when the monk declared he still felt nothing.

"Then, if you will be so kind..." Korin said as the other monk helped him to his feet despite his protests.

They made it back to his chambers with no further mishaps. After laying the child in his bed, both monks insisted on treating the slash on his arm before leaving with a promise to inform the Prior about everything.

"Tell him I shall see him personally after I have had the chance to talk to the child," Korin said grimly before bidding them both a good night.

He closed his door with a weary sigh before turning to the small enigma in his bed—and froze.

The monks had lit several lamps throughout his room before binding his wound, so the room shone as bright as a sunlit day, clearly illuminating the pair of pink-red eyes that stared back furiously.

"Didn't waste any time did you?" the boy spat before Korin could open his mouth.

He had only seen eyes that color a handful of other times in his life, the first so long ago that had what he had witnessed not been so horrible he probably would not have remembered it at all. A scream—so inhuman that even his soul had trembled when he had first heard it—tore across his mind, and he was back there again, pushing through a crowd that seemed endless, unable to look away from the image of a writhing newborn baby lying atop a pyre completely engulfed in flames.

The villagers had waited until he was away, stolen the pale, red-eyed infant from the monks who didn't entirely believe him when he had said the child wasn't an incarnation of evil, and proceeded to purge the world of this "evil" the only way they knew how—a cleansing fire. That had been the day he had nearly given up on mankind.

His eyes locked with the boy's, perhaps now understanding a little bit of that anger. He would not fail this child.

Feeling that moving any closer would be a mistake, the monk stood his ground. "I'm not sure I know what you mean," he replied carefully.

If anything, those disconcerting eyes narrowed with more fury. "Disgusting liar!"

The boy's fist had already buried itself deep into his belly before he could even register that the child had moved. Gasping frantically for a breath that was no longer there, Korin instinctually grabbed onto the tiny shoulders before him as his body toppled forward. At the moment of contact, his mind exploded with a brilliant, white light a half-beat before his body was suddenly thrust back against the door, his back striking with enough power that he was sure bones had cracked.

As Korin slid bonelessly against the door to the ground, different scenes began to flash across his eyes, at first hazy and colorless, then growing sharper and less monochromatic. Even so, his dazed mind could still only make sense of one thing, something that was present in them all—a young girl with hair like the brightest flame.

Then the images were gone, and he found himself on the floor and slumped in an awkward position against the door of his room, struggling to breathe and blinking blurry eyes. He could barely focus on the small figure across the room struggling to stand on unsteady legs.

He knew.

"You are—a girl—" he wheezed.

For a moment, the child froze, eyes wide in naked shock. Then as Korin struggled to sit up, the *girl* was racing towards him, and the disoriented monk found his arms rising instinctively up in defense. Yet, instead of a little foot, the door was crashing into his back, threatening to make him fall forward onto his face. Some little lucid corner of his mind realized what was happening, and his hand frantically shot out after the legs that were disappearing through the door, managing to only grab air.

"Wait!" he croaked, failing to climb onto his knees as he fitfully began to cough, gasping for a breath that still hadn't really been recovered and allowing his body to once again fall to the floor.

Countless centuries of praying and his answer had just run out the door.

Maybe the gods really did hate him.

6

Hahri wasn't one to be weighed down, figuratively or literally. That's why it was taking him a considerable amount of time to get used to the feeling of being smothered that had encased him from the first moment his new sour-faced companion had looked into his eyes. The closer Issai was to him physically, the tighter those invisible arms seemed to squeeze his body. Luckily for him, the violet-eyed boy made a conscious effort of keeping as much distance between them as possible without aggravating his own phantom pain. Strange, that they both experienced similar discomfort, though the effects and cause were different.

The only time he had felt any relief was when he and Issai had briefly touched souls back at the inn, but he doubted that Issai would so readily comply to more soul-touching even if he knew. It was more in the grumpy boy's character to use such knowledge for some future blackmail. The feeling was annoying but not so much that he would willingly give his new companion a leg up. That wouldn't be in *his* character.

However, he couldn't really complain about this stronger link between them despite the unpleasant side effects. All help was a double-edged sword anyway. Even now his chest was beginning to tighten with every breath, which was why he continued to dig through the pile of junk in the corner of the cellar rather than breaking the neck of the figure that silently moved towards him from behind. He hadn't even heard the doors above open.

"You know, you could make a fortune if you hired yourself out as an assassin," Hahri commented without turning around. "We'd be financially set for eternity."

"I'd off you for free," Issai growled as something landed at Hahri's feet. "What are you doing?"

Hahri turned and eyed the sack at his feet. "Treasure hunting. Looks like you were more successful, though. Any trouble?"

Issai shook his head as he began to shrug out of his pack. "For once. Except for the Traveler's District, the City Guard hasn't noticeably increased. Either we killed everyone that was any kind of witness or tomorrow we'll really find out just how much trouble your stupidity has brought us. The night was almost too still."

"My 'stupidity,' huh," Hahri groused, pausing from his inspection of the bag Issai had brought to glare up at him, "and that wasn't an *army* you left behind back in Daisha. Don't think you're the only one that can point fingers."

Issai's eyes seemed to flash even in the darkness, but he said nothing as he propped himself against a couple of grain sacks in the opposite corner near the faint glow of their sole oil lamp and began to rifle through his own pack. It was clear *that* discussion was over.

Hahri just shook his head, torn between amusement and exasperation. Sometimes it was hard to remember that Issai was just as ancient as himself when he sulked like a child. He grinned. Well, if Issai wanted to be childish than he could be childish as well.

He snatched the map peeking from the bag Issai had given him and sauntered over to where the disgruntled boy was beginning to sharpen one of his knives. Ignoring the death glare, he plopped himself down beside Issai so close that he was almost sitting on his lap and spread the map so that it covered both their legs. This near, it was beginning to hurt to breathe, but Hahri thought the pain worth the sight of the silent fury flashing across suddenly darkened eyes. His companion had recognized the implied challenge and in the same instant realized that he had utterly lost this battle. Whether he moved away or not, Hahri had driven him to either choice.

Hahri smirked, but then blinked in confusion when instead of biting his head off, Issai closed his eyes with a sigh and muttered, "It's spreading."

Issai raised now empty hands from beneath the map and slid a finger across a cluster of dots north of Nisei. "Which of these cities have you been to within the last century?" he asked.

I guess playtime is over, Hahri thought wryly, leaning closer to the map. "On this side of the Sohran River, only Ahshi. Until a couple of years ago, I haven't been in this region for about five centuries. I heard a rumor in Aigo that an Old Soul had been found in Shoul several years back, but nobody in town seemed to know much more than that. I thought it best to move north towards the throneseat and see if I could squeeze any more information out of people before actually visiting Shoul. After coming up short in Ahshi, I crossed the river to Niya, and suddenly everything was about the 'Violet-eyed Old Soul.' I left for Daisha after that."

"I see," Issai said frostily, causing blue eyes to roll in exasperation.

His new companion was way too sensitive; he'd have to remember not to use that name again. Luckily the petulant boy had already turned his eyes back to the map and missed the gesture.

"I guess as good a place to start as any is Subu," he said after a moment. "It's been about a couple of lifetimes since I passed through, but I remember a fairly large marketplace."

"How long is a 'couple of lifetimes'?" Hahri asked slowly. He had seen small cities rise and fall in less than a hundred years. There was a very good chance that Subu would not even remotely resemble what Issai would remember if the time he had visited was that long ago, and after the trouble they had found in this city, he preferred to avoid entering unnecessary areas as much as possible.

"Why?" Issai asked, his voice layered with suspicion and some other emotion he couldn't quite decipher.

Hahri sighed mentally. It seemed not even touching souls was enough to erase the lingering distrust between them. Well, one-sided distrust anyway. At this point, Hahri was completely certain his new companion was trustworthy, despite the constant stream of death threats. However, he knew with just as much certainty that Issai wouldn't be Issai without that distance. He wondered if the Violet-eyed Old Soul would ever be capable of opening himself up completely, even if only to him. After all, there were some things Hahri himself knew that he would never be capable of again.

"Because these days, towns change pretty quickly," he answered with a shrug, deciding against any smart remarks; he'd already had his fun earlier, and he really didn't need Issai knife-angry right now. "I was just thinking that before we leave, we might want to dig around for a bit of information about the northern cities we don't have any current information on. No use wasting time checking out unsuitable cities. Those *Shi* we ditched back in the forest still haven't made an appearance yet. Despite what you may think of me, I don't crave any more unnecessary excitement."

"So you did notice," Issai said with just a hint of surprise.

"Notice what?"

"That none of the men that attacked us last night were *Shi*."

Hahri processed that for a moment. "I assume you mean the swords?"

Issai nodded. "You've been caught," he said softly, fixing him with eyes so intense that Hahri imagined he could feel the heat.

It was not voiced as a question, but Hahri answered anyway, "Yeah, by both the gut-eating and blood-drinking psychos, but it's been a couple of centuries since the last time."

The sudden black expression on Issai's face said he knew what Hahri had intentionally left unsaid. His long success of remaining hidden from the *Shi* was mostly due to the fact of the infamy of the Violet-eyed Old Soul. It seemed that nowadays most of the *Shi* forgot that there was more than one Old Soul in the world, and it was obvious from the deep bitterness and hatred scarring Issai's soul that he had not been as lucky.

Were the *Shi* still doing those types of sadistic things? At the very least, the ones that had ambushed Issai in Daisha were still careful of spilling an Old Soul's blood outside of the ritual. He wanted to ask, but there were some things better left unsaid—at least at this point of the game.

He decided it was time to change the subject. "I think we should still leave before dark like we planned, information or no information. Though I don't like it, it'd probably be better if we split up until we're ready to leave the city. We shouldn't press our luck any more than necessary—I like my guts just where they are thank you."

"Agreed, but even without any current information, I still think our next stop should be Subu. What you asked before—it's been about sixty years since I was last there, but I doubt much has changed over the decades. Subu was surrounded by mostly cattle and sheep farms, and the size of their marketplace reflected that. From what I understood, they were one of the main suppliers of meat to Nisei. It was one of the reasons why I decided to stop for a while back then. Did you happen to notice any of the goods being sold in your vision?"

Sixty years—which meant that Issai had died fairly young both times. He wondered if the *Shi* had been involved. He eyed his companion speculatively. *Or is he like me?*

"What are you staring at?" Issai demanded sharply, breaking him out of his thoughts.

"What?" Hahri focused on the reawakening anger once again visible in violet eyes. Forget the bow analogy he'd made earlier, Issai's temperament was worse than a spitting cat whose tail had been stepped on. "Oh—sorry, sorry just thinking," he quickly placated, once again deciding against teasing the irritated boy. "What was that you asked me again?"

Though his eyes hardened even further, Issai repeated his question about the vision fairly calmly. Well—it seemed Hahri wasn't the only one trying to keep the air between them civilized. It was a hopeful sign for the future.

Hahri shook his head. "The vision was too hazy for that kind of detail. I could see the layout of the stalls, the crowds, but nothing more specific than outlines of shapes I was already familiar with. However, one particular stall was unique enough that I'm sure I'd recognize it on sight."

Issai nodded absently, his eyes softening a bit as his attention turned inward for a moment. Then he pushed the map from his legs and said, "We can't do much more until morning. I'll take first watch if you think you can be quiet long enough to sleep."

Ignoring the slight jab, Hahri smiled widely and impulsively planted his head onto the other boy's outstretched legs before he could get up. He braced himself for either a knee to the head or the sting of a knife against his throat, but all he heard was an angry sigh through clenched teeth. Not being able to help himself, he glanced up curiously at the dark-haired boy, but Issai's head was turned towards the cellar doors, his face twisted as if he had swallowed something disgusting and was determined to keep it down.

Hahri was almost shocked. At the very least, he had expected Issai to yell at him, and now, to his chagrin, he realized his teasing had backfired on him. He would never be able to fall asleep with what felt like the equivalent of a horse sitting on his chest. He took a deep, painful breath and considered. He'd just have to do something about it later; maybe he could pretend to roll away in his "sleep."

"Make sure you wake me for a turn," he said, but Issai still didn't look at him, the tightening of his jaw the only sign that he was still listening.

Hahri sighed mentally into the silence and concentrated on taking slow breaths that hopefully didn't alert the other boy to his discomfort. The night was shaping up to be one of the longest he had ever endured, and as usual, he had no one to blame but himself.

IN ALL RETROSPECT, Hahri was surprised that nothing else had happened to them so far. He'd half-expected to find an army waiting for them outside the city walls, but as they made their way past the wall with the usual stream of travelers, not so much as a bird blinked in their direction. Nothing better than going out the front door, so to speak, when everyone else waited in ambush for the thief to slip out the back window. At least that was his reasoning.

Nevertheless, Issai had been so on edge that Hahri had only nodded without the usual acerbic comment when the other boy had suggested they run as much of the way as they could to Subu. He was many things, but suicidal was not one of them.

Once they neared the city, Hahri had insisted on scouting around the perimeter alone before they actually entered. Despite what had happened in Nisei, it was still possible that no one knew him as an Old Soul. He was once again shocked when Issai didn't argue.

An hour later found him crouched within the tall weeds near the road, bored and if he could admit to himself, slightly worried that he hadn't spotted anyone suspicious—at least not in a *Shi* or vendetta kind of way. His luck had never been that good, and if the last few days were indicative of Issai's... He had learned long ago that it was never good to stay still for long.

He contemplated on whether or not he should just slip into the city for a peek at the marketplace without going back for Issai to save a bit of time. If it was indeed the correct marketplace, would his vision still be valid if the petulant boy was not with him?

However, that idea was immediately shot down when he suddenly realized that the dull pain of their bond was slowly fading even though he, himself, had not moved in the last few moments. He had been so intent on watching the flow of travelers that the relief had not registered.

Issai was moving away from him.

Cursing, Hahri raced off towards the place he had left his companion, and still, the tightness in his chest continued to fade. He altered his course towards the west, increasing his speed until the landscape became a series of multicolored lines.

Only when the invisible hand began squeezing his lungs again did he slow his grueling pace to a jog. He was getting closer—no, the other boy had stopped.

He found Issai on the highest hill overlooking a spattering of cattle farms on the west side of the city, far from the place he had left him. Though Hahri had not asked him to stay put, he also had not expected him to wander so far, given how paranoid the violet-eyed boy was to being seen.

Maybe he's not the only one that's paranoid, Hahri thought wryly as he slowly approached the tree Issai was leaning against.

The other boy didn't look at him as Hahri settled into the grass beside him. Instead, Issai's attention was focused on something below. The look on his companion's face was something Hahri had never seen him wear. His eyes were pensive, almost solemn.

Though he had settled a good couple of hand-spans away from Issai, the tightening in his chest still flared to a painful level. Yet, instead of being annoyed by it, it was almost comforting, like an infuriating relative that you would never believe you'd miss until they were taken away from you and you realized that you hated the silence even more.

Or maybe you're just a masochist, Hahri thought sardonically.

Faint voices sounded in the wind, and he turned his gaze from Issai's face to the point where the other was staring. A small gathering had formed at one of the closer farm houses, some entering the house as others left, their hands burdened with various possessions.

An eviction, perhaps? Wondering what exactly had caught the other boy's attention, Hahri turned back to him, but the words froze on his tongue when he saw the fury now smoldering in his violet eyes.

"Issai," he questioned tentatively, "what's wrong?"

Although his expression didn't change, Issai's reply was soft. "An old man just died at that farm. I've seen this very scene played out more times than I can remember. That house has held that man's entire life, everything he worked for, loved, surrounded himself with because to him every bit was a thing of value, held memories, was comforting to him."

His eyes flashed. "And yet, he hasn't even been cold long enough for a style's shadow to touch the next hour-line and almost all traces that he ever lived have already been snatched away by the very people who should have cared the most about his existence. It took an entire lifetime for that house to be as it was until his final breath and only the blink of an eye to be wiped clean of him."

He paused, and some of the anger died in his eyes as his gaze flickered momentarily to Hahri, then back to the scene below. "It's sad really, that in the end, all a mortal's efforts are really as pitiful as that. Lucky for them that they will never realize it. I often think that this is also part of the gods' curse on the Old Souls, for us to live so long that we can't help but realize how pitiful mortal existence is even as we yearn for it."

"People often spend their entire lives destroying every connection they come across even though that connection is the very thing they want more than anything. Perhaps that very flaw is what it truly means to *be* mortal," Hahri said with a shrug. He stared at Issai thoughtfully before adding, "You knew him didn't you?"

"I helped him build that house long ago. It was a job. Then I moved on."

The smaller boy nodded. He understood that only too well. To an Old Soul, people could only be remembered faces. Anything else was simply too dangerous—in every sense of the word.

"I watched the crowds for a while," Hahri said after a moment of silence. "Skirted around both the east and west perimeters of the city. Nothing really stood out, so I thought I'd take a quick peek at the marketplace, maybe save us a little time, but—well—when I realized you were moving away from the city..."

"I can take care of myself," Issai snapped, finally turning to look at him. The remaining anger had faded from his eyes to be replaced by the familiar irritation.

Hahri couldn't help but feel a little disappointed. The pensive, almost melancholy Issai of before was something he had never seen. It had been the most honest conversation they had exchanged. Those few words had given him a bit more insight into the person beneath all the anger and bitterness.

Hahri huffed in annoyance that wasn't entirely feigned and said, "That's not why I—oh never mind! I must've been briefly infected by some of your paranoia."

It was probably better to let Issai believe that he was rushing to aid him in an attack rather than admit he was afraid the other boy had decided to bail on him again. A riled Issai was always easier to handle than an offended one, and they really couldn't afford to stay idle for long.

His remark had the intended effect. Issai stood abruptly, his hands twitching as if they longed to either strangle or go for the knives. However, before Hahri could make another scathing remark, the air around him shifted minutely, becoming almost undetectably heavier. It was a change that human beings had long forgotten how to perceive.

Not so for an Old Soul.

"Issai," Hahri said quietly as he stood. He casually brushed himself off as he looked into the distance out of the corner of his eye.

"I know." No emotion, just acknowledgment. Hahri might as well have been commenting on the weather.

The surrounding hillside was empty, but it was an illusion. It was already too late. The predators had found their prey. The air was beginning to buzz with an almost frantic displacement.

Hahri turned to his companion and was not at all surprised to see two knives clutched in his fists.

"Should we..." He gestured towards the city at their backs.

"No—don't you sense it? We're already surrounded."

That startled him. As a matter of fact, he hadn't. Even forewarned, Hahri still sensed nothing unusual behind them. He was a little miffed. How could he have missed them on his earlier surveillance? He glanced back sharply at the multitudes of cattle pens and properties spread below them. Unless—

As if reading his mind, Issai stated, "They aren't coming from within Subu or even the farms. They've split their forces and are coming around both sides of the city from the north."

"And you know this how?" Hahri couldn't resist asking.

Issai shot him a *look*. "I just do."

Real enlightening, but Hahri had no more time to puzzle out the intricacies of the ancient boy as the first line of mounted men appeared over the rise of a distant hill. His eyes narrowed until he could make out individuals. Each carried what looked like a long-staff.

Definitely *Shi*. He counted twenty men, and some of his tension eased. Maybe things weren't as bad as he had feared.

Then as if on cue, another line of men appeared directly behind the first, then another and another until Hahri lost count. They moved in a box formation, several rows of cavalry in front followed by those on foot as if they were the king's soldiers on a long march to war, though they wore no discernable uniform.

The hairs on the back of his neck rose. Hahri had never seen *Shi* behave like this. They hadn't been this organized even in Daisha, and still, Issai had barely escaped with his guts still intact. The game had changed somehow, apparently sometime when his back had been turned for him to have missed something this big brewing. Whose side were the gods on anyway?

He grabbed Issai's arm urgently. "We can't fight this.

Forget Subu. We'll have to run, to the east—to Kodahn or Aideya or—"

Issai shook his arm loose. "I told you, we're *surrounded*. I feel movement coming from the east as well—a lot of movement. They were waiting for us. That's the only thing that makes sense. It's like every stray *Shi* decided to band together for this one big gamble. Somehow they knew we planned to come here, and they laid their trap accordingly."

He pointed to the swiftly advancing *Shi* to the south. "If the numbers are anything like *that*, we'll never make it through, even if we ran at top speed. Remember, back in Daisha, even though I had a head start, one of the mounted *Shi* managed to knock me to the ground. We don't have the advantage of the forest here. We'll be run down. Our only choice is to go west."

"Towards the Sorahn River?" Hahri asked incredulously. "You do know what season this is, don't you? Even if we can make it without running into any more ambushes, we would never make it across those rapids alive! The nearest bridge is in Ahshi, and it's a floater. They pulled it to the shore for the summer floods even before I left Niya for Daisha! Assuming there aren't *Shi* waiting for us there too! Why do you think they aren't bothering to advance on us from the west? I'm betting you remember the old language of the Forgotten Ones —Sorahn, 'the devourer.' The river is a better wall than any army of men!"

Time was running out. He could already see the first line of *Shi* marching on the edge of one of the northern farms.

If anything, his tirade only seemed to make Issai's jaw clench more stubbornly. "Better to drown than face capture again," he growled. "At least the rapids offer us a slim chance of escape. Here, we have no hand left to play, and *I will not be caught again*. What those bastards did to me the last time…"

Hahri forced himself to look away from him even as his heart sank to his feet. He didn't want to know what horrors swam in those eyes. He could not allow guilt to cloud the issue. Not now.

"We'll never make it across," he insisted, feeling the advancing *Shi* like the swing of an executioner's sword. "Can't we at least try to run—"

Suddenly he froze, nearly choking on his tongue as he was struck by a realization. Issai was right; he *was* an idiot, one of the jaw-dropping varieties. Forget drowning, they had a third option, one he couldn't believe he hadn't thought of earlier. The shock of seeing so many *Shi* moving like a real army must have made his brains leak out of his ears. The only problem was convincing the other boy it could work.

He caught and held Issai's eyes and asked seriously, "Do you trust me?"

For half a beat, Issai looked as if he had been slapped before he just—stilled. That was the only way

Hahri could think to describe what he was seeing. To say that the other boy was staring was a gross misnomer. You had to have some kind of emotion to stare, and what was now—*looking* back at him was something not quite human.

The air left his lungs as if he had been abruptly punched in the gut. This was not the pseudo-boy he enjoyed teasing, the Old Soul that was constantly walking the fine line between irritation and an unfathomable rage. This wasn't even the boy who could kill as ruthlessly as himself.

Between the space of a breath, an epiphany was born, one that should have made his senses scream *danger* instead of making him feel an irresistible urge to step closer. Hahri realized this was the first time the Violet-eyed Old Soul had shown him his true face—the face of an ancient creature masquerading as human. This was *Issai*. Until this moment, he had only known "Senn."

Looking at what thousands of years of life had created, Hahri couldn't help but wonder how anyone could view immortality as anything other than a curse —and what he had ever done to make the gods hate him so much they thought he deserved it.

For this Old Soul to show his true face now of all times—he must have royally and utterly screwed up. It was a question that should have never been asked, an unspoken taboo committed equal to the one Issai had committed back in the forest. However, unlike Issai, Hahri didn't believe this deliberate trespass could be as easily rectified as one committed by accident.

Still, if he didn't act soon, he might not ever get the chance. If they both died here, it was very probable that Issai would make sure they would never meet again. He had deciphered enough of the ancient boy's personality to understand that much. The curse had to end. He had to take the gamble. Time had run out.

Before Issai could react, Hahri shot forward, barely pausing as he lifted and threw the other boy over his shoulder like a sack of grain before sprinting towards the east where he knew another army of staffs yet unseen awaited them.

7

The thing that bothered him the most, Korin realized, was that he felt no pain. The moment he had begun to breathe more easily, the impact trauma in his back had also begun to fade. With the force that he had hit the door, he *should* have broken something, or at the very least shown the first signs of bruising.

However, not only did the monks declare him unmarked after careful examination, but the sword wound on his arm that they had also insisted on tending to had drastically changed as well. He had been shocked to see it scabbed over and looking days instead of moments old. He had been hurt countless times in the past, and nothing even remotely like this accelerated healing had occurred.

His world had drastically changed, and here he was,

ignorant of the new rules. How long had he waited for this day, prayed for this, and now that the gods had given him his first hint to the answers he so desperately sought, instead of feeling elated, he was drowning in unease.

Ever since that little girl had disappeared, he had been unable to think straight; his entire being seemed to hum as if it had absorbed and trapped the shock waves of his Gods' Voice. Though nowhere near the pain he had felt when he had tried to carry the child to his chambers, it was similar and just as disruptive, like a persistent itch he would never be able to scratch. If he did not find a remedy soon, he feared he would go mad within a tenday.

As it was, Korin wondered if he had wasted too much time already. His chances of finding her were rapidly fading with every beat even as the intensity of his newfound discomfort steadily increased. That he *had* to find her was the only thing he was certain of at this point.

Throughout the endless centuries of his lives, he had never reacted to anyone so strongly, so obviously unnaturally. Had that fleeting image of a redheaded girl he'd received signify that the red-eyed little girl was similar to him? Had she been reborn as he had with all memories of her previous life intact?

Whether he liked it or not, his path had irrevocably changed course.

Although dawn was only a couple of hours away, Korin didn't think he could spare even that much time no matter how beneficial the daylight. As soon as the monks left his room, he began to quickly gather what little possessions he had into a pack. He would need food, water—he wondered if the Prior was awake. He had to give some sort of an explanation before—

"You are leaving?"

Korin turned in surprise, his cloak halfway knotted at his neck. A tall, silver-haired man stood in his door-way, his stance hesitant as if unsure of his welcome. He immediately bowed his head before beckoning his visitor inside. Already, the gods seemed to be helping him.

"Prior Tourn, good, I was just on my way to see you," Korin said as he finished securing his cloak. "I do not know how much my Brothers have told you about our unexpected visitor."

The Prior sighed, looking every bit his seventy years. "Just that the child is responsible for tonight's commotion—" He paused, as if not sure he should continue. Then, "—that touching his skin causes you both pain when no one else is similarly affected."

There was an unspoken question in his eyes, as well as a hint of fear. Although Korin had no answers as to the cause of the strange affliction, the fear, on the other hand, was something he understood only too well. Luckily, he didn't think anyone else had seen the color of her eyes. While some of the older superstitions had been lost to time, there were those that still believed red- or pink-eyed children to be the offspring of demons or various malevolent spirits rather than just a strange whim of the gods. Taken together, it only led to a very troubling picture. The last thing he needed was for the waters to get any murkier.

"Trust me when I say that the child is not what you think, though I do believe it is the gods' will that I find her. The signs given me allow for no other course."

"'Her?' I was told the child was a boy."

"Yes, I thought so too in the beginning, but the child is undeniably female. She may be even older than I first thought."

If anything, the Prior looked even more troubled. "I saw the damage to the statues. How could a little girl accomplish that?"

Korin smiled wryly. While packing, he had finally noticed that the sword he had propped against the wall next to the door was gone. Somehow she had managed to snatch it back right under his nose on her way out. His Brothers had surely mentioned it to the Prior, so hopefully, the older man wouldn't ask about it now. The man had enough on his plate as it was without him adding to his worries needlessly.

"I have a feeling that is going to be the least of my worries. The sooner I find her, the sooner I can try to make sense of all of this."

"Where will you go?" the Prior asked. The question was said a bit offhandedly like his mind was on something else, or it wasn't what he really wanted to ask.

Korin decided not to question him about it. "For the moment, I plan to wander the city. Somebody must have seen the child. Even if she has left, perhaps the gods will see fit to send me a messenger to point me in the right direction. Whatever that girl is looking for, she did not find it at this temple. She may seek out another. If I cannot find any leads here, I shall try the temples at Kairash or Rihott."

"Or you can just stay here," the Prior suggested. "In time, she may return on her own."

Korin shook his head. It was already becoming increasingly harder to stand still. "Even now, something within me has become restless. I am afraid it means my time on this earth may finally be coming to an end. I must find the girl before that happens. I believe this is the task I have been waiting for all these long centuries."

The Prior regarded him for a long moment, his fingers absently smoothing the wrinkles in his robe. Korin had forgotten that even Prior Tourn became uncomfortable with him when so blatantly reminded of how long Korin had truly lived.

"Will you return?" he finally asked, some of the tension melting from his shoulders.

The ancient monk smiled. "If the gods will it. Everything before me has once again become uncertain. All I can do is follow the path that has been placed before me and hope in the end all the answers will be waiting."

The older man nodded though his eyes were still troubled. "Just be careful, my brother. I have heard many whispers of late that war may be brewing. Several of the local lords have been sending out their garrisons beyond the city for unknown purposes, and many foreign guardsmen have been seen passing through the city. I don't want you to be inadvertently caught up in whatever is stirring."

ONLY WHEN KORIN had been walking the streets and alleys for some time, talking to various shop owners and peddlers who seemed most likely to have seen his missing "boy," did it occur to him that the Prior had been concerned with more than his safety. Like many Priors before him, it was possible that he had not wanted him to leave the temple. How often had the old man lamented on the state of the city, how he feared things may begin to spiral downwards again.

Upon his first arrival to Aideya, despite his misgivings, Korin had agreed to the Prior's plea of demonstrating his Gods' Voice for the masses. The Prior had hoped to remind the less scrupulous that though the gods no longer walked the earth, they were still watching, that the gods had sent one of their most powerful servants to see that justice was done.

While the city was by no means crime free, it had gotten a little better during the five years he had taken residence in the temple, using his gift to occasionally dispel the worst of the violence during his daily outings among the masses. Hopefully, he had done enough for everything to balance out on its own in time.

He didn't like the idea that the temples he visited could possibly come to rely solely on his work, or worse, have that very expectation from the beginning. That's why he stayed at each temple no longer than ten years and sometimes left even earlier. He was no god, and more often than not, he found himself reminding his fellow Brothers of that fact. He was a servant, no more, no less.

Perhaps it was better that circumstances had forced him to leave his current temple sooner than planned. If it was one thing he had learned throughout his many lives, it was that the gods had reason even in what seemed like chaos.

The ancient monk sighed in frustration as he rested for a moment on one of the stone benches that circled the city's main sundial, watching the people around him going about their daily business as he sipped from a water skin. What he would give for a little more of that reason right now to settle the chaos his mind and senses had become. Even now, his entire being was protesting his current immobility in the form of the vibrations within him flaring stronger to a point beyond mere annoyance.

As if that weren't bad enough, it was beginning to seem as if the little girl had simply dropped out of the sky last night. Korin had thought that surely *someone* had noticed what looked like a ten-year-old boy wandering around alone, especially if this little boy was carrying a sword, but the child might as well have been a phantom for all the information several hours of searching and questioning had produced.

"Brother Korin."

He started, almost falling off the bench when his body reflexively turned towards the unexpected voice at his ear. A scruffy, redheaded boy of about ten stood behind him, failing to contain his laughter as he watched the monk try to steady himself. "Geen—"

Over the years he had lived in Aideya, Korin had earned the respect of a small group of very young street kids that had essentially adopted him as their older brother when they realized that his interest in helping them was genuine. However, most of the older kids would have nothing to do with him or any other monk. To this day, he still did not know where any of them slept. Trust only went so far with children born to the streets.

The boy climbed onto the bench beside the older man and sat back onto his haunches. "Heard you're lookin' for a kid," Geen said, reaching into Korin's partially opened pack and pulling out an apple. Whenever he walked the streets of the city, Korin always brought a pack full of fruit to hand out to the children. Geen had never been shy about claiming his share. "Brown hair, kinda reddish eyes? I might know some'in, 'specially if you haven't found 'im."

"You know the boy then?" Korin asked hopefully.

He almost sighed with relief. Finally, things would start moving along again. That thought instantly brought him up short. Since when had he become so impatient? For the first time since this had all begun, he felt his heart flutter with fear. Just what was happening to him?

Geen shook his head. "Nobody does. Must be from someplace else or somebody's kid. We just thought you should know that them slavers from Nihara and Yuzu've been sniffing for prey again, case your boy might've been snatched. None of us's missin' as far's we can tell, but one of the older boys said he saw them Norin bastards over by the veggie market early this mornin' loadin' barrels into their wagons and leavin' real quick, so they must've caught *somebody*, right?"

Korin felt his stomach sink to his knees. First, the Prior warns him of foreign guardsmen in the city, and now both the Norin clan and the Mahze clan were seen in the same city! Just what exactly was going on? No, more importantly, was the reason he couldn't find the girl because she had been abducted by slavers after running from the temple last night? He was only one man. How could he ever hope to rescue her from slavers, even if he did have the Gods' Voice?

"Your friend didn't happen to hear where these wagons were going did he?" Korin asked urgently.

He shrugged. "He didn't say, but nobody else saw them wagons this far up'n the city so probably wasn't Kairash or Maida. Probably goin' home."

"And the Mahze clan?"

The redhead wrinkled his nose. "Now that's really got kids scared. We see 'em skulking around at night, but every time somebody tries to follow 'em back to where they're stayin' it's like the night swallows 'em up or some'in. All's I know they were still here last night."

He wasn't sure what to think about that. With any luck, he wouldn't have to for a long while. One problem at a time.

"Thank you, Geen. You have helped me more than you realize." Korin dug a couple more apples from his pack and gave them to the boy. "Take these to your friends. It seems I may be leaving Aideya for a while. I fear something dangerous is beginning to stir in the wind, so I want you children to be especially careful from now on. Tell the others to stop trying to trail anyone they may think is part of the Mahze clan. Brother Kal will still be here in the city every day so don't be hesitant to approach him."

Geen slid off the bench and looked down at the apples in his arms then back at him. "Maybe you could bring oranges next time," he said before sprinting off into the crowd.

Korin immediately felt guilty. Although this wasn't by far the first city he had left behind, he couldn't help but feel he had somehow betrayed the trust of all the people he had promised his aid and counsel. Unfortunately, the world was just too heavy for one man's shoulders. At least he tried to tell himself that.

Grabbing his pack, he turned towards the marketplace. At least this was something he could do. One person at a time amounted to a lot in the long run. Perhaps one of the other stall owners knew what city the "vegetable peddlers" had planned to visit next.

Unfortunately, after talking to several people, he once again found himself at a dead end. Most of the local farmers who owned a stall paid little to no attention to the constantly changing faces of non-natives who stayed only a tenday or two at a time. His only concession to his conscience was that at least he was able to spread the word to everyone he questioned that there were slavers "hunting" within the city again even if it seemed he had just wasted precious time.

As he was passing a group of peddlers, pondering his next move, he would have missed one of them calling out to him had the man not grabbed his arm. "Sorry to bother you, Brother, but I think I might be able to help you. Though I don't know the peddlers you speak of, being of Nihara, if they are heading back home, most like they'd make a stop over in Rihott along the way to rest the horses. My farm's a bit south of Rihott, and if you don't mind waiting an hour or so as I finish up my business, then it would be no trouble for me to drop you off in Rihott on my way home. Mind, you'd have to ride in the back of my wagon as I've only got the one horse..."

Mind? Korin could've wept for joy. It was still a long shot that the girl was with the slavers and that they were indeed on their way back to Nihara, but he had to admit that it was the best clue he had at the moment. Walking around Aideya had gotten him no closer to her, and the vibrations within him were still getting worse by the moment. Perhaps that, in itself, was a sign from the gods that he was on the wrong path, that he needed to leave the city. He didn't know, but after the frustrations of the day, he was willing to go on a little faith.

He bowed his head. "I am in your debt."

As promised, less than a couple of hours later found Korin riding in the back of a small, uncovered wagon next to a couple of sacks of beets and wondering if he was, in fact, still thinking lucidly. Yes, he was on his way to Rihott, but he had no clue what he was going to do once he got there.

He had never dealt directly with any slavers, so he had no idea what to expect, or really, how to recognize them once he got there. There could be dozens of vegetable peddlers in the city carting around wagons filled with barrels. What was he going to do, sneak onto the wagons, wagons that were probably heavily guarded, and knock on all the barrels while trying not to be seen in hopes of hearing the cries of children?

Suppose he did, the gods forbid, hear cries. How would he ever hope to set them free? The slaver clans had long ago infiltrated the Guard, so going to them was always risky. Using his Gods' Voice to incapacitate any guardsmen would only alert others. He had yet to find a way to silently use his gift.

Korin tangled his fingers in his hair and yanked in frustration. How had his path become so twisted so quickly? Only last night he had been silently reading amongst the likenesses of the gods, praying for enlightenment. Instead, he had only received more questions, and what was beginning to seem like a hopeless task.

However, hopeless task or not, he was a servant of the gods, and if this were the fate chosen for him, then he would see it to its end, even if that end was himself. He had already lived more lifetimes than any man could ever hope to experience. Eternal death was something he was long overdue for anyway. He was the last person who had the right to begrudge the gods for that.

There was always reason in chaos.

It was an hour into nightfall when they finally reached the outskirts of Rihott. By this time, Korin was so edgy that he could barely force himself to sit still. The closer they had gotten to Rihott, the lesser the vibrations within his body had seemed to hum, which convinced him even more that the strange affliction was the gods' way of showing him whether or not he was on the right path.

The streets of the city were almost deserted, even along the Traveler's District, though the taverns were as bright and boisterous as usual. Still unsure about how best to proceed, Korin had the farmer drop him off in front of an inn he had often frequented in his last life. He had known the owner well, and if the man still lived, it was a good place to go for information. He could plot rescue scenarios all he wanted, but even the best-laid plan would be for naught if the slavers weren't even in the city.

The ancient monk smiled in relief when a familiar, though slightly grayer head turned in greeting at the door. "Welcome, Brother." The innkeeper's eyes fell on the pack slung over his shoulder. "Just stopping for dinner, or will you be needing a room?"

His gaze flickered back to Korin's face, and then he suddenly gasped and jerked back a step as if he had suddenly been stabbed.

"Hello Ruyek," Korin said, smiling gently. No matter how many times he had lived this particular situation, the reactions were always the same. "It's good to see you again."

"Brother...K-Korin?" the man stuttered, his eyes wide in disbelief.

When the ancient monk nodded, Ruyek collapsed to his knees as if he were trying to prostrate himself before him. After the innkeeper had dropped his hands to the floor, Korin realized with horror that that was exactly what the man was trying to do and that they were also starting to attract the attention of the inn's other patrons.

He rushed over to Ruyek before the man could press his face to the floor and asked if he was all right in a voice loud enough to carry into the adjoining common room.

As he raised his old friend back to his knees, Korin whispered urgently into the trembling man's ear, "As I told you before, I am no god for you to bow in worship." Over the other's shoulder, he saw Ruyek's wife rushing over to them from the stairs. He continued hurriedly, "I think it best if we continue this conversation elsewhere. I do not wish for others to know I am Korin just yet."

To his relief, the innkeeper nodded and rose onto shaky legs just as his wife reached them. "Ruyek! What happened?" she demanded, her eyes swimming with growing fear.

Before Korin could reply, her husband said, "Nothing to worry about; just felt a bit dizzy for a moment. It's already passed."

"You should sit for a while anyway," she said, eyeing

Ruyek skeptically before glancing over at Korin and nodding a greeting. "I will tend to our guest."

Ruyek hastily shook his head. "This Brother is here on Temple business. Could you and the children handle the customers for a moment while we speak upstairs?"

Her eyes became troubled again as she looked between the two men, but she nodded anyway and without a word, headed to the door to greet a couple of new patrons.

"Come," his old friend said quietly, "we can talk in my personal rooms."

Ruyek led him up the stairs to the third floor and into a familiar sitting room where in his past life Korin and a few others had often gathered for a night of camaraderie.

After accepting a mug of heated cider, the two men settled across from each other at the family dining table. "What gave me away?" Korin asked as a way to break the tense silence.

The innkeeper had avoided looking at him directly since they had entered the room, but at the question, he finally raised his gaze. "It was the eyes," Ruyek said without hesitation. "Every time you looked at me, it was as if one of the gods was looking through them at me in judgment. The same is true as you sit before me now, no matter that the color of them has changed."

Korin grimaced. It was as he suspected. "I am here merely to serve. Only the gods truly have the right to judge. It is in that service that I have come to Rihott tonight."

Some of the tension in the older man's shoulders ebbed, making Korin wonder what the other man had thought his arrival signified. His friend had obviously been thinking the worst, whatever that may have been for him or his family.

"Then you've come to minister to our city again?" Ruyek ventured. "That'll make Prior Sett happy. He was so devastated after your—death."

Korin shook his head regretfully. "I fear my path lies elsewhere. I have come here in search of a child."

The innkeeper blinked in surprise. "And you think I might have seen this child? Is that why you came here and not the temple?"

"No, not the child, but perhaps her abductors."

Ruyek's expression turned thunderous. "This wouldn't have anything to do with that caravan that rolled through a few hours ago, would it? Some of the local farmers were not at all pleased to see them."

Korin clutched the mug in his hand more tightly. "Please tell me that they have not left..."

"I heard they rented a stall down at the marketplace for a couple of days. Some of them are probably still down there guarding what didn't sell today if they plan to have another go at it tomorrow."

The ancient monk slumped in his chair. "Thank the gods." He leaned towards the other man and said seriously, "Listen very closely, Ruyek. If this caravan is the same vegetable peddlers I have pursued from Aideya, then the children of this city are in danger. They are not mere farmers but men of the Norin clan of Nihara."

Comprehension dawned in the other's eyes. "Slavers."

"I believe the little girl I seek might have been abducted last night in Aideya after leaving my current temple. I must find her at all costs."

"This child, who is she?"

Korin contemplated how to respond for a moment before deciding that here, the complete truth was best. He was in no position to cut corners. "Perhaps one that shares my fate."

His friend's eyes widened. "You don't mean..."

He nodded. "That is why I must find her, and if in the process I can save a few more unfortunate children from a terrible fate, then that is even better."

Ruyek fell silent for a moment. "Maybe I can help," he said slowly. "I have a few friends in the Guard, as is my youngest son. They will at least know where any caravans have settled their wagons for the night, and if I may be so bold, the experience in raiding one that will likely be more guarded than most."

Korin shook his head regretfully. "Slavers have been known in the past to kill the children out of spite when cornered. If they were to suspect the Guard was moving against them—"

The innkeeper smiled in a way that made him look exactly like the man Korin had last seen eighteen years ago. "Who says it'll be the Guard? Maybe a band of thieves will decide their caravan looks like a goldmine. The gods know that enough of them plague this city so an attack wouldn't make anyone suspicious. A thief stumbling across a bunch of children may even set them free as a distraction for his escape. Maybe it'll even make those pieces of scum think twice about trying to take children from Rihott again."

"I will be unable to use the Gods' Voice to help if we are discovered," he warned. "I will offer up my own life rather than risk harming the children with my gift. Also, the noise would undoubtedly point a finger straight to me, and as an extension, to the Temple. I would not have my Brothers in the path of any inevitable retaliation triggered by my own choices."

"Can't say *I'd* want to accidentally experience that power of yours," Ruyek agreed with a shudder. "I heard you had some of those criminals bleeding out of their eyes after you flattened them. Still, my offer stands regardless of that decision."

Korin was torn. He had not expected that his old friend would want to get involved in something so dangerous. Thus it was an angle he hadn't even considered on the journey from Aideya. Now, armed with a few more facts, his head knew that this was something he really could not do alone, but he had also lived for thousands of years and was no longer capable of deluding himself into thinking that this whole crazy endeavor couldn't end badly. A thousand years was a long time to have to carry the burden of blood-stained hands, especially if it was the blood of friends.

It was the humming within his body that ultimately reminded him that he could not afford to fail here. "If I agree to accept your aid," he said reluctantly, "then it must be done tonight. I dare not wait any longer. If the slavers manage to leave the city, then I have almost no hope of rescuing them."

The innkeeper rose from his chair. "Then come. Let us find us some thieves."

8

———

t first, all Issai could see was streaks of green, moving as if he were flying above some strange sea. For half a beat, he had been utterly bewildered. Then something thick and black flew up onto his face, plunging him into darkness, and he suddenly realized what exactly was digging into his stomach.

He was beyond livid. That *idiot* had—

He opened his mouth to snarl the other boy's name, but then his body lurched forward, and he nearly choked on the wad of cloth that entered his mouth when he inadvertently gasped. He tried to raise a clenched fist to bat the infuriating cloth away, but a heavy weight seemed to be pushing against his arms. His fury dissolved into shock when he found he could barely even move them. What in the name of the gods was going on?

In a panic, Issai wrenched his head to the side, and then his eyes nearly bugged out of his head. There were *Shi* everywhere, lined up and still as if they were lifelike statues blurring past him, some with their arms and legs raised in mid-stride, as Hahri raced through the open spaces between them. Issai only had time to blink twice before the still soldiers disappeared, only to be replaced with an equally still landscape of fields of high grasses and trees.

A chill ran down his spine that had nothing to do with the cold air slicing past him. He wanted to scream at Hahri to stop, but it was all he could do to suck enough air into his lungs through the pressure that was crushing his upper half against the other's back. Instead, he settled on smacking the other boy as hard as he could manage on his lower back with a fist that, thankfully, was still clutching a knife. What he *should* have done was ram that same knife into the bastard's back, but Issai was in enough pain already as his fist's sharp impact flared instantaneously in his own back.

What he didn't count on was his face slamming hard into Hahri's back as the other stumbled, coming to a bone-crushing halt that sent both of them crashing to the ground into a chaotic roll. The world was definitely moving again, alternating between blues and greens as Issai struggled to stop himself.

By the time his body came to a stop with the sky swirling madly across his blurred vision, Issai was certain he had broken every bone in his body. He gagged and turned his head to the side, spitting out a mouth full of blood and dirt and who knows what else before collapsing back onto his back.

For a long moment, all he could do was close his eyes and concentrate on getting enough oxygen to his abused lungs as every inch of his body hummed with pain. He could feel warmth leaking from his nose, but at this point, he was beyond caring.

That is until what felt like a *Shi's* staff slammed into his right side. Something heavy fell beside him as Issai grunted in shock, his arms curling protectively around his ribs even as his eyes flew open in enough time to see the fist coming at his face. Pure centuries-honed reflexes were the only thing that saved him from probable oblivion as Issai jerked his face out of the way before his fuzzy mind could even realize the danger. His hands twitched in his usual automatic response, and only then did he realize he was no longer holding his knives.

Then a voice started ranting unintelligibly somewhere above him and the panic he was beginning to feel died instantly. His ears may have been ringing too loudly to make out any words, but the voice was unmistakable. Not moving became a viable option again.

Gradually, discernable phases began to filter through the haze. "*Stupid* idiot...do you want to die that badly? I should have...should have...drowned you in those stupid rapids instead! Of all the crazy..."

Issai slowly opened his eyes again and was greeted by the dirty and blood-stained face of his companion, Hahri's blue eyes blazing mad and his nose bleeding same as his. His hair was a nest of tangles and grass, and his clothes were torn in several places. The ancient boy looked as though he had been on the losing end of a particularly brutal tavern fight.

He absently noted that Hahri was also nursing the same side where, he realized now, the other boy had apparently kicked him. That irritating connection between them could get very interesting in the future if they decided to get into any more fist fights with each other. He frowned. *Or anyone else for that matter.*

"Like I knew that was going to happen," Issai muttered, then spat in disgust as more blood trickled into his mouth.

Rolling his eyes, Hahri untangled him from his cloak and carefully helped him sit up despite his protests. "Don't worry; I don't think anything's broken."

Issai moved his arms and legs experimentally anyway. "You mean besides our noses?" he replied sarcastically as he wiped at the blood beneath his nose with the hem of his tunic. "Hopefully your ribs are since mine feel as if something's been chewing on them. Just what the hell did you think you were doing? No, forget that. Where in the three hells are we?"

All around them lay grassy hills with a small spattering of solitary trees. Not a farm or road was in sight. He didn't recognize any of the landmarks around them.

Hahri shrugged. "Somewhere between Kodahn and Rihott."

Issai stared at him. "You're joking."

"Does it look like I'm in a joking mood?" he demanded. "We would be in Rihott right now if you hadn't tripped me up back there."

"But—" He was staggered. "That's around thirty spans! You couldn't have been running for more than a few moments!"

"I told you about this before. Speed is my specialty. Weren't you paying attention?"

Issai was just too astonished to take offense at the chastising tone. "How could everything just—stop?"

The ancient boy laughed. "Of course it didn't. It's just we were moving faster than our eyes could perceive movement. At least that's what I think."

Issai considered. "Yeah," he said slowly, "I guess that makes sense, though it's still unsettling. I wish you would have told me what you planned to do beforehand. Perhaps then I wouldn't have been so impatient for answers."

"Yeah right," Hahri scoffed. "You would have argued, and we definitely didn't have the time. Just admit it already; it's in your nature. The important thing is that we're still alive with nothing worse than a broken nose, and speaking of which, do you think you can heal yourself without passing out?"

Issai bit back the first thing he wanted to say and considered. It was a good question, after all. "I don't know. I've never tried it on an injury that wasn't life-threatening. After what happened in Subu, I don't think we can afford the risk."

"Can you at least stop the blood?" Hahri persisted. "It's *your* nosebleed, so anything I do to myself would be incredibly pointless. I'm still waiting for my body to crash, and losing blood is not going to help matters any."

Issai looked at him sharply. "What do you mean 'crash'?"

Hahri grinned at him sheepishly. "The same thing that happens to yours after you heal, except I don't pass out. Which, I'll admit, doesn't really account for much since I won't have the strength to move for a few hours. Why do you think I don't always run that fast? I could have made it to Rihott, but that would have been my limit."

"You didn't think I needed to know about this earlier?" Issai accused angrily, suddenly remembering the identical pain he had felt in his back the instant he had punched the other boy during the run. "We're in the middle of nowhere with an army in pursuit, and you're telling me that forget running, any time now you won't be able to even stand?"

Although Hahri had not lost consciousness along with him back in the cave, how did he know the same would be true for him in regards to the other's exhaustion? Their reactions to each other so far seemed to be on opposite sides of the same pole. The probability of them both collapsing was something he hadn't even considered.

His anger didn't even seem to faze the ancient boy. If anything, it seemed as if he was no longer paying attention, his eyes focused inward. Issai's anger was quickly being replaced with irritation. Maybe the bastard's fatigue was already starting.

He contemplated giving the other boy a shake, but Hahri's eyes re-focused on him before he could even lift a finger. "You know," he said, "now that I think about it, I should have collapsed as soon as I tried to pick myself up after I stopped rolling. Even now, sure I'm tired, but no more than if I had just come off a regular, but long, run. I haven't run that fast since that time I needed to catch you after you decked me. Before—"

"—before that connection started between us," Issai finished for him, that sinking feeling he had gotten from his earlier thoughts growing. "You didn't collapse that time either."

"I wasn't expecting to. It took me only a moment to catch you. True, even running that short amount of time I should have been exhausted, but after we touched souls—"

"Right," Issai interjected uncomfortably. "It's an interesting theory, but I healed my arm after all of that and fell unconscious as usual. Why would I not be similarly affected?"

Hahri held up a hand between them. "Just let me finish. I didn't expect to collapse that time in the forest, but we both know something did change at that moment. When our souls touched and you pushed me away, that was the first time—that was the first time I felt—pain."

He said it almost grudgingly, but Issai said nothing. He had a feeling he knew why it was so hard for the smaller boy to admit such a thing—and also why he had felt he should. Repaying a debt was never easy...

Hahri wiped at the blood trickling over his lips with a grimace and continued, "The nearer I am to you, the greater the pain. I can't even begin to guess why, or if you're even affected the same way, but for now, that's not important. What is important is that the only time I have felt complete relief was when we touched souls again back in Nisei—and just now when I carried you."

Issai went completely still. "Are you feeling pain now," he couldn't help asking.

"Yes." He couldn't read the expression in the other's eyes, but something about it still set him on edge. This conversation was quickly heading into dangerous waters.

"Are you trying to say that you think the connection between us is getting stronger?" Issai asked quietly.

"How did you know *Shi* were coming at us from the north and east?" Hahri shot back instead of answering.

Already feeling incredibly unbalanced and a bit lightheaded from probably both shock and blood loss, Issai was not prepared for this seemingly out of the blue rejoinder. He had forgotten this particular quirk of Hahri's, so before he could stop himself, he answered honestly, "After the second time we touched—souls, I can somehow sense the distortions in the air more clearly. The air was practically roaring at me from behind. My skin crawled with it. I thought it was something that would disappear since our souls were no longer touching, but it never did."

"Well, there's your answer. Care to reconsider the healing?" Hahri grinned suddenly, which looked plain wrong coming from such a dirty and bloodied face. "Even Old Souls need blood, and it doesn't look like your nosebleed is planning on stopping anytime this century."

Still, Issai hesitated. Although he had already placed his life in Hahri's hands once when he hadn't even known him well, it didn't mean he was itching to do it again.

Hahri sighed. "Look, it's all right even if you still pass out. Give me an hour's rest, and I can carry you the rest of the way to Rihott, no problem."

"But the *Shi*—"

He snorted. "If those *Shi* make thirty spans in a day then I'll eat your knives."

"Yes, the knives. You do realize that since you're the reason I lost them in the process of eating dirt, you're going to help me find them."

Hahri looked back at him dubiously. "You and your stupid knives. You're just lucky that you didn't manage to cut your own balls off during all of that."

Instead of the usual anger, Issai was almost surprised when he voiced the thought that came, unbidden, to his mind, "Just think about what you said for a moment before you go wishing such travesties on me." To drive his point home, he pinched himself hard on the arm and watched the other boy wince in surprise.

The look on Hahri's face when the insinuation sank in was enough to make Issai laugh for the second time in a tenday. Maybe having this loud-mouthed Old Soul around wasn't so bad after all.

"Now that's just sadistic," Hahri complained, but he was smiling, too.

However, all mirth was lost instantly when Issai found himself spitting out yet another bit of blood that had trickled into his mouth. That, more than anything else, finally decided him.

"All right," he said, wiping irritably beneath his nose, "I'll try the healing. Just make sure you catch me if

I start falling forward. It would be annoyingly ironic if I were to wake up with the damn thing broken again."

Hahri scooted closer. "Maybe I should hold your arm or something, in case the contact is needed."

Issai opened his mouth to protest—he still was uncomfortable with people in his personal space, much less touching him—but he forced himself to nod. Right now passing out was the greater evil. After being completely blindsided in Subu, it would be stupid not to take every precaution.

He did his best to ignore the slight pressure on his arm and the relief to his own separation pain that the contact brought him and focused on the throbbing in the center of his face. He idly wondered if his eyes had started to blacken as well, but dismissed it when he remembered that Hahri's had not.

He concentrated on feeling out every aspect of the injury, the edges of the fractures, the torn tissue, and the ruptured blood vessels and released his silent command. As before, all the warmth left his extremities and converged on his nose, followed by the usual temperature discomfort and finally, relief.

He waited.

"Now that was just weird," Hahri abruptly said inches from his ear, nearly causing Issai to jump out of his skin. "For a moment, the pain caused by you being so close went away, and I started to feel kind of numb.

That didn't happen the first time when you healed our arms."

Issai realized two things at once, that the other boy was studying his face closely as he talked and that he was still conscious to notice this. No, not only just conscious, but only feeling slightly more fatigued than before the healing.

He turned his head away with a scowl and raised an appraising hand to his nose. His fingers smeared a bit of blood on his upper lip, but nothing was currently streaming out of his nostrils, nor was the nose, itself, tender.

He wiped the remaining blood off with the back of his hand as he looked back at his companion's face. Hahri's nose was no longer a red ruin of flesh but straight and un-swollen. With a start, Issai realized that, in a way, Hahri had become a strange kind of mirror—at least as far as his own injuries were concerned.

"Okay," he said with a smirk, "now you can help me find my knives."

9

The situation was near to hopeless, just as Korin had feared.

Ruyek's son, Shimil, and another guard had snuck over to spy on the slaver's caravan. Their grim faces when they had returned to the inn said it all before they even spoke. The only remotely good news they had had to report was that the two men no longer held any doubts that those particular peddlers were, if not slavers, then something other than vegetable farmers.

The caravan had settled themselves for the night in one of the southern pastures of a nearby sheep farmer. It was composed of three, relatively tall, hide-covered wagons tethered together to form a triangle. The wagons were nowhere near any boundary fences or anything else that could be used to conceal any of the twenty men Ruyek had managed to recruit. They were set up in the open as if they *expected* an attack. Not even the grasses were high enough to hide more than a man's boots. Sneaking up on them unseen would be next to impossible.

Unfortunately, that meant there was no way of knowing just how many, if any, men were within each wagon before attacking, or where the barrels Geen had mentioned were stored. However, that was the least of their worries since Shimil had counted twelve guards posted in pairs, swords in hand, protecting every exposed, outer side and back entrance of each wagon and at least three more within the open-aired center the triangle of wagons had formed.

The friends Ruyek had assembled consisted of three bowmen, five street patrol guardsmen, and the rest part of one of the City Guard's many foot units. After a short debate, it was decided that there was no getting around the fact that they would have to wound as many from a distance as they could before openly charging the wagons. Korin would follow closely behind those of the foot unit and along with Shimil, try to infiltrate the wagons during the melee.

They had snuck onto the sheep farmer's property from the northern end and were now situated behind a small barn, the closest structure in the line of sight of the caravans. Ruyek had stayed behind with the wagon they had arrived in, waiting to haul them back to Rihott.

Korin fidgeted uncomfortably as he listened to all

the last moment instructions whispered among the disguised guardsmen. He was dressed as they were in dark trews, tunic, and cloak with the hood up and over the top portion of his face for concealment. A thin, linen scarf had also been wrapped loosely around his mouth and nose until only a narrow patch of skin was visible on his face. He had not worn anything other than his loose-fitting monk's robes since he was a toddler, and he could not help but feel a bit claustrophobic in the unfamiliar clothing.

Someone nudged him, and he focused his eyes on the figure beside him. "Ready, Brother Korin?" Shimil whispered, his hand clutching his short sword so tightly that his whole arm trembled. He suddenly wondered how old the young man was and felt ashamed that he had not thought to ask sooner. Shimil had not been born during the time Korin had known his father. He didn't even look sixteen.

Korin gathered himself and nodded more calmly than he felt. "May the gods help us," he prayed with a quiet breath and watched the glint of the first three arrows streak across a faint, moonlit sky.

It was pure luck that this was happening today during a crescent moon and not a tenday later in the darkness of a moonless sky. It was just enough light to guide the eyes of the bowmen, but enough darkness to conceal their features.

His heart clenched when cries of pain shattered the

silent night, immediately followed by the twang of more arrows being fired. Slavers or not, deserving or not, he loathed being forced to cause others pain.

"Go!" a voice hissed behind him, and he was forced to leave his guilt behind as he was shoved after the already charging guardsmen.

Korin caught a glimpse of several moving shadows on the ground as the first of his comrades crashed head-on into the raised swords of the enemy before he was tugged sharply to the right and wide of five men engaged in a fierce battle.

"There! Under the wheels!" Shimil panted, and they both dove beneath the farthest wagon against the cacophony of clashing steel, curses, and moans.

Korin couldn't believe that they had gotten this far without being challenged, and determined not to waste this obvious answering of his prayers, he crawled towards the rear of the wagon without waiting to see if the other teen followed. Before he could reach his goal, he was abruptly pulled back by the end of his cloak with a panicked, "Brother!" His head jerked back, and that's when he saw it.

"There's a small hatch under here!" Korin whispered excitedly, already reaching for the wooden latch.

Shimil grabbed his arm. "There could be men within still waiting in ambush," he warned. "Let me try to peer into the rear opening first."

Feeling incredibly foolish at his near blunder, Korin

dropped his arm and nodded. He watched nervously as his friend's son carefully crawled to the rear, and after observing what he could see of the situation beyond the wagon, Shimil slowly emerged from the end and raised himself only enough to take a quick peek inside before crawling back to Korin's side.

"Looks like we two thieves struck gold," he grinned. "Nothing but barrels in this one."

The ancient monk sucked his breath in sharply, then without a word, he unbuckled the latch and allowed the small hatch to fall open.

"Go on; I'll stand guard down here."

Korin nodded and then hoisted himself up into the dark wagon. Squinting within the near total blackness, the monk could barely discern the outlines of five rows of tightly packed barrels that filled the front half of the wagon. Nothing larger than a mouse could possibly hide amongst them so he could see how Shimil could be so confident of its safety with just a single glance. Korin lowered his hood and the scarf covering his face and set to work.

The first barrel he experimentally shook gave a very distinctive *slosh*, and he almost panicked. Only the street children had seen any of the Norin's faces. Had he targeted the wrong caravan after all? Had they unwittingly caused harm to innocent men? He swallowed against the tightness rising in his already dry throat and forced himself to check the next barrel. There was no use in berating himself before he was absolutely sure he had mucked everything up.

He shook the barrels on either side of the first one, and something unnamable clenched in his chest when they too appeared to contain only liquid. Now seriously alarmed, Korin forced himself to carefully jostle one of the barrels on the second row.

Nothing sloshed.

He did it again, and his heart nearly stopped when he heard a scrape from within. As quietly as he could, he wedged the tip of a dagger one of the guardsmen had loaned him into the lid crease and began prying the wooden cover up slowly. The lid had surprisingly few nails keeping it shut, and within moments, he had it lifted enough to peer inside.

Although he had expected what he would find within, Korin was still unprepared for the horror that engulfed him when he saw the small face of a little boy looking up at him with eyes crazed with terror and a gag tightly wrapped around a frantically moving mouth. Hands and feet were bound together, then to each other, by thick coils of rope. It was one of the most pitiful and heartbreaking sights Korin had ever seen. He immediately reached in to try to cut the boy's bonds.

Upon seeing the dagger, the boy's eyes bulged wildly, and he began to struggle frantically against the ropes. "Shh, little one," Korin whispered urgently. "It's all right.

The gods have sent me to help you. Can you please be still for a moment so I can cut the ropes?"

Unfortunately, the child was too hysterical with fear, and no amount of gentle coaxing from the monk made the child stop thrashing. Feeling the short noose of time tightening around his neck, Korin decided to leave the boy for the moment and open the other barrels. If he found more children and had more success with calming and cutting their bindings free, then perhaps seeing other children free and unharmed would allow the boy to finally calm down enough for him to cut his bonds.

He pried the lids off every barrel that did not slosh with liquid and revealed several more terrified little boys and girls, all ranging in ages of about five to ten. To his immense relief, none of the others gave him trouble after his assurance of rescue, and one of the oldest girls even offered to help the first little boy he had found while he searched more barrels.

Only when Korin had freed the last child from a barrel and turned to organize them near the hatch did it hit him, and hit him hard.

None of the children had been the red-eyed girl.

10

He was going to kill him.

Issai could already picture it, the widening of those cerulean eyes as they slowly glazed over with shock, the opening of that infuriating mouth that could no longer utter a sound as he plunged his knife into his heart and sliced to the side through the lungs to steal his breath. After the last couple of hours he had endured, he was convinced the matching pain he would suffer would be totally worth it.

However, for the time being, Issai had to settle for merely kicking Hahri hard in the back of his knees and watching the other crumble rather disgracefully to the cobblestone street with what he swore was a squeak. Through a sheer act of will, he managed to stay on his feet when he felt the same blow.

A young couple passing on the other side of the

street paused to gape at them, and Issai hurriedly crouched at the fallen boy's side as if to help him up before the other could begin his howling. He winced when his damaged ribs protested the movement. To his relief, the couple moved on. He really shouldn't have done anything to attract attention, but...

The look in Hahri's eyes was smoldering mad.

Issai returned the glare without batting an eye. "*That* was payback for my bruised ribs," he growled before Hahri could open his mouth. "I don't care if you *are* feeling the same pain as me; it's still your fault for kicking me in the first place! Nothing more enjoyable than walking ten spans with several thousand knives stabbing into your chest with every step."

As much as he hated to admit it, it was all he could do to keep himself upright and walking instead of falling to his knees in tears of agony. Issai was beginning to think some of them may have cracked after all.

"Of course nothing is ever *your* fault, right," the ancient boy snarled back as he stiffly picked himself up. "And here I was trying to suck it up because I was feeling a little guilty about it. That'll definitely never happen again."

Hahri began stalking up the street again, but then immediately slowed his pace until Issai fell into step beside him.

"I'm not going to kick you again," Issai said irritably.

"The mood you're in, I'm more worried about getting

knifed in the back," Hahri replied dryly. "That's why I told you to heal yourself before we set off again, but no. You were too paranoid about passing out, never mind that you didn't before. How much more evidence do you need before you accept something as *fact*?"

"Fact? Neither one of us knows exactly what this weird connection between us is doing to us, let alone why. We both could have lost consciousness the second time. The fact of the matter is that we just can't make assumptions at this point of the game, so no matter how small the risk, I won't do something that may allow a *Shi* to capture me if it can be put off until later."

Hahri sighed. "All right, point taken. Let's just hurry up and check out the marketplace. If it still isn't the right place, then we can just grab some supplies and head up to Aideya next."

The smaller boy stumbled on a loose stone and immediately grabbed his right side with a grimace. "I really hope you plan on healing yourself sometime soon," he said plaintively. "Forget the *Shi*, if we get jumped by the regular city scum, then neither one of us will be worth much in a fight. There's a point when payback starts becoming pure masochism."

Issai scowled but said nothing as he was reminded that they both had been forced to abandon their packs in Subu when Hahri had abruptly carted him off. If Rihott wasn't the city they sought, then they would have to waste more time buying supplies. One of the few things they both agreed on was that they should avoid staying in or around cities as much as possible.

Neither one familiar with Rihott, they opted to follow a man pulling a small cart of apples rather than rely on Issai's new heightened sensibility to movement. Within a city, which in itself was a single moving entity, the ability was almost useless. Issai could just as likely lead them to a large tavern filled to bulging as to the marketplace.

Issai's skin steadily began to crawl more and more as they moved farther into the city until, finally, he was forcing himself not to rub at his arms, keeping them ramrod straight and his fists clenched at his sides.

"Something wrong?" Hahri asked softly. Of course, he would notice.

He shook his head. "Too many people," was all he said, but the answer seemed to satisfy his companion.

The crowds were beginning to thicken as they rounded a bend, and Issai could see the beginnings of merchant shops at the end of the street. He moved closer to Hahri and muttered out of the corner of his mouth, "Recognize anything?"

Blue eyes looked at him sideways. "No, but the vision seemed to be focused in the center of a bunch of peddler stalls, nothing permanent like a merchant shop."

Issai nodded and turned his attention back to the mass of people moving around and against them like a river current, eyes alert for anything remotely suspicious. The roar of a hundred voices and just as many different smells were now assaulting him from every direction, so only when someone elbowed him sharply on his uninjured side did he turn and notice that Hahri had been trying to get his attention. The look on the other boy's face was enough to halt whatever bit of irritation or anger that had been trying to claw its way to the surface.

An invisible hand seemed to squeeze his throat. "This is it?" he asked, hardly daring to believe.

"Without a doubt," Hahri said, his voice trembling with excitement. He pulled Issai away from the center of the street until they moved outside of the flow of market goers and into a space between two meat stalls. "Do you see that linen awning over that fruit stall?" he said, and Issai's eyes followed where his finger pointed and widened a bit in disbelief.

It was hard to miss. Which he suspected was the owner's intention, no matter that it was the most idiotic thing Issai had ever seen and that was saying something given he had lived for thousands of years. Someone had either stitched or painted a scene of apples, oranges, and an assortment of berries with hands and feet. Their hands were clasped together until they had formed what looked like a dancing circle, and all of this against a backdrop of an orchard next to a farmhouse. He didn't know whether to laugh or gag.

"Now I understand why you seemed so confident you'd recognize the right marketplace."

Hahri, on the other hand, did laugh. "Even blurry, there was no way in hell I wouldn't recognize something so ludicrous. I don't care how bad my sales were, I'd starve before resorting to something like *that* to attract buyers."

Issai snorted at his partner's words and turned his eyes back to the other stalls. "So this is the right place. What now? I know you said we were looking for two people, but without even knowing what they look like, it would be like looking for a single eyelash at the bottom of the sea."

Hahri shrugged, his expression undaunted. "For the moment, let's just go stand in front of that ridiculous fruit stall and see what happens."

Not really happy about the thought of standing in one place for any length of time but having no better plan to offer, after making sure his hood and bangs still covered his eyes, Issai reluctantly followed Hahri back into the crowd. Several people of all ages stood gawking at the absurd awning as well as those who were actually perusing the offered fruit. It was relatively simple for two teenaged boys to unobtrusively insert themselves into the group.

As Issai pretended to examine an apple while Hahri scanned the passing crowd for anything out of the ordinary, the conversation of two young women behind him caught his attention.

"...no, not that incident in Kodahn. It was here! Just this last night! Some thieves attacked a caravan! Apparently, a lot of gold and some of their food stock were stolen. Word is that some of 'em were even hurt right badly, too."

"No wonder there's been so many guardsmen pokin' around lately..." the other woman added. "I was scared that some more brigands had escaped their cells again or even that all those rumors of a foreign army trying to invade were really true, but thieves! That's just as bad in its own way."

And there's one right over there, Issai thought in amusement as, out of the corner of his eye, he watched a dark-haired boy of about ten a few stalls down filch an entire plucked chicken right from under the nose of the seller and the three patrons examining the different types of fowl the stall offered.

The boy was dressed too cleanly to be a street child, but not near well enough to be of noble stock. Perhaps he was from a family fallen on hard times; Issai had seen that often enough. Even the rich were not immune, much as they liked to think themselves gods among men.

Curious despite himself, Issai's gaze followed the child as he moved off into the crowd and instantly froze when he met the eyes of two men staring at him from the end of the street. His first thought was that perhaps these were the people they were looking for, but then he saw the long-staffs in their hands, instantly shattering that theory. Realizing they had been noticed, the men immediately began pushing their way through the crowd towards them.

"Shit!" he hissed, causing the woman directly behind him to gasp in shock as he grabbed Hahri's arm and began tugging him in the opposite direction without pausing to explain.

"Hey—Issai—what are you—!" Hahri sputtered as he struggled to keep up.

The fire in his ribs had flared white hot, so it was a moment before Issai could draw enough breath to bite out, "*Shi.*"

The word that was spat from Hahri's mouth caused Issai enough of a jolt that he almost tripped over his feet. How long had it been since he had heard that particular expletive? Never mind that, how was it that Hahri knew it in the first place? It seemed the two of them needed to have a very long overdue conversation. He glanced over his shoulder and saw one of the *Shi* had gained a bit of ground. That is, if they managed to get out of this newest predicament with their current bodies still intact.

The street curved into a public courtyard surrounded by more merchant buildings where several water wells flashed into view. A few people were hard at work drawing buckets of water to the surface. Most turned to gawk at them as they raced past, Issai still pulling Hahri's arm as his eyes frantically scanned ahead for the best path. That was when he finally noticed the dark line that had formed at the opposite end of the courtyard, effectively blocking every path in that direction.

With a curse, Issai skidded to a halt and dropped Hahri's arm. Another breath and his knives were in his hands. He turned towards the merchant shops to his left and swore again. The buildings had been built so close together that, unless they were a rat or cat, then there was no way they would be able to squeeze between them. A quick glance to the right showed him the same thing. Only one option left to them now.

He turned behind him and found Hahri already glaring in that direction. The people in the courtyard, realizing the impending danger, were already rushing back towards the marketplace, some even abandoning their pails in their haste. The initial two *Shi* had already made it into the courtyard, standing a few lengths away from them, their long-staffs held threateningly before them. That, in itself, would not have been cause for alarm as much as the half-dozen *Shi* that filed in beside them.

"What, are *Shi* in every city now?" Hahri said sarcastically through his teeth. "The world has surely gone to the gutter fast since my last life."

The line of *Shi* moved slowly towards them like the advancing frontline of an army.

"Now aren't you glad I made you help me find my knives," Issai said, his lips stretched into a grim line.

Hahri rolled his eyes. "Fine. If we make it out of this still in our same bodies, then I promise not to harp on them—as much."

Then the ancient boy shot forward faster than Issai could keep track, and the first *Shi* was already down before he could even move. He sensed the group behind him charging, but he only spared them a brief glance to gauge their positions before dashing forward himself, one of his knives stabbing into a *Shi*'s chest before the man even realized he had been attacked. He slashed out at the *Shi* to his left with the other knife, but he was barely able to graze his arm before the *Shi*'s staff knocked him hard in the chest.

Issai saw blackness for half a beat as a gut wrenching pain reverberated throughout his entire body. He involuntarily staggered back and briefly saw Hahri become more substantial than a black blur as he too stumbled, doubling over his own chest before desperately leaping out of the way of a long-staff aiming for his head.

Then Issai saw the two staffs descending on his head from behind and knew with a sick certainty that he would not be able to dodge them even as he forced his abused body to move.

"*STOP!*"

The command rang in his ears impossibly loud at the same time a force like the lash of a whip slammed into his back, knocking him into several *Shi* hard enough that his already-battered ribs screeched with agony. Another jarring impact in both his back and right side instantly followed, and then the world around him fell silent except for a faint ringing in his ears.

Groaning with pain, Issai forced pain-teared eyes open and was met with the blurred, unconscious face of a *Shi*. He automatically flinched away with an oath and cried out as pain engulfed his chest when he hit the cobblestones once again.

He must have blacked out for a moment because the next thing he became aware of was a hand touching his forehead. Eyes he hadn't realized were closed flew open in a panic, and his hand shot up in a familiar arc at the shadow looming over him. His fingers hit something soft, and Issai realized he didn't have a knife.

As Issai frantically struggled to sit up through the agony, something bubbled up in his throat, as if he were about to be sick. He stopped struggling, turned his head to the side, and coughed violently, spewing warmth from his mouth.

Struggling to breathe, he heard an unfamiliar tenor voice say almost hysterically, "I'm sorry; I'm sorry! The gods help me, I am sorry! I never meant to hurt you so terribly...I cannot believe you are..."

At first, he was confused. Why would a *Shi* be apologizing for hurting *him*? Then, as he wheezed painfully, the figure leaning over him began to slowly come into focus, and Issai saw a blond-haired young man staring down at him with worried, dark eyes. A man wearing the white robes of a monk...

"Who are you?" he rasped out, then tasting something metallic and salty, spit in disgust when he realized his mouth was once again full of blood. He wiped his lips with the back of his hand. This was quickly becoming a reoccurring condition he would just as soon live without.

However, before the monk could answer, Issai heard someone else coughing wetly somewhere to his left, and he once again struggled to sit up. Hahri! This time, he managed to stay sitting up and turned towards the coughing. The other boy was on his knees, but barely, one arm wrapped protectively around his chest while the other held himself aloft enough to keep his face from the stones as he, too, coughed up a bit of blood.

"Another one..." the monk voiced in disbelief. "Do not move," he told Issai as he stood and rushed over to Hahri.

Issai didn't understand why the monk sounded so surprised, but now wasn't the time for questions. The man was obviously not a *Shi* in disguise, or else he would have run screaming at the first sight of an Old Soul's blood. Nevertheless, monk or no, he didn't like the fact that both he and Hahri appeared so vulnerable before a stranger.

Careful not to jostle his ribs further, he slowly slid onto his knees, an arm emulating Hahri's around his chest. Pausing to suck in a couple of painful breaths of air that was now almost shockingly cold, Issai slowly rose to unsteady feet, biting his lip hard as a fresh wave of agony crashed into his chest when he tried to straighten.

"You masochistic idiot!" Hahri wailed. "Don't try to stand up! I'm about to *die* here!"

Unfortunately, Issai's almost nonexistent sense of humor chose that inopportune moment to rear its ugly head, and he found himself alternating between chuckles and the gasps of pain they caused at the other's indignation.

"Yes, please do not move," the monk fretted as he tried to coax Hahri to lie back down. "I already sent one of the patrol guardsmen to fetch a few more of the Guard. They will help you to—"

Issai nearly toppled over as Hahri cursed loudly. He and Hahri might as well cut their own stomachs open for all the good the Guard would do them. Keeping himself bent protectively over his ribs, he looked around wildly for his once again missing knives. Only then did he notice for the first time the fallen bodies of every *Shi* that had appeared in the courtyard and remembered the reason why his ribs were currently a shattered mess. And why was it suddenly so *cold*?

His eyes shot suspiciously over to the monk who was currently backing away from a furious-looking Hahri that had somehow managed to get to his feet. "Did you do this?" Issai demanded, drawing the attention of the blond back to him.

Startled, the monk looked between the two boys before he said, "What do you mean?"

Still hunched over his ribs, Issai cautiously stepped closer to the other two. "I remember a loud voice right before something knocked me flat."

The monk shifted nervously. "That was the Gods' Voice."

Hahri gasped, and Issai instantly looked over at him. Hahri looked as if he had been kicked by a horse.

"You're—Korin the Watcher, aren't you?" he accused in an almost disbelieving voice.

The blond flinched as if he'd been slapped but then nodded curtly. It was Issai's turn to feel as if he'd been horse-kicked. He knew that name, a name passed on along the ages of a godly figure whom he had always assumed was pure myth.

He locked eyes with Hahri. "He's..." Issai began, but he immediately saw in the other's stare that it was unnecessary to finish. They both had had the same thought. Perhaps the blond monk was the person they were intended to meet here.

Hahri stiffly shuffled his way over to Issai before he turned to Korin the Watcher and said, "Look, my name is Kye, and this is Senn. I think you're the one we came to Rihott to meet, but if you don't help us leave before the guardsmen arrive, you'll have to wait a very long time to find out why."

The monk's eyes narrowed. "Are you asking for Sanctuary from the Temple?" he asked bluntly.

Hahri started to shrug then winced with gritted teeth. "Whatever works, but I think you might have the wrong idea about us." He toed the nearest fallen *Shi*, which happened to be the only one Issai had managed to kill. "These bastards weren't just normal thugs taking advantage of two boys, nor were we out to take advantage of them."

"We can't afford to be seen by anyone else," Issai added. "As it is, we can barely stand. I hope to everything divine that your temple is not far."

"It is, but I do not think that will be a problem. If you think you can walk just a bit more, I have a friend who lives a couple of streets over past this courtyard. He has a small cart he sometimes uses to haul coal from the Merchant District." He paused and stared at the two injured boys for a moment, before he continued, "I shall see you safely to the temple; we shall talk more then."

The two ancient boys hobbled after the monk, shivering and holding on to each other for support even though Issai knew Hahri must be near to passing out because of his proximity to him. He almost immediately spotted his forgotten knives relatively close together near one of the wells. They must have gone flying the moment Korin the Watcher's Gods' Voice—whatever that was—had struck him.

Apparently, his companion had also noticed the lost items. "Brother Korin, do you think you can pick up Senn's knives for him?" Hahri asked in a voice too innocent for the smile that accompanied it.

The look the mythical monk gave them when he saw the blood-stained knife Hahri pointed out would have been enough to make even a demon feel guilty.

Issai closed his eyes with a grimace; the gods were sure to curse them with misfortune until the end of time.

"Just swing around the back of the main building, if you do not mind," Issai heard Korin say through the squeak of the wheels around him, and he could have cried.

As if on cue, he felt the warm body pressed uncomfortably against his back start to squirm, and he had to bite his tongue—hard—to keep from snarling at the other. He knew the smaller boy couldn't help it, that his restlessness was a consequence of his Old Soul nature, but it was hard to think rationally when the agony in his chest was jarred to an almost unbearable degree.

That Hahri had managed to stay so still for more than half an hour was a minor miracle, so he really didn't have much room to complain. Especially when he, himself, was struggling to stay motionless and was virtually blind under the thick, wool blanket the monk and his friend had thrown over the two of them after they had situated themselves in the back of the man's cart. It had been smaller than he had expected; the two boys had had to lie on their sides and press themselves as close together as possible against the back, their knees bent, just so Korin could have enough room to sit with his knees up against his chest beside them.

Issai had half-expected Hahri to complain about having to be so near to him for such a long time, but to the other boy's credit, he didn't complain once even though the agony of the situation must have been ghastly for him. He supposed he should be happy that their new benefactors hadn't suggested stuffing them into a couple of grain sacks to keep them hidden until they reached the temple, and it wasn't as though being so close to the other boy was causing *him* any extra physical pain. The natural bumps caused by the uneven stones as the cart was pulled along the streets were a different matter. Frankly, he was surprised that they were still conscious, though that wasn't necessarily a good thing.

A few moments after the monk had spoken, the cart came to a stop, and Issai felt the monk stir beside them.

"We are here," Korin said, and the blanket was abruptly lifted off them.

Everything around him was still dark; night had fallen sometime during their journey. Issai felt some of the tension leave his body. After countless centuries of running and hiding, he always felt more comfortable in the dark.

He tried to sit up and immediately hissed in pain before he could rise more than a finger's length. He froze when he heard the whimper behind him.

"Don't," Hahri moaned, his voice layered with so much exhaustion and pain that it was almost unintelligible.

Issai carefully turned his neck until he could see his companion's face. Even in the darkness, he could see the other's pinched expression as if he were struggling not to scream. His bangs were darkened with sweat and plastered to his forehead. Beads of sweat had also tracked dark grooves down the sides of his dusty face, looking like trails of blood in the darkness. He wondered if he looked as bad but somehow doubted it.

He turned back and met the worried eyes of the monk. "Brother Korin, can you please move me away from him?" he asked. He felt Hahri twitch.

Korin frowned down at him. "Why?" he asked, sounding puzzled. "Neither one of you should—"

"I'm hurting him," Issai interjected with some heat. "Just move me away."

Until they learned more about this mythical monk, that was the only explanation he would give. Fortunately, the blond didn't question him further, although his eyes narrowed in something akin to suspicion. Issai was just too tired and in too much pain to puzzle it out. Time enough for questions later.

Still kneeling, Korin reached an arm behind his neck and the other against the crook of his knees and slowly pulled him away from Hahri. He then carefully turning him onto his back until Issai rested heavily on the monk's arms. Though Korin had moved him as gently as possible, something sharp dug deep into the soft tissues within his chest, and for one long, eternal breath, his vision blurred white while his entire being seemed to explode with pain. He heard a moan but was not sure whether it had come from Hahri or himself.

After a couple of labored breaths amidst Korin's frantic apologies, Issai was finally able to wheeze out, "Please—get us—somewhere—private."

They were out of time. Issai was already struggling to keep from blacking out completely, to keep his gaze focused on the other's shadowed face. He didn't know if that last jolt had finally tipped Hahri into the darkness, but if they both blacked out, then he was afraid that neither one of them would wake up in the same body.

After everything they had been through in the last couple of days, Issai was not about to let that happen.

The blond monk slowly rose to his feet, lifting Issai as if he weighed no more than a fire log. "I think the other boy is unconscious," Korin said to his friend. His voice sounded as if it was a span away. "Be extremely careful of his ribs when you lift him, but hurry. I think they both may be bleeding inside. They need..."

The monk's voice disappeared as the stars began to spin into a dark ocean of bobbing points of light. Issai could feel Korin moving, but it took every bit of his concentration to keep from closing his eyes. Various lights seemed to flash on and off across his field of vision until they, and the agony in his chest, became the focus of his whole world as even every noise faded from existence.

11

It was neither a sound nor a sensation an indeterminable time later that allowed Issai's mind to detach itself enough from the pain to partially stray. It was the realization that he tasted something bitter. Once his fuzzy mind grasped that enough to wonder why, a whole host of other things suddenly came to the forefront. He realized that his tongue felt a bit fat and heavy, that his eyes were mildly stinging, and something cold and moist rested against his forehead. He blinked several times, but he couldn't seem to make sense of what he was seeing in the dim light.

Confused, he tried to raise his head, but the various dark shapes within the illumination started to spin. He quickly shut his eyes as a wave of nausea washed through him. It was a long moment before his head stopped spinning and he felt it was safe to open his eyes again without the threat of vomiting. His body was beginning to feel lighter, the pain in his chest not nearly so consuming, so that he was finally able to focus his blurry eyes enough to see that he was staring at a wall made of gray stone.

Before his mind could puzzle that out, he heard movement to his right, and his head turned automatically towards it. A dark shape filled his vision, and Issai instinctively jerked away in alarm before he could even comprehend what he was seeing. His chest exploded with pain, and he cried out as he was once again lost in a torrent of agony.

It was the voice that ultimately snapped him out of it, vaguely familiar and calling out a name that he thought he should know. Issai focused on that voice until the pain once again released its stranglehold on his mind and body, and he was able to breathe more easily. When even the pain began to fade into the background to be replaced with a kind of numbness, his mind cleared enough for him to want to know who was talking to him, and he forced his eyes open.

"Stay still...you are safe..." the voice crooned softly as a man blurred into focus.

Issai stared at him for a long moment, taking in the shoulder-length blond hair, the dark eyes, and white robes, certain he should know him. Then movement beyond the man caught his eye, and he saw a figure lying on a cot along the opposite wall from him. When he noted the tangle of auburn hair spread limply across the white cloth of a pillow, it was as if the sun had finally risen, pulling his mind with it from the darkness.

Hahri!

Then hands were on his shoulders, pushing him down like two heavy stones as he struggled to sit up. The damp cloth on his forehead slid down momentarily over his eyes before he dislodged it with a violent shake of his head that caused his vision to blur once again.

"Senn!" a voice cried above him. "Stop! It's all right. Please calm down. You will hurt yourself!"

The shock of hearing that name made Issai fall still, and he finally focused on the man holding him down. "Brother—Korin?" he asked slowly, bits and pieces from earlier in the day surfacing in his mind as if through thick mud. A courtyard...*Shi*...his chest on fire...a man in white robes kneeling over him...riding in a cart with Hahri pressed up against his back...

"Thank the gods you are finally talking sense," the monk said as he slowly released Issai's shoulders and fell back into a wooden chair that had been pulled up alongside his cot. "You were in a trance for so long that I was afraid that even the darkroot tea would be unable to ease your pain enough for your mind to return."

Well, at least that explained why his mouth tasted like the inside of a guardsman's boot. Issai grimaced as his mind seemed on the verge of floating away. He had a distinct feeling that he was forgetting something significant, but he just couldn't focus his meandering thoughts long enough to figure out what. It was almost as though he was half-asleep and wide awake at the same time, his mind warring between the two states so rapidly that he could barely hold on to the individual threads of his thoughts.

"And Hah-Kye?" he asked, luckily catching himself before he could stick his entire foot in his mouth. His eyes flickered over to the still form across the room.

The monk sighed, wringing his hands absently in his lap. "Your friend is still unconscious. I am afraid that his injuries were far worse than your own. I had one of the healer-monks look at you both, but there really was not much he could do for broken ribs except to try to ease your pain and make sure you were no longer in any position to injure yourselves further."

"Where are we?" Issai asked, his words slightly slurred as he tried to talk around his currently thick tongue.

Violet eyes took in his surroundings—not that there was a whole lot to focus on. The only furniture in the tiny room were the two cots and a small table at the foot of the one he rested on where his belt, knife holsters, two money pouches, an oil lamp, a couple of earthen cups, and a water basin rested. There wasn't even a window.

"This is the room I was given within the temple," Korin said. "Only a handful of people know you two are here if that is what you are worried about. The Temple takes its offers of Sanctuary very seriously. No one will enter this room unless I invite them." He smiled wryly. "I fear my presence is a bit daunting to even my fellow Brothers, so they do not usually seek my company. I shall watch over both of you tonight. The only thing you need to worry about now is rest and healing."

Healing— With a start, some of the haze around his mind lifted as the word triggered a memory. Issai suddenly remembered exactly why he had been so adamant on getting Hahri and himself someplace private and secure and why he had struggled so hard to keep himself conscious.

He closed his eyes and tried to concentrate on feeling out the extent of the damage to his chest. It was hard to focus around the tea-induced numbness of his body—exactly how much had that monk given him?— but luckily he was still feeling enough pain that the remedy had not completely fuzzed out his ability to think and feel lucidly.

Had the monk not been sitting next to him, Issai would have cursed violently. It was no wonder that he was having so much trouble breathing. The bones in his chest were a cracked and ruined mess. Splintered fragments of his ribs had sliced or embedded themselves into the surrounding tissue, causing an alarming amount of blood to pool into his abdomen.

Although his lungs had miraculously been spared

any serious damage from any of the bone shards, the impact of smacking into those *Shi* so hard after Korin's Gods' Voice had sent him flying had caused enough trauma that his left lung was swollen to almost twice its size. It was also beginning to fill with fluid and trace amounts of blood. It was a mortal wound, and he suspected that Korin the Watcher knew this very well and had dosed them accordingly with the darkroot tea in hopes of giving them an easier passing.

Left alone, neither one of them would survive the night.

Which left him only one choice really. He would have to ask Korin to help him with the healing and pray that he was not already too late.

Issai opened his eyes and turned to look up into the monk's black eyes. "Can you move the blankets down a bit?" he asked. "I need to see my chest."

The blond shifted nervously in his chair. "Do not worry about that right now," he soothed. "Just rest."

Issai sighed in growing frustration. It seemed Korin the Watcher was just as stubborn as Hahri, though in a decidedly more annoying manner—as though he were a father trying to allay the fears of his young son. He just didn't have time to play that particular game.

"Just do it!" he snapped causing the other to flinch at the unexpected harshness.

The monk held out his hands between them for a moment as if trying to placate an animal on the verge of attacking before he carefully moved the thin blankets down to Issai's legs. Either the healer-monk or Korin had stripped him of both his outer tunic and undershirt so that his chest was laid bare in all its blue and purple glory. He frowned. There wasn't a single patch of skin from his collarbone down that was still its original tanned color or not swollen grotesquely as a result of the internal bleeding.

"You should not see this," Korin muttered softly. He had gone back to wringing his hands, so tightly that his knuckles had turned white.

"I know we're dying," Issai retorted crossly. "I don't need your pity or coddling right now monk. What I *do* need is your unconditional help if I'm to have any hope of changing that."

He was wheezing by the end of his outburst. Issai really hoped the monk would just do as he asked and wait to ask questions later. Breathing was getting harder by the moment, but that fact didn't stop the angry desire to punch the older man in the face when Korin looked down at him as if he were hopelessly naïve. Had he been able to move, he probably would have done it.

Issai forced down his anger with effort. Now was not the time. "I need you to move Kye's cot right up against mine," he continued in a calmer voice. "I need to be able to grasp his hand."

"Why?"

Issai bit back the first two responses he wanted to

snarl back at the infuriating monk but settled on, "Because I'm going to try to heal us."

To his further infuriation, Korin sat rooted to his chair, looking at Issai with a thoughtful frown as if he was trying to decide if he was still sane. At that moment, the man was extremely lucky that Issai didn't have a knife in his hand.

"We haven't much time," he gritted out. "I can already feel my pain increasing. We both know what caused this injury. Bring him here if you don't want our deaths on your conscience. I don't have enough strength remaining to do it alone."

For a moment, Korin looked stricken, but then he closed his eyes and sighed. "All right, but I do not understand what you think you can do," he said, but to Issai's immense relief, he did as asked, removing the chair before sliding Hahri, cot and all, over to him.

Through it all, Hahri didn't even twitch, not even when the iron cot released an awful screech as it was moved across the stone floor. Now that his companion was closer, Issai saw just how much the other boy was struggling to breathe, his chest barely rising as Hahri took short, choppy breaths.

Issai slowly moved his hand over to the other's forearm, ignoring the pain even that slight movement caused, and slid it down along the other's clammy skin until he was able to grasp Hahri's limp, cold hand. His hand almost instantly began to tingle as if blood was only now beginning to flow through what had once been deadened flesh. It reminded him a little of how he had felt as they touched souls in the inn. He took it as a hopeful sign.

He closed his eyes. "Whatever you do, don't try to separate our hands," he warned.

From that point on, Issai completely ignored the monk, even when the man began his relentless questions when it appeared to him as if Issai was doing nothing but lying on his cot with his eyes closed. The numbing effects of the tea had worn off enough to make his mind's assessment of the damage much easier to hold onto when he finally released his mental command to heal.

It was as if a staff had suddenly slammed into his chest again and had opened a hole large enough for his remaining blood to seep out, leaving him to freeze in the wake of the wave of agony that thundered over every nerve in his body and stole the breath from his lungs so he couldn't even scream. As Issai gasped after a breath that was no longer there, his chest seemed to spontaneously erupt in flames for one eternal moment of agony before he found himself curled on his side, coughing up something molten hot and thick and struggling not to drown in it.

One beat, an hour, days, years—he didn't know—passed in agony as his entire being convulsed. Then nothing more was coming up his throat, and the next cough was followed by a painful gasp that finally delivered nothing but air to his starved lungs. Issai focused on taking several more deep breaths until his breathing slowed to a more normal rhythm and the ache in his chest faded to a dull throb. When even the throb disappeared and a bone-deep weariness settled into his body in its place, he slowly opened heavy eyes and was met with a pair of shadowed cerulean eyes staring back from about a hand-span away.

"You look like shit," Hahri croaked, his voice sounding as if his throat had never seen a drop of water.

Issai's lips slowly curved up. "Likewise." He made a face as he tried to lick his dry lips and tasted blood for what seemed like the hundredth time that day. "Next time I refuse to heal something right away, remind me of this," he grumbled.

"Well then, apology accepted," his companion replied cheekily. "Now, can I have my hand back?"

Issai felt a sharp squeeze on his hand, and he was astonished when he realized that he had not let go of Hahri's hand even after all of that. He stiffly opened his fingers, wondering just how hard he had been gripping the other's hand when he felt them ache sharply as they straightened. His hand dropped limply to the bed as he momentarily felt lightheaded, but the spell passed almost as quickly as it had come.

He looked down at his bare chest, and minus the blood he had just spewed all over himself, his skin had returned to its original color. The swelling had also vanished. He pressed his fingers into his chest experimentally, but he wasn't even tender. The only thing that seemed to still be hurting was his throat which didn't surprise him at all considering he had expelled what seemed like his entire blood volume only moments before.

Issai turned his attention back to Hahri, his eyes roving over the parts of the other boy's chest that were not under his blankets. He couldn't see even a hint of a bruise. Only splatters of the blood he must have also spewed up remained on his chin and chest.

"Are you hurting?" he asked.

"I am now that you let go of my hand," Hahri complained, "but compared to the agony of pulverized ribs, it's not even worth mentioning. You must've just given me my soul back."

Issai sucked in a sharp breath. That moment of light-headedness had occurred right after he had let go of the other boy's hand. The thought made him uneasy. Was that why Hahri felt pain whenever he was close to him? Was he unconsciously trying to steal the other's soul?

"You might be right," he said slowly.

"I was just joking," the ancient boy said with wide eyes.

However, a noise at the front of the room saved them from what was quickly turning into an awkward moment when they both simultaneously turned towards the sound. Korin the Watcher sat sprawled against the wall near the door as if his legs had unexpectedly crumbled on him and he was still too stunned to react. One of his cheeks, as well as the front of his once pristine robes, were splattered with blood. Issai had completely forgotten about the blond monk. The look on Korin's face as he stared back at them was a mixture of shock, horror, and suspicion.

"Right," Issai said with a weary sigh.

Now that he was sure that they both were healed and out of imminent danger, he wanted nothing more than to finally pass out. Judging from the way the monk was staring at them as Korin slowly began picking himself up from the floor, Issai didn't think he could dismiss the older man so easily this time.

With a massive effort, Issai managed to sit up on the cot and maneuver himself so that his back was resting against the stone wall. It was extremely uncomfortable, but it was better than the helplessness of being prone. He wasn't surprised when Hahri crawled over to his cot with only a hint of fatigue in his movements and settled next to him on the side closest to the monk. How ironic that the one closer to death was now the one who was stronger.

A large, blood-red spot on Hahri's upper right arm caught his attention then. Issai squinted at it briefly in the dim light and confirmed that it was indeed an impact wound and not any of the blood the boy had spat up. He glanced at his own arm, but it was uninjured. The injury was fresh, so it wasn't as though Hahri had obtained it before they had met. Why did the bruise not manifest on Issai's own arm? He had certainly felt the kick he had given Hahri to the back of his knees earlier, so that strange connection was definitely not one-sided.

Issai pinched the bridge of his nose, feeling a headache coming on with all the force of a sledgehammer. Screw it. He was just too damned tired to worry about such a weighty topic right now. Especially when they still had Korin the Watcher to deal with.

Looking over at the small table, Hahri reached over and took the two cups, sniffing one suspiciously before handing the other to Issai. "Water," he said simply before taking a sip.

Issai was grateful. He too sniffed the contents of his cup before taking a mouthful to rinse the remaining blood in his mouth and spitting it onto the floor. With all the blood currently staining the stones, he figured a little more wouldn't matter. He downed the rest in one gulp before turning his attention back to their benefactor.

Korin continued to study them for a long moment with an unreadable expression before he finally spoke. "To heal yourselves like that—just who are you two?" he asked calmly, yet Issai could clearly see the monk was slightly trembling. Though he was back on his feet, Korin made no move to approach them.

Issai and Hahri looked at each other for a long moment before Issai nodded to the other boy slightly, handing him the reigns. Hahri was the better talker, after all.

"Have a seat," Hahri offered. "This may take a while."

Korin shook his head. "Go on."

Hahri shrugged. "Some of it is pretty straightforward. Senn and I are Old Souls."

Silence.

Then, "What do you mean, an 'Old Soul'?"

If Hahri had not been sitting so close to him, Issai would have fallen over.

"You have got to be kidding me!" Hahri exclaimed, staring at the monk as if he had suddenly sprouted another head. "Word was that Korin the Watcher was a being who knew just about everything concerning this world, and you're telling me that you've never heard of an Old Soul?"

It was the other man's turn to scoff. "Only the gods know *everything*. I may have lived on this earth for thousands of years, but that hardly qualifies me to have the mind of a god."

"Wait—did you say thousands of years?" Hahri interjected. "You're immortal then?"

Once again the other man snorted in disdain. "Perhaps it is better that I do not know this, but what exactly have you heard about me?"

"Just that you appeared in many different time periods and places all around the world to offer your counsel and sometimes, punishment with your Gods' Voice. To hear some people talk, you were the one that created fire. However, I've never talked to anyone who could say they had met you."

Hahri turned questioningly to Issai, but Issai shook his head. "I haven't either, but I remember people would sometimes say that you were an ageless being that had the ability to change your appearance at will while others claimed that a person was chosen by the gods each generation to become Korin the Watcher."

Korin closed his eyes and groaned. "I think I am starting to understand why even the Priors sometimes fear me." He dragged over the sole chair in the room beside the cot Hahri had abandoned and practically fell into it. "How do these misunderstandings even get started?"

Hahri laughed dryly. "We wonder the same thing all the time. So, you're saying that none of that is true?"

"No. I am born, and I age just as normally as any other person. Nor do I have an unusually long lifespan. The only difference is that I am slightly stronger than a regular man, and at my death, I am simply reborn with all my prior life's memories intact."

Issai's breath caught painfully in his throat. The look

of utter disbelief that flashed across Hahri's face probably mirrored his own.

"I think you just answered your own question about Old Souls," Issai said quietly before the other boy could open his mouth.

Issai knew the moment the blond monk understood because he went very still like a rodent under the eyes of a viper.

"We told you we came to Rihott to meet someone," Hahri said into the thick silence, his almost emotionless gaze fixed on the other man. The ancient Hahri had surfaced again. "I wasn't entirely certain it was you until this moment. We were compelled to come here because you are just like us—an Old Soul." He turned to Issai. "Things have become just a little clearer now."

"A little bit," Issai agreed slowly, trying not to look at those hated eyes, "but it still doesn't tell us *why*."

"I tried to touch you," Korin said hesitantly, fixing Issai with troubled eyes. "When you started to fall into a fit and began coughing up blood, I reached down to try to hold your body down, but I suddenly felt a heavy pressure fall onto my back from above like a large, invisible foot was attempting to crush me to the floor. I backed up all the way to the wall, but the massive pressure did not stop until well after I had been forced down to the floor."

Issai frowned. "I don't know why that happened. I've never had anyone besides Kye near me when I've healed myself, so I don't know if only Old Souls are affected by it."

If anything, the monk seemed even more troubled. "Even now, I still feel a very slight pressure weighing down on me—even more so now that you two are sitting together. Is it that I am just reacting to another —Old Soul?"

"Right now I am so exhausted that I probably couldn't sense a fly buzzing around the room," Issai said, "and I don't recall sensing anything different when we met you in the courtyard. Still, I was in agony, so I just might not have noticed."

Hahri turned to Issai. Issai was relieved to see the emotion had returned to the boy's eyes. "I don't really sense anyone but you," he said, "but I'm pretty exhausted myself, so I really can't be sure either."

"How do you sense him?" Korin asked Hahri. Issai noted that he was nervously wringing his hands again. For someone who had lived for so long, the monk was unusually like an open book from his posture to his expressions.

Hahri's eyes hardened. "Why do you want to know?" he demanded.

"I am sorry," the monk immediately said, "but I am just trying to understand all of this. For centuries I thought I was the only one who carried this heavy burden, and I have gone from temple to temple praying to the gods to help me understand what it was I was supposed to do."

Hahri snorted. "Not going to happen. You can pray all you want, but I don't think the gods are inclined to do anything except watch in amusement as we stumble around."

Though Issai agreed wholeheartedly, he didn't think he would have said it so bluntly to the monk's face.

The glare Korin directed at Hahri would have melted iron. "You, of course, are free to believe what you will," he said coolly, "but I believe the gods have already given me a sign—first through a little girl and now with this serendipitous meeting."

"What do you mean a little girl?" Hahri asked.

"She is the reason why I wanted to know what you sensed from Senn. I met her for the first time in my temple when she damaged some of the statues of the gods within the chamber of worship. Point of fact, she is the reason why I am in Rihott in the first place. I am originally from Aideya."

"So you sensed something from her?" Hahri speculated.

"Quite literally. When I confronted her, she attacked me with a sword, and I was forced to use the Gods' Voice to keep her from killing me."

"You used *that* on a little girl?" Hahri said in disbelief.

Korin winced. "Not quite to the extent I used in the

courtyard today. She was merely rendered unconscious. When I tried to lift her from the floor, I felt a force slam into me as if I had been struck by lightning, and from then on, I could not touch her without feeling pain."

Issai and Hahri exchanged a startled glance. This could not merely be a coincidence.

"This girl, is she here in this temple?" Issai asked.

The blond monk suddenly looked agitated. "No. After saying some confusing things, she ran from the temple and disappeared. I spent an entire day looking for her within the city, but no one had ever seen her. Then after talking to one of the street kids in Aideya and he mentioned that the Norin and Mahze clans were seen within the city, I feared she had been abducted. I followed the Norin caravan here, and last night, with the help of some friends from the City Guard, we were able to rescue the children they had abducted and hide them here in the temple."

Issai nodded thoughtfully. "Some women in the marketplace were talking about thieves attacking a caravan."

Korin smiled. "My friend's idea. To keep the Temple from any potential trouble, some of the men talked loudly of their disappointment of finding only children and not the large amounts of gold they expected from a caravan so highly guarded. The Norins probably thought the 'thieves' released the children to vent their frustration at such a disappointing mark. Unfortunately, the girl was not among the abducted. The slavers had been my only lead, and now I am at a loss of where to search next. I had been searching for her here in the city when someone informed me of a commotion near the community wells."

"What makes you think she's even in this city?" Hahri asked. "Why not return to Aideya which you know was her last location?"

"Because from the moment she fled, there has been a humming within what seems like my very soul that was getting progressively worse until I arrived here in Rihott where it lessened to a steadier, bearable vibration. The sensation has been at the same level until about a couple of hours ago. It's slowly starting to get worse again. If she was here, then I fear this change signifies that she is on the move again."

"I hate to say this, but you're probably right about all of that," Hahri said grimly, "and judging from everything that happened between you, she is probably an Old Soul as well."

"We were observing everyone in the marketplace for a bit before we were spotted by the *Shi*, so perhaps we saw her," Issai said.

"What are sh—" Korin started to ask, but Hahri held up his hand quickly.

"They're all those men you flattened in the courtyard," he interrupted hastily with a quick glance at Issai. "I'll explain all about them later."

Issai shot the boy a dirty look but continued on as if he hadn't noticed the exchange, "About how old does she look? What does she look like?"

"Oddly enough, she is disguising herself as a boy for reasons I cannot fathom. As a boy, she looks about nine or ten, but she may be a bit older. Her hair is cut short and ragged, brown like the color of a saddle, and her eyes are a pale red, almost pink."

"Now that's unusual. With eyes like that, it shouldn't be too tough to find..." Hahri trailed off at the glare Issai was sending him, but he wisely did not continue.

"She's probably dying her hair with leather dye," Issai added, struggling to keep the anger out of his voice as Korin looked from one boy to the other in confusion. He knew he shouldn't take his anger about the whole "Violet-eyed Old Soul" mess out on Hahri, but it seemed the boy was constantly poking that particularly painful sore point without really meaning to. "I have never seen a person with that eye color that did not also have hair as white as an eggshell—"

Issai's eyes suddenly widened.

"What?" Hahri asked.

"You said she had a sword, right?" Issai directed at the monk.

Korin nodded. "It was one of those narrow, slightly curved blades."

He turned back to Hahri and said, "I don't think the

person we were supposed to meet was Korin the Watcher after all."

"You don't mean—"

"Korin's missing little girl, I'm almost positive I saw her in the marketplace when we were standing in front of that ridiculous fruit stall. It was her all along."

12

Hahri paced the length of the room like a caged animal. He had been doing it almost from the moment he had woken up, and it was beginning to grate on Issai's nerves. They had been arguing for almost as long, trying to decide their next move while Korin was away attending to business with the City Guard concerning the mess he had left behind in the courtyard yesterday.

Admittedly, most of Issai's irritation stemmed from how quickly everything seemed to be spiraling out of his control and not with his companion's antics. Why were all of these Old Souls suddenly coming out of the woodwork when he had lived thousands of years without knowing if any others actually existed? Had meeting Hahri somehow been the catalyst? It was an idea that didn't sit well. It suggested that the gods really were forcing them to play a game—a game where only they knew the rules as well as the ultimate goal.

The only thing they had managed to agree on was that they had to find their initial target again. At least this time Issai knew it was a little girl and knew what she looked like. Where to start looking was a different story. With so many *Shi* out for their guts, Issai no longer felt they could risk moving from city to city as haphazardly as before.

Hahri blew out a frustrated breath. "Let's just touch souls again, like we did back in Nisei," he said, going over to where Issai still sat on his cot and plopping down beside him. "We might get a better result this time since we both know who we are looking for, and you at least know what she looks like."

Issai frowned. "I'm not sure I like the idea of doing something like that here where anyone could walk in on us. The door doesn't lock; I checked."

"Then we'll just wait for Korin to return and have him stand guard."

He raked his hands agitatedly through his hair. "I don't really like that idea either."

"You allowed Korin to see you heal," Hahri pointed out. "I don't see how this is any different."

"I had no choice then. It would not have mattered if he had betrayed us at that point. We were dying anyway. This soul-touching business puts me on edge more than my healing ever could. We still don't even understand why we can do it in the first place. Until we know more about the monk, I would rather he not know that we can do this."

"This wouldn't have anything to do with that comment I made earlier about you giving me my soul back does it?" Hahri asked suspiciously.

Issai swallowed nervously. He really didn't want to discuss it right now, at least until he had had some time to think things through without the air of danger so thick around them. He had hoped that the ancient boy had forgotten all about the incident.

When he remained silent, Hahri huffed and grasped his shoulder. Issai instantly tried to pull away, but the cerulean-eyed boy squeezed his hand harder until Issai stilled tensely, although he stubbornly kept his gaze fixed on the wall before him.

"Look," Hahri said, "my being this physically close to you is making me feel like I'm being embraced too tightly. It's extremely uncomfortable, makes it a little hard to breathe, but it's nowhere *near* what I felt last night when I was a couple of gasps away from death. You aren't stealing my life from me, Issai, so stop worrying about it so much."

Issai looked at him sideways. "You can't know that for sure," he insisted. "There's a reason why you feel pain being so near to me when at the same time, it brings me relief from the pain of separation. Perhaps— that time in the forest—when we—"

He paused, suddenly horrified at the possibility that his thoughts had uncovered.

Hahri tensed in response to whatever he had seen on Issai's face. "When we *what*, Issai?" he demanded.

He turned, shrugging off the other's hand, and faced Hahri fully. Issai tried not to flinch away from those ancient eyes as he continued, "When we touched souls for the first time, perhaps we didn't break apart—not completely anyway. What if the pain we are feeling is because we are somehow trying to reclaim the part of our soul we left behind and each of us is unconsciously resisting? It would certainly also explain that strange connection we have when it comes to injuries."

"All right, maybe you're right and we *are* tugging on each other's souls, but that doesn't mean you're going to swallow me up like some soul-eating monster if I get too close. Or Korin for that matter. We don't even feel that kind of connection to him. You keep saying that we don't know enough about what's really going on to reliably speculate about anything, and I completely agree with you on that point. However, I also think that we need to do everything we can to gather more information, and right now that means finding Korin's missing girl. Touching souls is the next logical step."

Issai closed his eyes and sighed. "Once again it comes down to choosing the lesser evil."

Hahri smiled, and his eyes warmed. "Well, if that's the way you want to look at it, then yes, but if it makes you feel better, I think that Korin the Watcher, the godly monk of myths, is more than a little afraid of us."

Issai's lips curved up slightly. "It does."

"Thought it would," the other boy said smugly. "I noticed this morning that he was very careful to stay as far away from us as he thought he could get away with, and he also twitched if either one of us made a sudden, unexpected move like he wanted nothing more than to bolt out of the room."

"Fine. As much as I hate everything about this, including staying here even longer, we'll do this your way. We'll wait for the monk to return to stand guard. We'll tell him we're using a technique to divine the girl's location, but," Issai glared at Hahri challengingly, "*we will not tell him we are touching souls to do it.*"

"Understood," Hahri agreed amiably. "At this point, I really don't care if he knows or not, but remember, we'll have to tell him about it some time. It may be important. If he asks, I'll leave the answering to you. Tell him whatever you feel comfortable revealing. I'll back you."

Issai turned his head away. "Thank you."

It was so quiet that it was almost unintelligible, but he felt Hahri jerk beside him. He didn't need to turn to know that the other boy was smiling.

IT WAS several hours before the monk finally appeared

with a look on his face that immediately set both boys on edge. Korin stood with his back against the door, silently staring at them so intently it was as if he was trying to steal their secrets directly from their minds. With a start, Issai realized that it was a very real possibility, given Korin was an Old Soul. Was all of the monk's earlier nervousness around them just an act to fool them into letting their guard down enough for him to pick their minds apart?

He stood up abruptly. "What are you doing?" he growled, flicking a knife into his right hand.

"Senn?" Hahri questioned, his tone more curious than alarmed.

The blond, however, seemed to want to melt into the wood at his back, eying the knife as though it were already sticking out of his chest.

"What—" Korin began, but the rest of the words seemed to get stuck in his throat. He licked his lips nervously before trying again, "W-What do you mean?"

"You've been staring at us pretty intently on and off since the moment we met. An Old Soul has many unique abilities." He held up his knife threateningly. "Have you been trying to steal our thoughts?"

He heard Hahri draw in a sharp breath beside him, but he dared not spare the other a glance, his entire attention focused on Korin's reaction to his accusation. The look of terror in the monk's eyes instantly melted into confusion. Issai relaxed his tense stance minutely.

"Your thoughts?" Korin echoed, his eyes still glued to the knife. "Is such a thing even possible?"

"You say this when you can knock a man flat with just your voice?" Hahri pointed out dryly.

The man looked so bewildered that even Issai had to roll his eyes. He lowered his arm and returned his knife to its holster. "I had to be sure," he said as he sat down beside Hahri again.

"You know, the little girl was very suspicious of me as well," Korin said slowly as he moved cautiously towards Hahri's empty cot and sat down. "Is there a reason why Old Souls have such mistrust towards monks?"

"Trust is a hard commodity for an Old Soul," Hahri said lightly, perhaps in an attempt to dissolve some of the heaviness in the room. "I can't speak for the girl, but our caution has nothing to do with you being a monk and everything to do with our past experiences."

"We simply do not know you," Issai added.

Korin sighed. "I suppose I cannot really blame you, especially after talking with the Guard today."

Issai was immediately tense again. "Did something else happen?"

The monk shook his head, though his expression was worried. "It's not so much that something happened as what *did not* happen. Those men that attacked you yesterday, they were gathered up by the Guard and imprisoned until they became conscious again. I have used the Gods' Voice in this city before, so the situation was nothing new to them. They knew I would show up eventually to give witness, so I was not worried they would seek me here. Only, this time they did."

Issai and Hahri jumped to their feet simultaneously. "Guardsmen are here at the temple?" Hahri hissed.

Korin waved his hands before him. "No, no," he placated, "they were here this morning, but I left the temple with them. Luckily, I was talking to the Prior when they arrived and not here with you. Some in the higher ranks were rather interested in you two. That is why it took me so long to return. I was interrogated rather thoroughly."

"Dammit," Issai spat angrily, then marched over to Korin and grabbed him by the shoulders. "What did you tell them," he demanded.

The monk flinched as though Issai had hit him, but nevertheless, his answer came quickly, "I told them the truth, that I had thought the commotion was a simple brawl that needed to be quelled. Since at least one patrol guardsman saw everyone go down before he ran ahead to alert the guard station, I had to concoct a story to explain your absence as well as mine."

"I hope for your sake that you did not mention the words 'Old Soul' to them," Issai interjected darkly, his hands still digging into the monk's shoulders.

Korin winced, but he made no move to push Issai away. His hands lay limply in his lap as he stared at Issai with wide eyes.

"Senn," Hahri said quietly.

Though Issai tensed even more at his companion's voice, he gave a curt nod and released the ancient monk's shoulders. He stepped back to Hahri's side but remained standing.

Korin released the breath he had been holding and unconsciously began to wring his hands. His eyes were fixed on Issai.

"You said that we are the same," he continued warily. "For countless centuries, I have lived among many different people, and yet, I have never truly belonged among them. I have stood on the edges of society and merely observed them. Thus I was given the name 'The Watcher' by the other monks. It's a name I despise because of its truth. I can only watch the ages come and go while everything around me changes into something no longer recognizable. Then you two come along, and suddenly, I have a peer again, something I have not had since my first life. Do you really think I would carelessly jeopardize this opportunity?"

Hahri shook his head. "I think you're misunderstanding something, but I suppose it really can't be helped since you don't know either of us at all. The reasons for our suspicions run so deep that they have become second nature to us, so it's something you'll just have to get used to if you plan to stick with us for any length of time. At this point, even if the gods, themselves, stood here in your place, we'd still be suspicious of them."

Korin sighed and pushed an errant lock of hair behind his ear. "We shall have to exchange stories someday. For now, I think you will be more interested in the story I told the captain of the City Guard. He wanted to know why I had left the courtyard, and I told him it was to chase after you two, that you had managed to dodge the path of my Gods' Voice and had feigned unconsciousness until the patrol guardsman had left and my back was turned. I said I searched until nightfall but was unable to locate you, nor had anyone else seen you. The Prior verified my intentions to talk with them this morning."

"So what became of all those imprisoned *Shi*?" Issai asked.

Korin shifted nervously. "They were released this morning, even before I arrived at the guard station."

If the ancient monk was expecting them to blow up at this news, then he would be sorely disappointed.

"'It was the street scum, we swear,'" Hahri quoted sarcastically. "Same old story. *Shi* are always within the Guard. That's why we avoid all of them like the plague. You can't be too careful."

The monk was looking confused again. "What is a 'Shi' exactly?" he asked hesitantly. "Will you at least tell me that much?"

"I can't believe you really don't know," Issai muttered

darkly. He sat back down onto the cot. "You tell him," he said to Hahri.

Hahri nodded and turned to the monk. "Somewhere along the ages, people found out about us," he said, "at least enough to know we 'enjoyed' a form of immortality. They got it into their heads that if they performed a special ritual using specific parts of an Old Soul's body, then they would become immortal as well. The trick is to capture us without spilling our blood because coming in contact with our blood outside the ritual is deadly—hence the staffs instead of swords.

"I've gotten away a few times by cutting myself in their presence, but that doesn't always scare them off. Seems some of them think that as long as a mortal isn't responsible for the injury, then there will be no consequence to touching our blood, and the ritual can still be performed. It's really a mixed bag of convoluted beliefs."

Korin looked horrified. "What kind of ritual?" he asked.

"You name it, they've probably done it," Hahri replied with a grimace, "but the constant theme in all of them is that they have to remove some part of our body and consume it completely while we are still alive. Guts are particularly popular."

Now the blond monk looked sick. "Where did—I mean how could someone even consider doing such a ghastly thing?" His face turned from pale to a bright red in the next breath, and his eyes grew thunderous. "I cannot understand how the Temple has never become aware of such an atrocity."

Hahri laughed, but the humor didn't reach his eyes. "You said so yourself; you are not all-seeing. Until this lifetime, *Shi* have been a very rare breed. Since most *Shi* want a chance at immortality all to themselves, they would usually attack singly or in small groups, the largest probably about twenty men and these men usually the grunts sent out by a lord that don't even understand why their lord wants us so badly. Not many people, at least decent people, are ever aware of any of this."

"Then it probably would not surprise you that I believe the men who attacked you are part of a slaver clan," Korin said.

Issai's eyes narrowed. "How do you figure?"

"Remember when I told you last night that my friends and I disguised ourselves as thieves when we attacked the Norin caravan? Well, one of the guardsmen that had been with me that night pulled me aside before I left the guard station and told me that the new prisoners claimed that their own caravan had been attacked by those same thieves, and they had merely been in pursuit when I interfered. As you and I both know none of that is true, I can only conclude that the Norins are still unaware of our deception and used that as a plausible excuse."

"Perhaps," Hahri said skeptically, "but Issai heard

ordinary people in the marketplace talking about the supposed theft, so the attack had already become common knowledge. Any *Shi* in the city could have heard the gossip. Besides, I have yet to run into a *Shi* who is also a slaver."

Issai nodded. "Nor I, but with the abnormally large groups of *Shi* that have been attacking us lately, it's definitely something to keep in mind."

"Nevertheless, even the thought of more slavers in the area makes me anxious to find my missing little girl," the blond said, "and after hearing about that *Shi* business…"

"Yes, about that," Hahri began, exchanging a meaningful look with Issai, "we think we might be able to help you find her exact location."

Korin leaned forward eagerly. "How so?"

"The same way we knew we would find one of you in Rihott's marketplace," Issai replied. "It's a—technique, I suppose, performed between us. Let's just leave it at that for the time being."

To Issai's relief, the ancient monk merely nodded and said, "What can I do to help?"

"Just make sure nobody comes into this room while we do this, and to be safe, don't come anywhere near us."

"And you can do this right now?" Korin asked, sounding hopeful.

"With what you just told us, the sooner we have a

destination, the better," Hahri said. "Your face has likely been seen by at least one *Shi*. No matter your reputation within the Temple, those *Shi* have to be suspicious of such a mythical monk. They'll definitely be watching you from now on, and believe me, you want to be far away from them if they decide your blood might be just as tasty as ours."

The monk shuddered. "Right. I'll just go stand over by the door."

Hahri smirked and leaned into Issai. "That was easier than I thought it would be," he whispered into his ear.

He then turned and drew his legs back onto the cot, situating himself cross-legged. Issai emulated him and offered his hands to the other.

"I'll try to keep a mental picture of the girl in my mind," Issai murmured, glancing over at Korin who was once again staring intently at them. "Just do what you did in Nisei, and we'll see what happens."

He closed his eyes and thought back to the scene of the little "boy" snatching the chicken from the stall. He tried to ignore the pins and needles sensation in his hands where Hahri grasped them, but it seemed more pronounced this time. It made him want to rub at them, almost to the point of making him unable to concentrate on the image in his head. He tried to ignore his hands altogether, splitting his attention between the image of the girl and his awareness of Hahri, himself.

Issai took a couple of steady breaths in an attempt to remain calm as his whole body slowly began to tingle, then to vibrate as if the whole room was shaking. A startled moment later, he realized that neither he nor the room was shaking; the very air was rapidly pulsing like a living heart racing in fear. He also could no longer feel Hahri clutching his hands, nor the linen blanket he was sitting on. Yet, through the pulses of the air, he could sense both of them sitting together on his cot as well as Korin standing across the room to the point where he could almost see them clearly in his mind.

Then that strange sense was expanding on its own volition, and it was as though Issai was suddenly watching the whole city of Rihott rush past him even though his eyes were closed. His awareness continued moving outside the city until farms and tree-littered grasslands flew by, and the shadows in the distance formed into mountains while the grasslands changed into long stretches of white wildflowers.

Before he could even process what he was seeing, the white-dotted landscape in his mind jolted to a halt and rapidly faded into darkness. Issai abruptly felt his body again, felt the iron grip of Hahri's hands as they painfully squeezed the bones of his fingers together, felt a pull from the very air around him that seemed determined to peel his skin from his muscles.

Disoriented, he instinctually jerked his hands free and fell back onto something a bit softer than the ground. His eyes flew open and met with the stone ceiling of the temple room. His entire body stung like a recently skinned knee, but when he looked at his hands, the skin was uninjured.

"Are you all right?" he heard a voice ask as if from across a field. It took him a moment to recognize it was the monk who had spoken.

Ignoring the other man for the moment, Issai struggled to sit up just as Hahri reached for him. "Don't," he warned, and the other boy immediately backed away with a frown.

"Are you in pain?" Hahri asked after Issai had righted himself.

He shrugged then gave into the urge to rub his arms, but the action brought no relief. "I don't know if 'pain' is the right word," he said. "Are you?"

"A bit," Hahri admitted. "I mean, other than the usual." He glanced at Korin briefly. "But as long as you're all right then that's a discussion best left for later. The important thing is that I was able to see our missing little girl."

"What do you mean 'see'?" Korin demanded, not able to stay quiet any longer. He approached the two teens hesitantly.

Hahri turned to him and grinned. "I guess you can call it a vision. I saw a little boy with dark brown hair watching you flatten all of us in the courtyard from one of the merchant shops. I wouldn't have known it was her except for the red eyes. She doesn't look like a little girl at all. She probably recognized you and decided to high-tail it out of the city."

Korin sighed. "Her knowing I am pursuing her will certainly complicate things. Did you see anything else?"

"Yeah, her surrounded by a field of white blossoms. You could see a mountain range to the north, and the kid appeared to be moving towards them."

Issai started. "I saw the white flowers as well."

Surprise flashed briefly in Hahri's eyes, but he merely said, "Can't say that I recognize the area, though."

"I do," Korin spoke before Issai could even open his mouth. "I was born there."

"Currently?" Issai asked.

"For this life, yes. The western outskirts of Kairash are the only place I have seen where those particular flowers bloom as you described, especially during this time of year. There are mountains visible to the north as well."

"I've never been to Kairash. Is it a large city?" Issai asked.

Korin frowned thoughtfully. "I suppose it is about the size of Rihott, perhaps a little larger."

Hahri rose to his feet. "Then we had better get moving. She was still traveling in the vision, so she may just be planning to pass through the city. For all we know, she may be planning to stock up and head out-kingdom."

Korin looked startled. "Out-kingdom?"

Issai stood as well. "Yes, we've already stayed too long. Can we get a few supplies from the temple?" he asked the monk.

"Yes, of course, but finding a wagon willing to take us to Kairash may take some time."

Issai frowned quizzically at the ancient monk. "A wagon? Why in the name of the gods would we need a wagon?"

"If the girl is already there, then how else are we going to get there quickly?"

Hahri smirked. "Just how fast can you run?"

13

"Please...stop..."

The plea sounded as if it was uttered by a man with his last, dying breath. Issai skidded to a halt and looked over his shoulder, panting a little now that his momentum had been broken. About a hundred strides back, Korin was collapsed onto his hands and knees with his head down, a quivering white mass half-hidden within the grass and weeds.

Wondering what could possibly be wrong with him, he turned back to holler at Hahri and cursed loudly when the ancient boy was nowhere in sight. He probably hadn't heard the monk at all and was still speeding ahead.

"Kye!" Issai bellowed. "Get back here!"

He then turned around and hurried over to the

fallen monk. Korin hadn't moved from his position at all, nor did he look up when Issai approached him.

"What's wrong?" Issai asked as he bent down closer to him for a better look.

Korin raised his head, the expression on his face pinched as if he was in pure agony and trying not to scream. Darkened strands of hair lay plastered to his scalp and cheeks while sweat streamed from his temples. He looked as if he had been running through the rain.

"...rest...I need..." he gasped, his sides heaving.

Issai scowled, understanding. Never mind Hahri, apparently, the blond monk's endurance was nothing compared to his own. As he straightened, he felt the other boy step up behind him, and the mild pain that had been building in his body almost disappeared.

"For someone who doesn't talk much, you sure can yell loud," Hahri commented cheerfully as he squatted down beside Issai and regarded Korin curiously. "Hmm...we've only been running for a little over an hour, and you look like you're ready to die. I guess endurance isn't necessarily an Old Soul trait."

"S-Sorry," the monk panted, struggling to sit back onto his haunches. Hahri reached over to steady him before he could topple over. "I have never...run...for such a...long period...of time. I just need...to rest...for a bit."

"We really can't afford to waste time resting," Issai

said bluntly. He stared at Korin speculatively. "I suppose we could take turns carrying him."

Hahri shrugged. "No skin off my back."

Korin looked aghast. "Absolutely not! I would rather...you leave me...behind! I could not possibly...ask you to..."

Issai pitched him over his shoulder and stood up before the monk could even finish his protest. The other boy came up behind them and suddenly laughed.

"I wonder if that's what your face looked like when I did the same to you?" Hahri teased as the older man sputtered.

"Shut up," Issai replied irritably as he tried to adjust the squirming blond more comfortably on his shoulder. "We've wasted enough time. Let's go."

After the excitement of the last couple of days, the rest of the trip was surprisingly uneventful. Resigned to his fate, Korin didn't even put up a token fight when they stopped in order for Hahri to take a turn in carrying him. Nevertheless, Issai sighed with relief when the first patches of white began to show underfoot, and the distant mountains began to grow larger.

When there was more white than green around them, he reached out to Hahri, who was a few paces ahead of him, and tugged his cloak sharply. Hahri immediately stopped and turned to look back at him quizzically. Issai motioned for him to set the monk back on his feet.

"Just how close are we to Kairash?" Issai asked once Korin had steadied himself.

Glancing around for a moment, Korin frowned. "Perhaps three or four spans away from the first farms. It's hard to judge once among the white blossoms."

"How's the buzzing in your body?" Hahri inquired.

"Better. We are definitely closer to her."

"Stand here for a moment and see if you can tell if she's moving farther away or just milling about the city."

For a long moment, Korin stared off to the east, frowning so hard that the lines and angles of his face sharpened, and he seemed to age twenty years in an instant. Issai shifted uneasily and glanced behind them. He couldn't remember the last time he had willingly stood so still in such an open, vulnerable place where their closest cover was a city still several spans away. Even the white flowers reached to only halfway to his knees—suitable cover for nothing larger than a cat.

Perhaps sensing Issai's unease, Hahri moved his gaze from the monk to completely sweep their surroundings a few times before looking at Issai questioningly, his body tensing minutely in response to whatever the ancient boy saw in him. Only then did Issai realize that he had unconsciously moved his body into a fight-ready stance, and he immediately straightened into a more relaxed state, feeling something that took him a moment to recognize as embarrassment. At least he hadn't taken out his knives. He wasn't in the mood for any of Hahri's teasing.

He shook his head before the other could open his mouth and muttered, "It's nothing."

An eternity later, Korin sighed and said, "The humming seems to be neither getting worse nor better, so I suppose there is an excellent chance she has stopped within Kairash."

"Then, let's not waste any more time here," Issai said, advancing towards the monk.

Korin hastily stepped back a few paces. "I don't need to be carried!" he protested, his reddening face betraying his embarrassment when both teens eyed him skeptically. "At your pace, we are less than a quarter-hour to the city's perimeter. I can run at least that much."

"Whatever," Issai growled. "Let's just go."

He shot out towards the northeast, not waiting to see if either Hahri or the monk followed. A few breaths later, he nearly tripped when something impacted the back of his head, and a white blur appeared directly in front of him and sharpened into Hahri's back, borrowed white robe billowing out as he ran almost close enough for him to touch. When a faint laugh reached his ears, Issai impulsively put on a burst of speed, intent on returning the favor—only to have the smaller boy suddenly blur and disappear.

Issai cursed, but any remaining irritation melted

into slight amusement as he slowed his pace back to his original speed instead of giving chase. He was beginning to understand that the reason why Hahri seemed to like to tease him so much was that he was so easily goaded. He supposed that he could blame his incredibly short fuse on that.

Or maybe even after all these centuries, I'm just incredibly naïve when it comes to people, he thought sardonically. *Scratch that—I know I am. Speaking of naïve...*

He looked behind him and was admittedly a bit surprised when he saw that the blond monk was only a few paces behind, his expression tight with determination, as his chest visibly heaved. There was no telling what the monk thought of their childish exchange, but to his credit, Korin said nothing as he caught up to Issai and settled into a pace alongside the "younger" boy.

They caught up to Hahri a few moments later, the other boy smiling entirely too innocently as he leaned up against a wooden fencepost marking the land of the first sign they had come across of the city ahead. Issai promptly walked up to the grinning boy and smacked the other hard against his head with an opened palm. His eyes watered when the force of his blow was instantly echoed against his own head. Crap—he had completely forgotten about that.

"Hey, I didn't hit you *that* hard," Hahri complained though, for some unfathomable reason, that stupid grin was still firmly in place.

Issai pointedly turned his back on him and focused his attention on Korin, who was eyeing them both with an indiscernible expression even as he still gasped for breath. "Do you think the girl is still in the city?" he asked.

Korin drew in a deep breath and replied, "I think so. At any rate, the humming...within my soul is...still about the same intensity. The main road...into the city is only a few...hundred paces more to the east...just over that hill, and the city itself...probably a half-hour more traveling...at a man's normal pace. I am sorry I cannot help...us much more than that."

Issai shrugged; he had expected as much. "Although you might have the better chance of finding her, we can save time by splitting up within the city." He looked sideways at Hahri as he said this and the other nodded.

"While Senn and I can find each other relatively easily, we'll need a place to meet up, discrete, but simple enough for someone who has never been to Kairash to find."

"...and somewhere that isn't the local temple," Issai interjected as Korin began to speak. "After your little demonstration in the courtyard, my bet is on the *Shi* watching every temple in the kingdom like a hawk."

Hahri nodded. "Yeah, some are likely inside 'worshipping' now with the masses as we speak. Having a crowd of witnesses never stopped them before. We should probably also stay away from anyone that you know here. They would expect you to make contact with someone, and we can't be sure they won't decide you're an Old Soul instead of a godlet and try to capture you instead of us." He pulled off his white monk robe and began stuffing it into his pack. "These are pretty much useless to us now."

"That might be a problem," Korin warned. "Remember, I was born in Kairash in this life. *Everyone* probably knows my face here, even if I have aged a bit since they last saw me."

Hahri paused in his task, then looked thoughtful. "Maybe—being in Korin the Watcher's birth city may not be such a bad thing." He turned to Issai. "If *we* were to be attacked by *Shi*, everyone would probably turn the other way and pretend they didn't see anything—probably think we did something to deserve it. However, if a 'divine' figure like Korin were to be attacked..."

Issai nodded. "Yes, it wouldn't be tolerated. Nevertheless, I still think Kye and I shouldn't be seen with you. Quite a few *Shi* know you were the last person to see us. As well known as you are here, it would be tricky to hide your location, and I don't want anyone to think we are together where they can more easily plan an ambush using Korin as bait."

"So the local temple is still a no-go for a meeting place," Hahri said. "What are some of the ritualistic places you visited daily that you can still visit right now without arousing any suspicion?"

The monk's eyes abruptly lit up. "Of course! At dusk, the Temple performs its Soul Purifications at one of three public bathhouses. This should more than adequately suit our purposes." At their blank stares, he elaborated, "As this is a private sacrament, rooms are set aside for us to accept petitioners. If I tell them that some nobles have requested me personally to perform the sacrament, then I should be able to secure one of the rooms for my sole use. I was singled out often like that in the past, so no one, including my fellow Brothers, will think twice about it."

"Can't say I've ever had my soul 'purified,'" Hahri said dubiously. "The whole thing always sounded pretty sketchy to me, what with everyone always acting like the whole thing was some big life-or-death secret. How long is the ritual supposed to last?"

Korin's mouth tightened slightly. "As long as it needs to," he answered, though a quick flash of emotion in those dark eyes told Issai that the monk wanted to say something else. The not-so-innocent sparkle in cerulean eyes also told Issai that Hahri knew this and was intentionally trying to goad the monk into saying that "something else."

Over the past couple of days, Hahri's disdain for the Temple had become abundantly clear, and Issai wondered how long Korin would tolerate that blunt disdain. Although his own feelings concerning the Temple would be best described as indifference, Issai saw no point in making that indifference known at every opportunity. What the monk decided to believe was his own business as long as he didn't try to drag him into it.

Before Hahri could open his mouth again and inflame the monk's ire any further, Issai interjected, "If no one will think twice about a Purification lasting all night, then this will not only solve our meeting problem, but we'll also have secured a place to stay for the night if we are unable to locate the girl today."

"I once had a Soul Purification last three days," Korin told him with a smile, "so one night won't raise any eyebrows."

"Wow, that person must have stained the waters of the entire bathhouse black," Hahri commented with a completely serious face, though his tone practically dripped with mockery. Issai didn't know whether to punch the ancient boy or admire his gall.

"I suspect yours would be stained red," Korin retorted coolly.

Apparently, Hahri was no longer toeing the line.

"No doubt," Hahri agreed with a small smile.

It seemed that the monk had nothing to say to that, or more correctly, he didn't know *how* to respond, his expression openly perplexed as he stared at the smaller boy. Issai just shook his head, refusing to get involved. Korin would learn soon enough that Hahri was more complex than he ever imagined. He knew that even *he* had not discovered all the different pieces yet.

Maybe he would ask Hahri later why the monk seemed to rub him the wrong way, especially when Hahri had initially had no problem filling the monk in on anything Old Soul related. Until then, he had more important things to concentrate on. His list of "things to ask later" was becoming alarmingly long lately.

"Kye..." Issai said warningly.

Hahri turned his head to him, and he was not at all surprised to see the ancient Hahri meet his gaze.

"Sorry," Hahri said simply, but something in his tone made Issai think that he was the only one the apology was directed at. Having that long overdue conversation was rapidly moving to the top of his priorities.

"Where is the bathhouse located?" Issai asked Korin.

Frowning a bit, Korin turned his eyes to him. "Well —it's summer, so unless something has changed in the years I have been away, the Purifications should still be held in the open-air bathhouse within the Residential District to the north. If you follow the main road as you enter the city directly north a span or so, you will eventually see it off to the left as the first few houses become visible. It is the largest structure in that immediate area, so I am certain you will be able to find it easily."

"There's just one potential problem I can see in the whole thing," Hahri stated. "Senn and I hardly look like a pair of nobles."

"If you wear your cloaks with the hoods up, I think it will be dark enough that no one will see you properly enough to be able to identify you later. Plus, as you said before, Soul Purifications can be very secretive experiences for some, particularly the nobility. Very few attend any such sacraments un-cloaked. Just tell the receiving monks I am waiting for you, and they will question you no further."

Korin reached for the pack at his feet. "I shall go on ahead and enter the city alone. I shall see if I cannot find one of my Brothers making their daily rounds within the city to request the room. Then I shall search for the little girl until dusk. Come to the bathhouse only at that time, even if you manage to find her long before the appointed time."

"Something tells me that even if we manage to locate her before you, it won't be so easy to bring her anywhere," Hahri said.

He nodded. "Just remember what I told you about her swordsmanship. If she is indeed an Old Soul as you say, then she has likely had centuries to hone her skill. Even after using my Gods' Voice, I had trouble subduing her. I saw her as only a child, and it nearly cost me my life."

"I underestimate no one," Issai affirmed quietly.

As Hahri moved past him, he grabbed the other's arm to stop him and leaned in to whisper, "Just pinch your arm if you've found her. Pinch twice if you think we should meet back up with the monk. I'll do the same."

Issai was a bit discomfited when he realized that

Korin had been staring at them in something like suspicion during their private exchange, but he chose to simply pretend he hadn't noticed. He could only hope the awkwardness between them could be resolved in the near future. Otherwise, he cringed to think what adding a girl who was a complete stranger to the mix would do to their already fragile ties.

The two younger teens silently watched the monk trek off towards the main road, and only when he had moved out of sight behind the aforementioned hill did Hahri say, "'Go on ahead,' he says. We can be in Kairash before he even reaches the road." He grinned mischievously. "What do you say?"

The corners of Issai's mouth lifted a bit. "That I'm not walking another half-hour. Let's go."

Fields and farmhouses blurred into streaks of colored lines as they—though Issai would never admit to it—raced each other to just a few paces outside the city wall and around to the main road. There, they easily blended with the influx of wagons, horses, and travelers on foot entering the city gates.

"I'll stake out the inns and taverns," Hahri announced once they had safely made it past the entrance guardsmen, "see if anyone mentions a young boy wandering around alone. She may have tried to rent a room."

Issai looked at him sharply. "Just keep the fights to a

minimum, and I better not find you drunk later. I'll try the Merchant District."

Hahri just laughed and joined the stream of people branching off to the left. Issai scowled at his retreating back for a moment, then moved in the opposite direction towards a row of public stables. He had no idea where the Merchant District was in this city, but the glut of people on foot moving in that direction was a good sign.

His head lowered, face hidden from the nose up beneath his hood, Issai discreetly slid his eyes over the people that surrounded and passed him on either side, scrutinizing any child that caught his eye as well as keeping an eye out for potential *Shi*.

He had just reached a wide brick archway opening into a long arcade of shops when a violent blow to the back of the head drove Issai to his knees. For a long moment, blackness swallowed his vision before the world just as suddenly flooded with a brilliant, white light that hit his dazed eyes like a second blow. Issai reflexively sucked in a breath too quickly and half-choked, half-coughed violently enough to threaten his already precarious balance on his knees. However, even as he leaned an arm forward to steady himself against the cobblestones, the throbbing pain in the back of his head began to ease into numbness, accompanied by a slight ringing in his ears.

Issai sucked in a few more shaky breaths before the

fog of disorientation had cleared enough for him to remember why he was currently on the ground practically kissing stone. He automatically tried to focus on the distortion of the air all around him even as his eyes flew open in panic, but his senses were still a jumbled mess.

Blurry, dark shapes that slowly sharpened into people moved all around him, but none of them were relatively close. Someone had definitely hit him, but now he was alone as the flow of the crowd parted widely around him as though he was a leper dying on the street, everyone trying their hardest not to look at him.

He carefully felt the back of his head while his eyes scanned the faces around him for any sign of danger. Issai was surprised when his hand came away clean of blood. He ran his fingers more firmly against his scalp, but he couldn't find any knots or spots of tenderness.

"Shit!" he cursed loudly enough to startle those nearest to him into scurrying away when he suddenly realized his mistake.

It was Hahri. Hahri was the one who had actually received the blow. He jumped to his feet, his head still mockingly throbbing with the remnants of pain that wasn't even his own but still threatened to send him pitching back to the ground as the world briefly turned upside down. He stumbled forward anyway, towards the west where Hahri had said he would be searching within the Traveler's District, hoping that the smaller boy had merely gotten into a tavern brawl. He kept to the edges of the crowds in case he suddenly had to make a run for it.

"Less than a half-hour and that idiot has already managed to find trouble," Issai grumbled under his breath as his eyes scanned for both Hahri and any potential *Shi*, the girl forgotten for the moment.

Perhaps it was because his attention was so riveted on the faces all around him that he didn't even notice the lone figure approaching him from behind until a pale hand had already grabbed his left sleeve and a quiet voice said, "You're looking for your friend, aren't you?"

Issai's reaction was instant; a knife materialized in his right hand as he pivoted on his left foot so quickly that the knife was already against the pale throat before he could slam the other person back against the perimeter wall of one of the public stables that were only a few steps behind them.

Wide, brown eyes almost dilated to pure black met his glare as he forced the hand clutching the blade to still. No, he needed this one alive. Issai took in his captive's entire figure and realized the person was a boy perhaps no older than his current body. His hair was a darker shade of blond than Korin's, but his skin was just as pale. Those features, coupled together with the dark eyes told him that, like Korin, this boy might also be a native of Kairash. This was the first city he had witnessed within the kingdom of Sarim that the majority of its people shared such pale coloring.

More importantly, the kid did not have any visible weapons in the hands that trembled at his sides.

Although he had never run across a *Shi* as young as this boy, Issai did not relax the knife's position, or the hand pushing his chest firmly back against the wall. "Where is he?" he hissed quietly, pressing the blade deeply enough into the soft tissue to feel the sting but still not enough to draw blood. They were probably attracting attention, so he didn't have much time.

The teen opened his mouth, but no sound emerged. He swallowed and winced before desperately trying to move his throat back away from the knife, but the stones at his back were unyielding.

Issai growled in frustration; he didn't have time for the kid to choke on his own panic. Aware of the eyes at his back, he relented a little by drawing the knife away from the other's neck and holding it against the boy's belly instead where Issai's body could conceal it.

"Where. Is. He?" he asked again, every word laced with the promise of violence.

The stranger swallowed nervously again as he eyed the knife pressing into the plain linen shirt he wore. "Hey, I just—I just saw it happen," he finally managed to stammer out. "Y-you get me? I saw you come in with a big group of travelers and then split off into different directions. Your friend was heading to the same area as me. A guardsman got him outside of the Green Valley Inn, said he was a pickpocket..."

"And like a good little boy, you decided to find me to tell me this because..." Issai shot back sarcastically.

Something in the violet-eyed boy's expression seemed to set the blond stranger even more on edge because he flinched away and tried unsuccessfully again to melt into the stones at his back. "I swear to all the gods that I had nothing to do with it! I just couldn't stand seeing it happen again and nobody—" His voice trailed off in a gasp of alarm as Issai pressed his knife deeper into the boy's stomach until the blade had cut through the linen and was pricking bare skin.

"See *what* happen?" Issai demanded.

The boy's eyes flitted from left to right. Suddenly, his expression seemed more nervous than afraid as he answered, "I've lived in this city my whole life, so this isn't the first time I've seen the man that arrested your friend. Kairash is their favorite hunting grounds after all —the Mahze clan, I mean."

Issai felt as if he had been kicked in the gut. As if *Shi* weren't bad enough, now it was slavers. He took a step away from his captive, though he didn't immediately put his knife away. The boy sagged a bit, the relief reflected in his eyes apparently threatening the stability of his legs more than the sight of Issai's brandished knife had. He all but fell against the wall behind him for support.

"Was he truly a guardsman, this supposed slaver?" It

didn't make sense. Hahri was much older than the prey the slavers usually targeted, nor was he dressed even remotely like a child of the nobility that could warrant a kidnapping in hopes of collecting a lucrative ransom.

Still eyeing Issai's knife warily, the stranger shook his head. "Probably not. The Mahze often pose as legitimate workers—guardsmen, sweepers, peddlers—but I suppose some of them might be exactly what they seem."

"And you know this because...?" Issai asked suspiciously.

The blond tensed. "L-Like I told you, I've seen that particular man attacking supposed pickpockets before. Plus, So—"

The boy choked mid-word, his eyes widening as the expression of wariness he wore inexplicably melted into something like terror. His hand clutched at his stomach where the knife had punctured his shirt earlier, and before Issai could blink, the boy was pushing past him back towards the human river. Issai instinctually made a grab for the other, but his fingers seized nothing but air.

Cursing, Issai gave chase, but once the crowd swallowed up the boy, he knew it was hopeless to pursue him any farther and stayed along the fringes of the moving mass of bodies. His time would be better spent concentrating on Hahri's location. At this point, if what the boy had said was true, he could be anywhere, even outside the city.

He gave his arm a couple of hard pinches, hoping it would illicit a response. He waited for a full sixty beats without any answering pain before deciding Hahri was either unconscious or bound and gagged, unable to reach any part of his body with his hands or teeth. Also, the separation pain he was currently feeling in relation to their bond had not noticeably changed in the last half-hour or so.

Issai continued his interrupted path towards the Traveler's District, cursing his thoughtlessness earlier of not asking the stranger for a description of the "guardsman" as the faces all around him begin to blur meaninglessly one into another. He kept an eye out for the escaped boy as well; perhaps he could bully some more information out of him.

However, nothing looked familiar; nothing looked suspicious. The only thing he seemed to be accomplishing was increasing the level of paranoia he felt as the crowds around him seemed to press closer and closer to him like a pair of giant, writhing hands determined to squeeze the breath out of him.

Too close—everyone was too close. If a *Shi* attacked him now, he would have nowhere to run, and the thick press of bodies would conceal the crime being committed. He was completely at the mercy of the currents of this human river, a mistake he could not afford now. Issai pushed, shoved, and waded through the moving bodies until he was closer to the edge of the foot traffic.

Then someone bumped against him hard from behind, and he whirled around before he had even completely regained his balance, both knives clenched in his fists—only to meet the astonished black eyes of the last person he had expected to see. The monk had probably just entered the city.

"Senn! You—"

Throwing all caution to the wind, Issai grabbed Korin's arm before he could finish and dragged them both out of the crowd. At this point, he no longer cared who saw him with the monk.

"Hah-Kye's been attacked," he said without preamble once he deemed them out of earshot of anyone else, "by one of the Mahze slavers posing as a guardsman if the local that told me can be believed. You'll have to hunt down the girl alone. If I find him before nightfall, then we'll meet at the bathhouse as planned."

"Should I not help you find him?" Korin asked anxiously.

Even as Issai shook his head, the steady ache within his body began to noticeably increase. He was out of time.

"Just find the girl," he said. "Keep the room for three days if you are able. After that, if we haven't returned or you're forced to leave the city to chase after her, then leave a message for us at the local temple where we can find you and every subsequent temple after that until we meet again."

"But, did you not say that meeting at the temple was dangerous? Would it not be better if I just waited at the bath—"

"Korin," Issai interrupted softly, "if after three days we haven't returned, then it's likely we'll be unable to meet again for several years."

"Why?" Korin asked in confusion.

Issai couldn't believe he still had to explain. "Because we'll be dead, monk, and it'll take Kye and me that long to grow up enough to be able to travel to find each other, and you, again."

14
_____

He couldn't understand it. The urgency that permeated every pore, that constricted his throat with every breath, but most of all, the fact that none of that had anything to do with the steadily increasing pain from their invisible bond being inadvertently stretched by distance. Issai knew that all of that was completely his own feelings and that confused him.

Was it really just a few days ago that he had wished this very separation? When had things changed so drastically that now all he could think about was finding that loud-mouthed brat again? Maybe it was a consequence of that last brush with death they shared, but it seemed as if Hahri had been by his side for ages when in reality, it had only been a little over a tenday since they had met. Maybe because of that, now that Hahri was gone, he felt so off-balanced.

Issai ran harder than he had ever run, tormented by the converging images flashing across his mind of Hahri and what those slavers could be doing with him and his own past experiences in the hands of all the *Shi* who had ever caught him. He raced across fields of white towards a city he had sworn only a few years before never to return to again, a city where he had left two *Shi* dead one particularly troublesome night.

Eight years ago he had walked into Yuzu in the dead of night, a city at the mouth of a river that had started his current life's journey through the Sarim Kingdom. How ironic that it might also mark his journey's end as Senn.

As it was, Issai feared he had already wasted too much time wandering the streets of Kairash trying to determine the direction Hahri was moving. The sudden wrench of pain from their bond had caught him completely off-guard as he had been staking out the central guard station, trying to decide if infiltration was a possibility. It had been incredibly frustrating that in order to hide his Old Soul identity, he'd had to navigate the streets at a normal pace when he realized that the pain was increasing too rapidly, meaning Hahri was moving too fast to still be within the city.

He *should* have caught up with the slavers by now, but the fact that his pain had only slightly lessened after running at his top speed for about a quarter-hour worried him. Had the pain not eased even that much, he would have thought he was heading in the wrong direction. From all credible accounts, slavers usually traveled by wagon no matter what cover they chose to present, and in the past, he had always been faster than even the smaller ones being pulled by multiple horses. The only thing he had come across faster than him was Hahri and—

—a single horse at full gallop.

Even carrying double, how many times had *Shi* run him down? It was about thirty spans from Kairash to Yuzu. If they ran their fastest horse to near foundering, then it was just possible to maintain such a hard gallop for, if not half the distance, then very near—more so, if they changed horses more than once. However, why would the slavers feel the need to do this?

A sudden, horrible thought almost made Issai stumble. A slaver's sole commodity was people. What if the *Shi* enlisted the help of the slaver clans with the promise of a lucrative payoff? Were they so desperate now that they were willing to share knowledge of an Old Soul's abilities with such a shady group? As far as he knew, it had never been done before, but with all the unusual *Shi* activity they had encountered in just the past couple of weeks, it was a very real possibility.

With that realization came another, more disturbing, thought. If Hahri's abduction was the result of *Shi* involvement and not just the ancient boy's own bad luck, then the probability that Issai was running straight into a trap was high. He had been so worried that the *Shi* would try to use Korin as bait that he hadn't even considered that he and Hahri were just as vulnerable when separated.

I should have at least sliced up that boy's face, he thought maliciously. *He was probably one of the Mahze sent to set the trap in motion, and I let him slip through my fingers without so much as a bruise...*

Not that knowing the whole thing was a trap would have made him even consider abandoning Hahri to his fate. Whether or not he understood why he felt this way or why this epiphany had happened now, Issai realized he was at the point where that was no longer an option and never would be again. Whatever fate he found at the end of this road, he and Hahri would experience it together.

Still, that didn't mean that the whole thing no longer made him feel uneasy. That was one feeling he was relatively sure would never go away, no matter how many centuries passed. He had walked alone for too long.

Issai had been running for perhaps another quarter-hour when a sharp pain abruptly erupted on his left arm, and this time he did stumble, twisting his right ankle as he frantically tried to keep himself from pitching headfirst into the ground at such a neck-breaking speed. A second sharp pain flared in the same arm even before he could regain his balance, startling him enough to make him lose his battle with gravity and earn himself a face-full of weeds. Cursing, he started to pick himself up but froze on his hands and knees when he realized what had likely caused the bursts of pain in his arm.

"Just pinch your arm if you've found her. Pinch twice if you think we should meet back up with the monk. I'll do the same."

It appeared as if Hahri's long past due answer had finally reached him.

Issai slowly rose up onto his knees and sat back onto his calves, ignoring the mild throb in his ankle for the moment. Now that he was still, the pull of their invisible ties was also more noticeably neither strengthening nor weakening. Wherever Hahri was being taken, it seemed he was no longer moving at high speed or quite possibly, not moving at all. Could they have already reached Yuzu? Or was the slaver's property not within the city itself? Issai had no idea, but he did know that he was at least a quarter-hour, if running at top speed, away from Yuzu.

Two pinches—judging by the separation pain alone, Hahri had to know how close Issai was to him, so why did Hahri want him to go back to meet up with the monk when...?

Issai was instantly livid. Did that idiot honestly think he would stop his pursuit and return to Kairash after coming so far? Even if Hahri thought his situation was hopeless, that was no reason for either of them to give up so quickly. Searching for a girl they had never met for the gods-only-knew what purpose was already bad enough. He could only imagine what it would be like to first, share Hahri's pain if the slavers handed him over to the *Shi* to be slaughtered, then having to find him again after his rebirth while his very soul screamed in agony. It would be beyond unbearable.

Issai pinched his arm several times with enough angry force to almost draw blood to let Hahri know exactly what he thought of the captive boy's wishes.

He had been sitting on the ground fuming for probably no longer than a couple hundred beats, and the pull within his being still had not increased. If the slavers had already reached their desired destination, then Issai needed to rethink his strategy. His best chances of rescuing Hahri had relied on him catching them while they still traveled when the number of men was significantly less. The gods-only-knew just how many slavers made up the Mahze clan or what kind of place Hahri would be imprisoned.

Even with their bond to guide him, Issai would still have to wander around for quite a bit using such a trial-and-error method. In that time, it was likely Hahri would either be handed over to the *Shi* and killed—if indeed the *Shi* were behind his abduction—or the slavers would do whatever unspeakable things they did to their victims.

Alone, Issai had virtually no chance of rescuing Hahri. There was really only one option left to him, and the violet-eyed boy wondered why the thought left him more with a sense of anticipation rather than fear as he stood. He carefully put weight on his injured ankle, testing, but other than a little soreness, he figured it was not injured enough to cause him any further trouble. He resumed, full speed, towards Yuzu.

He was not surprised when almost immediately, he began to feel a series of double pinches, each becoming more painful as he neared the city, but Issai completely ignored them. Things must be pretty dire indeed on Hahri's end. Feelings akin to panic were beginning to grip his chest, but recognizing that they were not his, Issai did his best to ignore them. Instead, his mind was back to supplying him with a fresh set of gruesome images of his companion's possible fate.

Half-expecting an ambush at any time, Issai was fairly surprised when he reached the main road into northern Yuzu without incident, slipping into a stream of mostly pedestrian travelers moving towards the perimeter wall. This close to the city, his separation pain was continuing to decrease, raising the probability that Hahri had been taken within the city after all. At the very least, he knew that Hahri was not being held at any of the farms he had just passed.

Issai had spent almost no time, all of it at night, walking Yuzu's streets, so nothing was really familiar to him as he continued south into the city via the central road through a Residential District towards what he hoped was the Merchant District.

The pain within his body had suddenly become harder to distinguish, as if Hahri had begun to move at about Issai's own pace. Not sure what to make of this new development, he continued on his current path, trying to see as much as he could through eyes half-hidden beneath his hood. He had not felt a pinch since he had entered the city, but rather than think Hahri had finally given up trying to persuade him in turning back, Issai worried it was a more sinister reason that had forced the ancient boy to stop. At least he knew Hahri was not being hurt.

A sudden rumbling from his stomach startled him a bit. He tried to remember the last time he had eaten and realized it had been back at the temple in Rihott what now seemed like a lifetime ago. After being lost for so long in the maelstrom of emotions he had never experienced before, feeling something as mundane as hunger was almost bewildering, like hearing an unexpected shout after a day of nothing but silence.

However, this too would have to be ignored for the time being as in an effort to travel as swiftly as possible, Issai had left his pack hidden within the flowers on the outskirts of Kairash. It was with these more sedate thoughts as his mind calmed down a bit, that he realized his skin was beginning to crawl more strongly in response to the increase of people moving nearer to him.

Men with their wives, children erratically circling the moving bodies of their mothers and siblings, the more elderly patrons of the city—Issai was fairly certain that those closest to him at the moment were ordinary people just going about their daily business. However, like that time back in the tavern in Daisha, there was also the irritating feeling of the weight of several eyes boring into his back.

This was perhaps the best chance he would get. Issai abruptly turned off the central road into what he hoped was an empty residential street. It was time he learned whether it was *Shi* or slavers he was dealing with. Sure enough, he had only gone about fifty paces down the street past several quiet homes before the impact of numerous boots moving heavily across the cobblestones resounded behind him.

Issai schooled his expression into one of warning as he stopped and slowly turned to face whoever was following him. Of those out in plain view, there were ten, most perhaps as young as their early twenties while the rest were older, harder to distinguish by age. He was also fairly certain a dozen more watched from within the shadows of the surrounding dwellings. Away from the press of the city crowds, Issai could feel their every movement like a thousand fingertips lightly sliding across his exposed flesh.

The men standing before him all carried long-staffs, raised and battle ready. Issai's stomach sank a notch. Slavers were notoriously famous for the stylized short daggers they carried as their weapon of choice, but right now he saw no evidence of any. A sliver of doubt began to creep in. Were these men merely *Shi* after all? Not all *Shi* were connected. What if these particular men had nothing to do with Hahri's abduction?

A slight narrowing of his eyes was the only indication of his rising anxiety as Issai said coldly, "Is there something you wanted?"

He couldn't help the way his body tensed into a more cautious stance when two of the oldest men suddenly moved forward a few steps. At the same time, he could feel movement a ways behind him, but he did not dare turn around. Alone and potentially surrounded, Issai had no choice but to rely on his Old Soul senses to get him through this unscathed. *Shi* or slavers—that distinction was still his primary concern for the moment.

"Our lord wants a word with you," one of the two advancing men announced.

Issai's eyes narrowed further in irritation. This still told him nothing.

"And who is your lord?" he asked, keeping his tone hostile.

"Mahze," the same man replied, a note of cockiness in his voice. "You get it, right? We're not asking."

Though the answer was the one he had hoped for, Issai did not relax his guarded stance. This was not a scenario he had considered. Ambush, even an open attack in the middle of the marketplace, but were these men going to actually allow him into their domain while still conscious? He had been prepared to confront then fake unconsciousness to infiltrate within their holdings in order to discretely gauge his best plan of attack once inside, but this rather unexpected scenario presented a better opportunity, at least on the surface. Or worse, given that he still had no way to know what he would be walking into, or if Hahri was even being kept in the same place he would be taken to.

He needed more information. "What business does the Mahze have with me?" he demanded.

The slaver shrugged. "Not my business. Don't care either. Now, are you gonna come like a good little brat, or do you still need a little persuadin'?"

Issai didn't move. "Where?"

Although practically every citizen in the kingdom knew of the various slaver clans by name, the fact of the matter was that the figureheads could be any of the highborn lords in each clan's respective city. Over the centuries, various family names had been suggested, but as far as he knew, none had ever been proven by the crown. Issai now deeply regretted he hadn't paid a bit more attention to the whisperings.

The two closest men's faces stretched in near identical, patronizing smiles. "Have it your way, brat."

The pain within had stopped increasing again. He was running out of time. Issai had both knives in his hands before anyone could move.

"Unless you want to dye the streets with your blood," he growled, "then I suggest you back off. I didn't say I wouldn't meet your lord. I only asked his location."

Eying his knives dubiously, the slaver sneered, "Don't press your luck, kid. There's more than twenty of us and only one of you. You should thank the gods our lord only wants to talk with you today."

Issai lowered his arms, but he did not put away his knives. Although this was somewhat the goal he had set out to accomplish, every instinct within was screaming for him to run for it while he still had the advantage. This was stupid; he knew how incredibly stupid this was, but he still forced himself to walk up to the group of men staring down at him, their hands trembling as though they couldn't wait to start beating him into a bloody mass of shattered bone. He had no other choice.

He stopped an arms-length away and said, "Although I can't imagine why your lord wants to speak with a traveler like me, I'm intrigued enough to play his game. Lead the way."

The slaver's grin widened, and it was all teeth. Issai

could sense several people rapidly closing in on him from behind, and he forced himself not to react, not at all certain if that last phantom blow to the head hadn't addled his brains after all.

"There's somethin' that almost slipped my mind," the man said, his voice almost gleeful.

Here it comes, was all Issai had time to think before he jerked sharply to the left, and in almost the same instant, the back of his neck exploded with pain, causing him to choke on a half-inhaled breath. He felt himself falling, his hands instinctually gripping his knives more tightly.

For a long moment, darkness swallowed his world as rivers of fire continued to flow from his neck and spread throughout his entire body. Then even that was eventually consumed by the darkness, and Issai was left with the sensation of being gently rocked, as though he lay adrift on a boat in the middle of a placid lake. Yet, even that slight movement was making his stomach churn.

He thought his eyes were open, but all he saw was darkness no matter how many times he blinked them. His muddled mind thought that might have something to do with the throbbing pain in his head. However, that still didn't explain the rocking, and why was it suddenly so hard to breathe?

Come to think of it, why were his arms hurting? He tried to lift his right hand to rub his shoulder, and alarm gripped his heart when he couldn't move either arm. It took him a few more moments of panicked gasps before he realized his hands were currently digging into his back and bound together. He tried to kick his legs and found that they were bent and drawn in against his stomach. They, too, were tightly bound together along his thighs and ankles as well as restricted by some sort of surrounding barrier.

Issai's heart began to thump almost painfully as panic seemed to squeeze his throat for a few torturous breaths that tasted of stale air while he struggled to remember where he was and what had happened to him. Unfortunately, except for the sense that his entire body had been hurting for quite some time, his mind drew a blank on the hows and whys.

He sucked in longer, slower breaths in an effort to calm his racing heart and forced himself to focus on the most predominate issue—his throbbing head. He vaguely recalled, after a moment of intense concentration, a violent impact and kneeling on the cobblestones of a street. He tried to concentrate more on this image, but it frustratingly seemed to fade before he could completely grasp on to the accompanying memory as if his mind had judged it unimportant.

He had been running, he thought, suddenly remembering the speeding landscapes of first, white blossoms, then open green hills. Why had he been running?

His head began to throb more insistently in response

to his efforts, and Issai thought, *Yes, I was definitely hit from behind, but why can't I—*

Shit! As if a dam had suddenly burst, memories thundered rapidly across his mind. He remembered facing the slavers who had tailed him, purposely trying to move only slightly away as he was hit from behind and—the rest was still a blank. Despite his efforts, it seemed he had been knocked unconscious after all.

Issai wiggled his fingers experimentally and encountered the same barrier as his legs, something that felt a bit like linen. Had those damn bastards rolled him up in a sheet of linen like a parcel to be delivered or stuffed him into a sack?

That would certainly explain the rocking, lack of fresh air, and his current fetal position. He was being carried on foot somewhere like a sack of vegetables, presumably to this, as of yet unnamed, Mahze lord. Bound and blinded—this was definitely a far cry from how he had hoped to enter the Mahze's domain. Although he had not moved his body enough to prevent complete unconsciousness as he had intended, at least he had regained consciousness before their arrival.

Whether that would prove to be a good or bad thing remained to be seen, and as he began to struggle to loosen his bonds, Issai couldn't help but remind himself grimly that fortune had never done anything other than spit in his face.

15

Korin felt torn.

For the nth time, he wished he had more aggressively insisted on helping Senn find Kye even as he scanned the passing faces in the market for anyone familiar, continuing his somewhat distracted search for his missing little girl. His distraction made him feel guilty. He had a task to complete, and there was no use fretting about things that were now beyond his control.

None of the monks he had spoken to had seen nor heard talk of a red-eyed child wandering around alone, so perhaps, as he had back in Aideya, he would have more luck questioning the street children. Although most of the street children he had known as a child were adults now, he hoped that some of them would still talk to him.

While he was careful to keep his face partially hidden beneath his hood, he feared that someone would still recognize him and begin spreading the word that he had returned. He had asked his Brothers to keep his arrival secret for the moment, but even then he wasn't entirely certain something wouldn't inadvertently slip out in conversation.

For a while, Korin had even felt as though he was being followed, seeing the same handful of initially unfamiliar faces in different crowds throughout the day, but as he had found and questioned the various monks of the city, the feeling had eventually disappeared. He had even wondered if some of his new companions' paranoia was beginning to rub off on him. Only a few people had approached him upon seeing his white robes to ask for directions to the local temple, but other than them and his Brothers, no one else had tried to talk to him; no one had recognized him yet.

Nothing would spook the girl like learning her pursuer was so close to finding her again, and Korin really didn't like the idea of having to leave the city to chase after her before the three days Senn had given him had passed. Especially since she would likely flee to the next kingdom rather than double back to Rihott or Aideya. If that happened and, the gods forbid, Senn and Kye were killed, then he knew he would have almost no chance of finding her on his own, and the vibrations within his soul would eventually drive him mad.

However, Korin realized that the bigger problem was what he would do if he did manage to find her. Without knowing the reason for her fear of him, he couldn't even imagine how he would convince her to at least talk with him. He wasn't even sure she knew of the existence of Old Souls, let alone that she could very likely be one. For all he knew, this could only be her second life.

Although the ancient monk saw many young people he recognized as he wandered up and down the narrow rows between the long stretches of stalls of the marketplace, none of them were the people he sought. A bit discouraged, Korin turned back and began to retrace his steps. Perhaps he would have better luck at the public wells or the Traveler's District.

His eyes automatically drifted across the faces he passed, then paused on a small, dark-haired child at the skirts of an elderly woman who was perusing a selection of fruit. Several other patrons were crowded beside and behind them, almost entirely hiding the child from view, but Korin could clearly see a small hand gripping the woman's skirt tightly as if afraid of being separated. He sighed and started to turn away just as the couple behind the child moved on, and a young woman quickly filled the spot. Within the space of a breath, the child's face had been revealed, head turned in profile, watching the couple depart.

Korin had only seen the red-eyed girl for mere moments that night at the temple, but that strangely angry face he had initially mistaken as a little boy's had permanently burned into his memory; he knew he would never forget it.

It was her.

Korin was so stunned that for a moment, standing frozen in the middle of the street, all he could do was stare as the small hand that had been clutching the woman's skirt carefully reached into the hand basket hanging from the old woman's arm and filched something from within he couldn't see. He remembered that Senn had mentioned she had been stealing food from a stall the first time he had seen her. The ancient monk didn't know whether to be appalled or just relieved that after all his searching, there she stood, only twenty paces away.

Suddenly the girl stiffened and whirled around as if someone had unexpectedly whispered in her ear. Narrowed red eyes quickly found and met startled black, and Korin forgot to breathe.

The girl slowly stepped around the woman with the basket and slipped between the two women behind her until she was clear of the small crowd; all the while, her eyes fixed on him warily like he was a wild animal that could attack at any moment. In her right hand was in all initial appearances a black walking stick that had not been visible earlier, but Korin knew better, unconsciously tensing at the sight of it.

She took a couple of deliberate steps towards him

and stopped. He felt his chest tighten in anticipation, half-expecting her to reveal the hidden secret in her hand despite all the witnesses around them, but she merely stared with that same wary expression and clutched the concealed sword more tightly.

Slowly, the blond monk raised his hands to his head and lowered his hood, his smile tentative, but before he could decide whether to approach her or not, she suddenly bolted, diving into the people streaming past.

"Wait!" Korin shouted desperately even as his legs moved to give chase.

After the long days of searching, the distance between them as they had faced off had seemed like nothing. Now that same expanse was the length of an ocean as he helplessly watched the small body move farther and farther away. Like a gentle breeze, she slipped in and out of the moving mass without jostling anyone while Korin stopped and stumbled and shouted, mindful of the stares he was receiving at the strange sight of a cloaked monk racing through the marketplace so recklessly.

It was almost evening. The crowds had already thinned considerably, but this seemingly good fortune only helped to widen the gap between them so far that he could barely keep her in sight.

"Stop, child! Please!" Korin called again, but his voice only seemed to add speed to her legs.

He could see the main crossroads up ahead

signaling the end of that portion of the Market District, see the girl dart sharply to the right towards the northern Residential Districts and disappear from sight. She was as good as lost if he did not catch her before she reached that urban maze.

A few panicked breaths later, he reached the crossroads and practically slid around the corner, eyes frantically searching for the girl, so he did not see the group of teens moving towards him until he slammed into them. Korin stumbled back but did not fall, an apology on his lips, when a flash of silver zipped across his vision, and a line of fire erupted down his chest. His body reflexively jerked back even as a strange *whoosh* resounded in the air before another hot line burned across his chest in a different place and continued across his left forearm.

A splash of red arced across the air in front of him, and behind that red was the flushed face of the little girl twisted in hate, one arm extended out to what seemed like an impossible length until he realized half the length was the narrow blade of a sword.

Behind him, someone began to scream.

Korin's knees slammed heavily into the cobblestones before he even realized he had fallen. He cried out as the skin of his chest seemed to split with the impact. He bent over in agony, cradling his arms to himself protectively, and that's when he finally noticed the blood. It stained the front of his once white robes in shocking scarlet streams of contrast and had already begun to pool in the cracks between the weathered stones beneath his knees.

He felt people surrounding him, touching him, but his shocked mind couldn't process what that meant because his entire being was focused on first, the blood-stained hands he held up before him, then on the writhing tangle of people down on the street, itself.

Because the one thrashing and cursing at the bottom of that pile was the girl, and she had just tried to kill him.

Several people were speaking to him, but none of the words made sense. A couple of men were tugging at his arms, and Korin brushed them away several times before he realized they were trying to pull him to his feet.

He shook his head in an effort to clear the fog. "I do not think I can stand," he protested with a grimace. He could feel the sticky warmth flowing down his belly.

"You're badly hurt, Brother Korin," a man said anxiously behind him. "We need to get you to the temple healers."

Korin turned his head sharply at the sound of his name and saw white robes identical to his own, the sleeves of both arms stained almost completely crimson up to the elbows as if they had been dipped into a vat of dye. He raised his eyes from the gruesome sight and was relieved to see a familiar face. He had just spoken with the young monk a few hours earlier.

"Wait—the child—"

"Don't worry. He's been subdued. The Guard will attend to him when they arrive."

"No!" Korin cried, grabbing the monk's sleeve urgently with his uninjured hand. "Do not give him to the guardsmen! The fault lies entirely with me because I frightened the poor child." He fixed serious eyes on the other monk even as his vision began to blur. "He is the one I told you about, the one I have been searching for. I will go to the temple, but please have the child brought along as well."

The monk looked between Korin and the violently struggling girl incredulously. "But—"

"Please, Brother," Korin whispered, closing his eyes as his vision began to swim even worse. "Do as I ask, and ask me no more."

ACCUSING red eyes stared at him from across the room, and once again, Korin pondered the reason behind that hatred.

The men who had brought her at his request had sat her on a cot, her back against the stone wall, and had bound each wrist with a thick rope to the metal railings on each side of the cot. Her legs had been stretched out and first, bound together at the ankles, then a longer rope had been tightly looped around both her legs and the cot several times until she could barely shift them.

Even from the door, Korin could clearly see the bit of blood that had seeped into the edges of the ropes coiled around her wrists. She had probably been struggling with her bindings up until he had opened the door. He cringed to think of what the skin looked like beneath the rope.

Although logically he knew the binds on her hands and ankles were necessary, Korin couldn't help the feelings of shame and guilt that were currently washing through him. None of this would have been necessary, none of this would have even happened if he hadn't botched everything back in Aideya to begin with.

At least he was able to convince the Prior to allow him to keep her here like this for the time being. The fact that his wounds had not been as serious as the blood had made them seem had helped his argument a great deal. Korin shivered slightly, remembering the way his blood had splashed through the air following the edge of her blade.

Had his cloak not wrapped around to the front like it did when he had stumbled back from his collision with the teens, she might have succeeded in cutting him in half. The sword blade had caught the thick fabric both times, dulling the force of each stroke but not completely stopping the extremely sharp edge from reaching his flesh. Both slashes were deep but had cut nothing vital. The gods had definitely been watching out for him today.

For now, things had settled down, but if the guardsmen tried to arrest her later, then he could always claim Sanctuary for her whether she wished it or not. Now that only the length of a room separated them, the ancient monk was not about to allow anyone to interfere.

The healer-monks had protested his movement, but Korin felt as though this was something that couldn't wait until morning no matter how much pain he would have to endure. He had already waited centuries for this moment.

He stepped completely into the room and shut the door, settling his back against it. It was better he kept his distance for now.

"I'm sorry," he said softly, "but this is the only way I felt I could talk to you."

Her expression did not change.

Korin shifted nervously. Where to begin? Now that they were in the same room, the vibrations within his soul had calmed significantly, but not enough to no longer be annoying. He had hoped that once he had found her, the disturbance would disappear altogether. The fact that it didn't worried him more than he wanted to admit.

"I cannot even begin to guess why you appeared in

my temple and did the things you did," he ventured. "All I do know is that from the moment we touched, something awakened within my soul. You felt it, did you not —back in my room at the temple when I grabbed onto you after you had hit me?"

"How did you find me?" she demanded, her voice tense with barely controlled fury.

Korin sighed wearily. At least she had finally spoken. "The answer is complicated. There are several things I shall have to explain first. My name is Korin, but most know me as 'Korin the Watcher.'"

He watched her expression carefully for any sign that the name meant anything to her, but as before, her expression did not change. He sighed again in disappointment. Why couldn't things ever be easy?

"You have never heard the name?" Korin pressed, just to be sure.

"I don't hang around temples," she spat. She pulled up hard against the ropes binding her wrists. "And for good reason."

Korin winced. "It's not my intention to hurt you. I do not know why you are so suspicious of monks, but I assure you that all I want to do is talk."

"So talk."

Perhaps the best course of action was to be blunt. "I asked you if you recognized my name since it would have made it a bit easier to accept the truth of what I am about to tell you. People call me 'the Watcher' because I have been watching over and caring for them for over four millennia now."

He expected some kind of reaction from her, a snort of disdain, a rolling of her eyes, or even outright disbelief. What he got was an explosion.

"You liar!" she screamed, her body convulsing as she strained against the bindings at her wrists and legs, the fury finally blazing freely from her eyes. "*They* sent you, didn't they! You're here for my torment too! When will it be enough? Why am I the only one who has to suffer like this!"

Korin stared, aghast, as the girl continued to thrash violently on the cot, still screaming her rage, though now without words. He didn't know what to do. Somehow he had botched it all up again. He hurried over to her side, and ignoring the stinging pain in his chest, he grasped her shoulders in an attempt to stop her thrashing. His fingers inadvertently brushed her face as she struggled, and he yelped and drew his hands away as a searing pain immediately shot up his hand and into his arm. He had completely forgotten about that particular affliction.

The girl also flinched away. "What in the three hells did you just do to me?" she hissed, eyes wide with not just anger, but fear.

Thank the gods she was no longer thrashing about.

"I'm sorry! I'm sorry!" Korin placated, wringing his hands guiltily. "I forgot the same thing happened in the temple when our skin came into contact. You were unconscious at the time, but I could not touch you without feeling pain."

"Why?" she asked, her voice trembling.

"I do not know," Korin replied, frustration coloring his tone. "That is what I am trying to understand. I have never reacted to anyone else like I have to you—not even with Senn and Kye."

"Senn and Kye?" The suspicion was back in her voice.

"I am explaining this all wrong!" Korin moaned, falling back against the wall and letting himself slide down the granite until he was seated on the stone floor.

He looked over at the girl who had gone back to glaring angrily at him. "Please tell me that you have heard of an Old Soul," he pleaded.

She stared at him for a long moment with an unfathomable expression. When the silence continued to stretch well beyond the point of becoming awkward, Korin didn't know whether to cry or start pulling his hair out at the roots.

"A couple of days ago, I met two teenaged boys in Rihott. They were both mortally wounded, and yet, before my very eyes, one of them healed himself and his companion with no method I had ever witnessed. It was as if he simply willed the wounds gone, willed the bleeding within to expunge itself.

"They are Senn and Kye.

"They told me they were Old Souls, that they had traveled to Rihott to meet me. That was the first time I had ever heard that name, so I asked what it meant. They told me it was a name used to describe people who are reborn time and time again with their memories of their previous lives intact."

Korin forced a smile. "I am one of these Old Souls."

Her eyes bored into him without so much as blinking.

"I suspect you are one as well."

She snorted. "Why are you following me?" she asked, her mouth twisted in obvious distaste as if the question cost her more than she wanted to pay. "To spin me this child's tale of Old Souls? I don't think so. What do you really want with me?"

Korin opened his mouth to answer, but any forthcoming words stuck in his throat when he realized that he really didn't know how. He had set out on this sudden quest with little more than a solitary hope and had instead gained a little knowledge from a completely unforeseen source in his unexpected encounter with Senn and Kye. He had been so focused on finding the girl that he had never stopped to consider what he hoped to learn from her. His whole being had just *known* that he had to find her at all costs. The problem was that there really was no good way to explain that certainty to this girl when he really didn't understand it himself.

Hoping to stall for time, the monk decided to ask a question of his own. "So I am wrong? You have no memory of any previous life?"

"I knew you wouldn't answer me," she said, her tone a strange mixture of amusement and something like bitterness. "Enough with this farce!" she snapped. "Just do what the gods have sent you to do to me if only to spare me more of your lies!"

Korin stared at her, perplexed. From the moment she'd laid eyes on him, it was as if she had expected some kind of plot, some kind of judgment from him as though it was all due course. Then, while she seemed to dismiss the concept of Old Souls, she had not denied his question of rebirth.

Frustrated, he buried his head in his hands. "'What the gods have sent me to do...'" He barked a humorless laugh. "I have spent many lives wishing for that very thing, for the gods to speak directly to me, to just give me even the smallest sign to explain the purpose of my seemingly perpetual existence."

He raised his head and looked at the deceptively young face still twisted in a very adult expression of anger. "Do you not feel it? A constant tremor in your very soul that seems to have awakened the moment I touched you back in the Aideyan temple?"

The girl's mouth hardened a bit, but otherwise, her expression didn't change. Korin took her silence as a good sign that at the very least, she was truly listening to him.

"It's all right if you do not want to answer. Kye also did not seem to want to discuss it when the subject came up regarding something similar between Senn and him, so I understand if you think I am being too intrusive. I just wanted you to understand that the affliction exists within me, and I believe with all my being that our meeting was the sign from the gods I have been waiting for after thousands of years of praying. *That* is why I have been chasing after you. I only want the chance to understand this connection we seem to have and to perhaps understand why I was born an Old Soul. Perhaps—we could help each other."

Korin had hoped that his sincerity would melt some of her anger, but if anything, her eyes only seemed to blaze more hotly.

"The gods have given me nothing but pain," she said through barely contained fury. "I want no part of them! If you really aren't going to do anything to me, then let me go!"

Korin gazed at her in anguish. "If you leave," he said quietly, "then I fear the separation will in time drive both of us mad." His expression turned pleading. "Just these past few days of so much distance between us have been almost more than I can bear. The strange vibrations within seem to be slowly shattering my soul. I can only guess that it is the same with you. At the very least, do you not wish to find some kind of relief?"

"That's why you should've just died on the street!" she snarled. "Seeing you in first, Rihott, then here in Kairash, I knew it had to be you that was making me tremble inside like this! I don't care if you're doing it on purpose or not. Dead, then the connection breaks!"

Her words stung. It felt as if an invisible hand had suddenly grasped his heart and cruelly squeezed until he almost couldn't breathe. It wasn't the first time someone had so blatantly wished for his death, and although saddened, he had always taken such sentiments with a grain of salt. The force of the pain he now felt shocked him, and he had to really struggle to keep it from his expression.

He forced his eyes to soften and managed to flash her a gentle smile. "I think I am starting to see the source of your hate towards me," he said, "but I do not think my death is the answer. I would likely be reborn as I have always been, and this strange affliction seems to be tied to our souls."

"You keep saying that you've lived many lives," she said. "Can you prove it to me?"

You might as well ask me to bring you the sun, he thought. *It would probably be easier.*

In the past, while a toddler, he had only needed to demonstrate his knowledge or his Gods' Voice for people to know him as Korin the Watcher. What could he possibly demonstrate to a girl who had never heard his name? At eighteen, his knowledge could easily be attributed to the mind of a gifted student, and although she had had firsthand experience with his Gods' Voice, that ability did not in any way offer proof of immortality.

He paused, considering. There was only one way he could think of to offer as proof, but it entirely depended on his assumption that she was truly an Old Soul who had lived hundreds of lives herself. So far, she had neither confirmed nor denied his assertion. The problem was getting her to admit it.

"Perhaps," he hedged. "It all depends on whether or not you are an Old Soul as ancient as me."

Korin braced himself for her inevitable blow up and was instead answered with silence. She stared at him intently with those disconcerting, crimson eyes as if she was trying to peel back the layers of his mind.

"And if I said I was," she finally replied, "how is that related to your proof?"

Korin released the breath he suddenly realized he had been holding. "Over the centuries," he said, "I have lived and traveled throughout every land on this continent. Many communities and later, kingdoms, have risen and fallen during that time, some that none today but perhaps Old Souls and the gods ever knew existed. Name me one of these lost peoples, and perhaps I shall be able to tell you something of them that no one born in these modern times could possibly know."

She stared at him for a long moment, her eyes pensive, before finally replying, "Within what is now the kingdom of Clite, a small group of nomads decided to settle along the northern shores of a lake about three thousand years ago. They eventually called themselves the Anorans. Tell me their fate."

"First of all, it was a waterfall that emptied into a monstrously wide river, not a lake," he answered without hesitation, "and I believe that around 350 to 400 years later the Talbuths moved into the land, wiped out most of them, and absorbed what little people remained. That was truly a terrible era in our history. The Talbuths destroyed many villages until the single entities that remained decided to band together to destroy them. Now, none of these communities and their customs are even remembered. There have been so many influxes of different peoples into that kingdom over the centuries that it is hard to say whether or not any of their progeny remain there today."

For the first time since he had walked into the room, the girl's eyes didn't reflect hatred or anger. The only thing Korin could see in them now was fear, and he suddenly realized. She finally believed him—who he was, what they both could possibly be. She believed him, and it was not something she had been prepared for. At that moment, he would have given his very soul to know what was in her mind.

"There is so much more that needs to be discovered," Korin said into the silence, "but without Senn and Kye to guide us, we can only stumble around blindly."

"They are the other supposed Old Souls you mentioned earlier, right?" The suspicion was back in her voice, but none of it shone from her eyes, only the fear.

It was as though that suspicion had become innate, a natural reflex born over endless years of experiences he could not imagine. Now that he thought about it, Senn and Kye seemed to perpetually radiate that same suspicion. Were all Old Souls like that, and if so, then why was *he* so different?

However, she was still speaking, and he would have to ponder it later. "Where are they now?"

"Hopefully waiting for me at one of the bathhouses in the city. Kye met up with a bit of trouble, and Senn insisted we split up in order for him to help his friend while I stayed behind to search for you."

"Wait—they *know* about me?" Her suspicion was quickly turning into alarm.

"They were the ones who told me you were likely an Old Soul as well. As I mentioned before, I believe they may suffer from a similar affliction to each other as we do. There is much that still needs to be discussed."

The ancient monk stood slowly as to not startle her.

"I do not want to leave you bound like this, nor do I want to force you to stay against your will. However, I truly believe that you should not leave this temple right now, either. Too many people saw you assaulting a monk on the street. This is my birth city; everyone knows me. I expect we will be hearing from the City Guard by morning, and it would be best to claim Sanctuary here until I can clear everything up. Plus, a few things Senn and Kye have told me regarding people who know of the existence of Old Souls make me fear for all of our safety."

He smiled at her sheepishly. "I guess what I am asking for is at least a couple of days."

"You mean stay here?" Her eyes narrowed. "Unbound?"

Korin nodded. "Just until we can speak with Senn and Kye. When I first saw you in my temple, it seemed as if you were searching for something. Perhaps this is your chance to find it. At the very least, we should try to cure this sudden affliction we share. Will you stay?"

"Unbind me, and I will consider it," she said. "Show me the truth of your words."

She was going to bolt. The moment she was free, she would bolt, and injured as he was, Korin would not be able to stop her. His mind understood this, but it was his heart with its newfound stirrings of hope that steered him over to the cot and had him unknotting the rope binding her legs. He then carefully removed the blood-stained ropes around her wrists, mindful of his fingers touching any of her skin.

Korin mentally winced when he saw just how badly she had torn and abraded the delicate skin around her wrists. Both were still slowly oozing blood. They had to have been painful, but she hadn't even flinched when the ropes had been peeled away.

Still, he said nothing as he straightened and stepped back away from the cot.

He waited.

After briefly inspecting both wounds and wiggling her legs a bit, she turned and regarded him with an unreadable expression. "I said I would consider it, monk. If I were you, I'd find your Old Soul friends quick before I decide I'd rather take my chances with the Guard than with someone as dubious as you. I haven't forgotten what you did to me in your temple or what you did to everyone in that Rihott courtyard."

Korin nodded, acknowledging the not-so-subtle hint that she still, after everything that was said, did not trust him at all. "I shall return as soon as I can. Until then, try to rest. I will send a healer-monk to attend to your wou—"

"*No.*" The word was said with such deadly intent that all he could do was hold his hands up in silent acquiesce.

"Then I shall leave word with my Brothers instead," he amended. "No one will bother you here." He gestured towards the basin and pitcher of water beside her cot. "At least clean your wounds."

He turned away and was about to take a step, but then he paused a moment and turned back to her. "Will you tell me your name?" he asked.

She turned her head to the wall, and Korin could only sigh sadly. Yes, no trust at all.

Although his mind was screaming at him that he was making perhaps the biggest, most foolish mistake of all his cumulative lives, the ancient monk calmly turned his back on the pseudo-child and forced himself to walk out of the room. All the while he felt the scorching heat of her eyes burning the possibility of that mistake into his back even as his soul began to tremble just a tiny bit more insistently, already beginning to mourn the distance.

16

When he saw that face was the moment Issai knew for certain the gods hated him.

Only moments earlier, he had been temporarily blinded when the sack had been wrenched opened without warning, and an oil lamp had been thrust down past the lip of the sack, stopping just short of touching his face before he could shut his eyes. He had hissed in surprise, then cursed when he realized he had just given away the fact that he was conscious.

A laugh had sounded somewhere above him, then he had toppled over against the linen as the sack was pushed to the side and upended, spilling him face-first out onto a cold floor of polished, pale stone. Gritting his teeth against the curses that threatened to spill from his lips, Issai had managed to roll to his side, then had watched through various-sized dots of bright yellow light that still flashed across his vision as a pair of legs came into view. He had immediately tensed, feeling his fingers twitch uselessly in a desire for his knives.

It was this way, trussed up like a captured hog after the hunt at the feet of an unknown person that Issai looked up and saw the face of a man he had last seen twisted in fear above the blade of one of his knives eight years ago. Rage like nothing he had ever felt before instantly flooded his mind. Had he been able, Issai would have ripped the bastard's throat out with his teeth.

"You've grown," the man said as a way of greeting, as if commenting on a nephew or cousin he hadn't seen for years.

He observed Issai's futile attempts of breaking his bonds with an amused smile before adding, "You left in such a hurry the last time that we were unable to be properly introduced. I am Lord Rahzon, master of the southern sect of the Yuzu Mahze clan. Of course, I had a different role when we met. And your name is?"

Issai merely glared daggers up at the slaver. Who would have thought that pathetic man he had spared on a whim in that dark alley would come back to bite him in the ass so thoroughly?

Rahzon laughed. "I see you're as rude as ever, but no matter. I don't really need your name anyway. The important thing is that I know exactly what kind of creature you truly are."

The slaver squatted down until his eyes were more at a level with him. Only then did his smile turn hungry. "Old Soul," he breathed, his tone layered with barely contained excitement. "Eight years I've waited to see you defeated at my feet, and to think that after all my planning, my failures over the years, all it took was another little boy to lure that once remorseless demon to me. Though he really isn't a *boy* is he?"

"What have you done with him?" Issai spat, so filled with rage that he thought his entire being would split open.

"Just as I expected. Mention the other brat and suddenly you find your tongue. Don't worry. You'll see him soon enough. My men brought you here much earlier than I expected, and the little party I have planned for you both isn't quite ready for you yet."

Despite himself, Issai felt himself go cold. That this man was a lord within a slaver clan was inconsequential. The only thing that mattered was that he was a true *Shi*, one who coveted an Old Soul's immortality—and once upon a time, Issai had spared his life. He had only until dawn to fix that spectacular mistake if Rahzon, like dozens before him, believed the ritual could only be performed at that specific time. Bait or no bait, it was probably the only reason Hahri was still alive.

Rahzon straightened once again, and before Issai could utter a sound, a boot slammed into his lower abdomen. He nearly bit his tongue in half trying to keep the cry of pain behind his teeth while the rest of his body curled in on itself. He was pretty much successful as only a sharp gasp was heard.

The bastard delivered another vicious kick to his middle, nearly making Issai hurl. "To think I once wanted to rub that smug look of yours into the dirt. This was much more satisfying," Rahzon crowed, nudging Issai's face mockingly with the filthy toe of his boot. "Without a weapon, it seems you're no different than the brats we sell here every day. I'll enjoy watching you scream as I rip out your guts and consume your immortality. Don't think I haven't forgotten how you nearly sliced my throat open."

"Idiots after immortality," Issai rasped, still a bit winded, as he echoed some of Hahri's earlier words. He looked up at Rahzon with a smirk and was rewarded when the slaver lord looked a bit discomfited. "Whatever you think you know about Old Souls will become your downfall because no power on this earth will ever make a mortal man immortal. Release us. I won't warn you again."

"Already pleading for your life?" Rahzon sneered. "None of your lies will work on me. Come tomorrow, you and your friend will start me on the path to becoming a god."

Rahzon raised his eyes and looked at a spot behind Issai. "Take him," he commanded, and only then did

Issai realize that others had been present in the room the whole time.

He wondered what the other slavers thought of their strange exchange. Many times, *Shi* had suddenly fought each other when it came time to perform the ritual, disputing who actually would receive the chance for immortality. Twice, all the *Shi* present managed to kill each other, and he had been spared the agony. Issai could only hope the same thing happened this time as well. Although he hated to admit it, perhaps Hahri had been right to be so fatalistic because things were currently as hopeless as they could get.

He was picked up by two stocky men he had never seen before, one on each end of his body, and carried out of the room like a log and down a long, narrow hall covered in dusty tapestries until they reached a dark-colored door that looked to be made of pure iron. The slaver holding Issai's shoulders grabbed an oil lamp hanging on a hook beside the door while the other fumbled with an enormous ring of seemingly identical keys before the door clicked, and the man with the lamp helped the other swing it the rest of the way open with a shove of his shoulder.

"Do you believe any of that crap?" the key holder asked the other as they slowly bore Issai down a set of narrow, stone steps that seemed to go down forever into the inky darkness. It was the first time either one of them had spoken.

"Nah. Someone's obviously pulling the lord's leg. Brat like this is only worth the strength of his arms, and this one looks pretty strong. A shame really that he'll be wasted on some crazy noble's game."

"Shh! Don't let Lord Rahzon hear you say that! He's pricklier than a room full of swords."

He looked down at Issai and grinned. "What do you say, boy? Reckon you'll bleed if we drop you the rest of the way down these stairs? Immortality my ass."

Issai smiled back. "Try it and see," he taunted, and for a moment, the violet-eyed boy thought the man would do just that as the key holder visibly flinched back at whatever he had seen in Issai's eyes, causing the other slaver to stumble a bit on the steps.

"Dammit! Are you trying to push me down the damn stairs with the kid too! I nearly dropped him!"

"Maybe we *should* chuck him down," the key holder said shakily. "Old Soul or whatever, this boy gives me the creeps, the way he's glaring at me now. Hurry up so we can get this over with!"

After what seemed like an eternity, they finally reached the bottom, and Issai's nose was immediately assaulted with a strong, musty scent faintly underlined with salt. He had entered the room backward, so despite himself, he craned his neck around as far as he could and squinted into the faint illumination the oil lamp provided.

All he could do was stare in horror at the sight that

greeted him. The stairs had led down to what looked like a natural cave, which explained the smells. The cave, itself, was not very wide, about the width of an ordinary common room of a tavern, although the darkness the light could not penetrate seemed to stretch on eternally. Distantly, he could both hear and sense the trickling of water, and there was a distinct damp quality to the cool air.

However, none of that was the reason for his horror. Both walls of the cave were lined with endless rows of small iron cages that continued on into the darkness where he could no longer see them, stacked five to each column, but even that was not what had ultimately captured Issai's attention.

At the end of the row closest to him where the feeble lamp light could barely reach, a still figure occupied the bottom cage. It was too dark to distinguish any features, but Issai only needed the Bond to know instantly that it was Hahri.

"You bastards!" Issai roared, straining against the ropes that bound him, but they might as well have been made of steel for all they budged against his efforts.

"Looks like you two'll have the place all to yourselves tonight," the slaver at his head jeered. "We sent off the other brats out-kingdom just this morning. Unless your friend's a crybaby, it should be nice and quiet."

Issai continued to struggle and curse as they carried him to the cage directly opposite to Hahri's. While the key holder shoved him as far as he could towards the solid back end of the cage, the other slaver grabbed his bound hands through a small, circular opening in the iron at his back and held them down into an indention only slightly bigger than the width of both wrists. Issai could feel a piece of rusted cold metal press firmly against the top of his wrists followed by a click that echoed ominously throughout the cavern.

Stocks, Issai realized with an inward curse. He was wrong when he thought things couldn't possibly get any bleaker.

The second slaver had a rough time keeping Issai's legs still enough to secure the metal piece over his lower legs, but they too were soon locked into place, and Issai's cage was securely locked.

Only when he could no longer hear the slavers' ascending footsteps did Hahri's voice croak out from within the darkness, "You certainly know some foul language." His voice sounded as if his throat hadn't seen a drop of water in several tendays.

Issai clenched his jaw against the laugh bubbling up from his throat. The last thing he wanted to do was laugh.

"Well, I couldn't slash their throats, could I?" he snapped back, suddenly wondering what had become of his knives. The thought of one of the slavers using them really ticked him off.

"Is that why somebody felt the need to dig their foot

in your stomach?" Issai couldn't believe it, but the ancient boy's tone was definitely amused. "And you accuse *me* of having a big mouth."

"*That* was strictly his revenge," Issai defended.

"Yes, that slaver lord said something to that effect," Hahri said, his voice sobering. "What was his name?"

"Rahzon." Issai spat the name like an expletive.

"He said you knew him."

Issai half-expected to hear accusation in the other's voice, but there was none. "Yes."

"What is he to you?"

"Probably the biggest mistake of all my cumulative lives."

"What do you mean?"

Issai tried to shift, but with all the additional bindings, he found he could barely move at all. His arms were already killing him, and he wondered if he was also feeling Hahri's share of discomfort.

As if that weren't enough, the smell within the cage was a torture in and of itself, the stomach-churning aroma bringing to mind a few horse stalls he had come across that hadn't been mucked out in years. He tried to breathe only through his mouth and nearly gagged when he could practically taste the filth in the air. After that happy experience, he could only hope that his sense of smell would die and die quickly because damned if he would breathe through his mouth again.

It was disgusting to think that countless children

had already had to endure the atrocities of these cages. Issai could well imagine the terror those poor souls had suffered sitting here in near complete darkness bound so painfully and surrounded by the filth of countless other victims, wondering what was to become of them. Perhaps it was equally appalling that after living through this scenario time and time again, the only emotion Issai could still feel, bound in his cage like an animal, was tired.

"We crossed paths about eight years ago in this very city," he said. "I was already being hunted, and I figured I could shake them better within the city, then double back the way I came. Instead, I ran into this bastard. At first, I thought he was either a pervert or a slaver, so I let him drag me down an alley and then stabbed him in the side."

"Let me guess, the *Shi* showed up right about then," Hahri interrupted dryly.

"Naturally," Issai continued just as sardonically. "It was then that I thought he might be a *Shi* after all and tried to slice open his belly before both sides could attack me, but that piece of scum must have had the luck of the wicked because he just barely dodged my blades. I gutted two *Shi* and incapacitated the third while the slaver was trying to pick himself off the ground.

"Every so often, I'll let a *Shi* live, if only to allow him to pass on the horrors I dealt to my enemies in the hopes that some may be dissuaded from pursuing us any further, or even not to start the hunt to begin with. I thought the bastard was merely a grunt; at no time did he give any indication that he was anything else. Slaver lords don't usually do any of the hunting."

"You couldn't have known."

Although he knew Hahri probably couldn't see it, Issai shook his head. "That doesn't change the fact that it was still stupid. This isn't exactly an inn we're staying at here."

"That's why I told you to turn back!" Hahri suddenly exploded. "Now you see exactly how hopeless the situation is! What is the sense of us both dying here?"

Issai was taken aback. He hadn't felt Hahri this angry since he had slashed his own arm back at that small cave. Talk about ironic.

"Do you really think I'm the type of bastard who would leave you behind in this gods-forsaken place?" Issai retorted, some of Hahri's anger creeping into his own voice. "Feeling every damned torture until the agony of it all drives me mad with the thought that I *might* have been able to prevent the whole effing thing!"

He pulled angrily against the iron prison around his wrists. "We're still not dead yet!"

"That's not it at all!" Hahri cried. "I didn't want you to come because this is all my fault! I was careless, not cautious enough back in Kairash. If I had been paying more attention, then that slaver never would have ambushed me. I gave that slaver lord exactly what he wanted!"

"Idiot—didn't you listen to a word I said earlier? That man is a *Shi*. He had us the moment we decided to separate in Kairash. I don't know how he knew we were headed there, but he was already prepared. You see, once I regained my head after that slaver knocked you unconscious, I went searching for you and was almost immediately waylaid by a kid around our age that said he had seen you abducted outside an inn by a slaver posing as one of the City Guard. He gave me the slip before I could get much more out of him. He was likely one of the Mahze."

"Are the slavers really that powerful now?" Hahri asked quietly. It seemed something Issai had said finally calmed the smaller boy down.

"I don't know," Issai replied with a sigh. "Some things Rahzon said were really strange. I got the impression that he intends to perform that sadistic ritual on us both himself, like he'll receive something extra from, in his words, 'consuming' two Old Souls. This doesn't sound like something he heard haphazardly over the years."

"That *is* strange. I've never heard of anyone talking about wanting to do the ritual twice."

"It makes me wonder if someone is feeding him this garbage directly. This could merely be a part of something larger. The *Shi* are moving against us in such large groups now that even ordinary citizens have started to notice."

"Yeah, I've heard all the whispers about war within the kingdom, itself, but it could all be just the speculation of those who can't possibly understand what they are seeing. We're all in the same boat; we just don't have enough reliable information."

"Perhaps I should just string Rahzon up with his own entrails and ask him directly," Issai added maliciously.

"If you manage that even in this situation, then I might just start worshipping you because nothing short of a god has a chance of making it out of here alive."

Issai snorted. "Nobody said it had to be during 'Senn's' life. Children grow up fast, after all."

Silence followed his comment, then, "You know, sometimes I wonder if you even have a sense of humor. Then you say things like that, things that if said by anyone else would be a joke, and I honestly don't know if you're trying to be funny or not."

"I'm not 'trying' to be anything," Issai returned irritably. "If you have time to analyze everything I say, then you should be thinking about ways of surviving this!"

"Let no one ever call you a pessimist," Hahri quipped. "Seeing possibility in even this kind of hell has to be some kind of god power."

"I'm no god. Quit being an idiot."

Silence descended between them. Issai tried to jostle

both the stocks on his wrists and legs, straining with all his strength against them even though deep down he understood anything he did was futile. Deep within the earth with only one possible exit of half an arms-lengths of iron that would only open with a key they didn't have —and only from the other side—the Mahze had constructed the ultimate dungeon.

"I know we aren't going to leave this place alive, you know," Issai admitted quietly to the darkness. Hahri said nothing. "But I'll be damned before I accept this willingly without giving those bastards a fight to the very end."

"Well, that's a given isn't it?" Hahri replied after a while. "Or we can always just mess up their plans. I don't know—bite our tongues and spit blood all over the place before we bleed to death so those bastards won't ever dare come down here again. Wouldn't it be a laugh if we use their own idiocy against them!"

"Have you ever bitten clear through your tongue?" Issai asked pointedly.

"No..."

"Well, then I have to say you're welcome to it because that is something I will never willingly do again."

"That bad, huh?"

"Very few things can compare to the pain."

"Do I even want to ask?"

Issai grimaced. "I was consumed with rage. I had

only been reborn for three years when *Shi* broke into my home, murdered my parents and older brother, and stole me away before I could kill them all. My previous life had ended just as badly, and I was just so tired of it all. Before the bastards could cut my throat, I bit through my tongue with the intention of spitting blood in as many faces as I could reach, but the pain was worse than I imagined. I almost was unable to do even that much, and it took longer to die than I had thought."

He shuddered. "It was pure agony, like I was continuously biting through my tongue until my last breath. I should have just let the bastard cut my throat—it would have been a lot less painful. I just hope all the scum I managed to stain with my blood ended up killing themselves in fear of the supposed agony of the 'Old Soul Curse' after that obviously failed ritual."

"Okay. Never mind that suggestion. You don't think Korin will try to come after us do you? For that matter, does he even know you're here?"

"I bumped into him as I was leaving Kairash. I think he had just arrived. I told him to wait for us at the bathhouse for three days and after that, leave a message at the temple and every successive temple should he leave the city until we find each other again. I made it clear he should focus on finding his missing girl. He'll probably have his hands full for a good long while to worry too much about us."

"Apparently, you don't know monks very well," Hahri said.

Issai could hear the smile in his voice.

In the proceeding hours, the memory of that smile became his lifeline.

17

"There was only one time that I died as a baby," Hahri suddenly said, probably just to break the tense silence that had fallen between them.

Issai lifted his chin from his chest. Those random topics again that seemed to exist solely to keep him unbalanced, but this time Issai was grateful for the distraction. It was probably closer to dawn than either of them wanted to admit, and the utter hopelessness of their situation had not changed, no matter how hard he had crammed his brain for a solution.

"I thought we couldn't get sick," Issai interjected dully. "At least *I've* never been stricken with illness."

"I'm pretty sure we can't. I didn't die of an illness. My parents killed me."

"What!" It was said so matter-of-factly that Issai wasn't entirely sure the ancient boy wasn't just trying to wind him up even as the very idea made his mouth twist with disgust.

"Don't get the wrong idea. It wasn't like that at all. It was completely my fault."

"If you had been older, I would've guessed that it was because you opened your big mouth one too many times."

"Well," Hahri said sheepishly, "that's exactly what I did."

Issai stared out into the darkness for a long moment. "You didn't."

"I did."

Even though Issai could barely see his companion's silhouette in the darkness, he knew the boy was grinning like a maniac.

"Idiot."

"Come on. You know how impatient I am. I couldn't help it. I told you before how much I hate childhood. Infancy is practically torture. In that life, I had a mother who had nothing better to do than make *gah-gah* faces at me all day. It was really sickening, believe me. So, one day I just snapped and told her exactly what she could do with herself if I had to look at one more of her stupid faces again. Well, you probably know how hard it is to talk with a throat that's not yet capable of talking, so it all came out pretty garbled. I think it was worse for her that way than if the words would have been spoken clearly."

He chuckled softly. "She freaked out more than I've ever seen anyone lose it. The way she was screaming and backing up into the wall, you would have thought I had come at her with fangs and claws. At that point, if I could have walked out, I would have, but I was only about six moons old and barely capable of crawling.

"As soon as my father came in from the smithy, they took me to the nearest stream and drowned me, convinced that I had been possessed by a demon and it was the only way to save my soul. They both were deeply religious people and believed all the old superstitions. I even tried to save myself by telling them that I was an 'Old Soul,' but as luck would have it, they had never even heard of an Old Soul."

Hahri sighed, and Issai could almost feel the weight of years in the soft sound.

"Needless to say, drowning sucked, so I never did that again, no matter how much crap I had to put up with as a baby."

Some of Hahri's behavior, especially his friction with Korin, was starting to make a bit more sense. Issai found himself wanting to know more, but shackled in a cage within a slaver's underground prison was definitely not the place to bring up such a potentially weighty subject.

However, he also didn't want the suffocating silence to return.

"Is that why you were so against trying to cross the rapids during that Subu debacle?" he asked instead.

Hahri barked a laugh. "Probably. My mind started screaming 'hell no!' the moment you suggested it. We might not have drowned, but it's not something I ever want to risk experiencing again. In a way, it's just as bad as being gutted."

Issai had nothing to say to that, and for a long moment, silence fell between them again. He couldn't believe how quiet his companion had been over the last few hours, and it made him wonder just how scared Hahri truly was if fear was, in fact, the reason for this abrupt shift in behavior. Even when the ancient Hahri emerged, he had not been this—still.

Issai rested the back of his head against the cool iron of the cage. Where were all these questions suddenly coming from? He had never been the contemplative or curious type, his primary rule not to let anyone get emotionally close to him and as a consequence, not to ever again have to understand what made that person tick. It was the only protection he had against the weight of the passing millennia.

Little by little, Hahri had been burrowing under his skin over the past couple of tendays, and Issai had to wonder how easily he had disregarded his most important rule by allowing it to happen, never mind if it had been consciously or not. Caring about someone was a dangerous thing; he had learned that lesson quite thoroughly early on. Just look where that bond had gotten him now, shackled inside a cage, about to be gutted yet again, all because he had deliberately walked into the hands of an enemy in order to try to save the one person he cared about in the world.

It was far too late for regrets. At this point, perhaps there was only one thing, one question that really mattered.

"Do you really believe we'll be born together in our next life?" Issai asked quietly.

He heard a sudden sharp intake of breath and marveled that he had actually managed to catch Hahri off-guard.

"You really do think we're going to die here," Hahri breathed. "When you said it earlier, I thought you were just humoring me." He sighed. "Remember when I told you that if you died, then I would die, and you were so angry that I knew this 'truth.' I only understood this when we touched souls for the first time, like something I had always known but had forgotten until that night. No matter if you die by injury or old age, I will die at the exact same moment, and because of that indisputable fact, I truly believe my soul will follow the bond that currently exists between us."

Issai frowned at the strange emotion he couldn't quite name resonating from the other boy. "I think I can sense a 'but' in there somewhere."

Hahri chuckled, but it was half-hearted at best. "Damn, when you bother to pay attention, you're actually pretty sharp. This is something that has been bothering me for a while now, ever since we nearly bit it in Rihott. When I lost consciousness while still riding in that wagon, I thought that was it, that the next time I opened my eyes, I would be a shivering, squalling mess the size of a loaf of bread.

"At that moment, I realized I was scared to die, something I have never felt, not even with my first life. While I was certain we would be together in death if you were the one dying, the same is not necessarily true if I die first. We react to each other differently, after all. I've yet to see any of my bruises appear on your skin. Whereas I'll bleed if you so much as pull out a splinter, I can crush an arm, and all you'll experience is the pain and even that, probably only for a short while.

"So does that mean you'll feel me die but not die yourself? Would my death break the bond between us? If I die first, will I have to spend more countless years searching for you? Now that we've come this far, that perhaps we're finally within distance to grasp the meaning behind our unending existence, I'm terrified we'll be separated again. After all, the gods have never played fair."

Issai was stunned. He had no idea Hahri had been struggling with such a heavy burden without even showing an inkling that something was weighing so heavily on his mind. Once again, Issai found himself wondering if the joker wasn't completely a mask after all. Just how much of his teasing and amusement was genuine? Not enough of Hahri's emotions bled over through the Bond for him to be sure, and if he were completely honest with himself, he was often so hung up on his own problems to notice anything else.

"I guess," Issai ventured, "we should make sure I die first from now on."

"Only you could say something horrid like that so seriously," Hahri groaned.

However, a boom sounded somewhere above them, and Issai's retort was lost somewhere between his throat and his tongue.

"You don't think..." Hahri asked, voice tight with anxiety.

Issai felt cold suddenly. His skin had just started to slightly prickle in response to movement nearby.

"Yes."

That word might as well have been a death sentence with all the panic that suddenly swelled within Issai's being. This time, not all of it was Hahri's. At that moment, Issai wished he could see the other boy, if only to have something other than his own dread to focus on, so he wouldn't feel so horribly alone.

He found himself straining with what remained of his strength against the metal surrounding his wrists, but he might as well have been trying to move a mountain for all the good his efforts produced. Yet, even knowing this, he couldn't bring himself to stop trying.

"Issai..."

Issai had never heard so much meaning inflected into a single word. It made him instantly stop his desperate struggles and look out into the darkness at the faint silhouette that was only a slightly different shade of black. There was more than fear and pain within Hahri's soul. Engulfing that was an emotion that Issai couldn't even begin to understand much less name. He couldn't let things end like this.

"We'll find each other," Issai said roughly. "Even if we die here and are reborn on opposite ends of the world, our next step will always lie with Korin in Kairash. No matter how long it takes, how many lives, I swear I'll wait for you there. You were right all along; this has to end. Both gods and men have played with us long enough."

Neither one said another word, even as the first faint footfalls reached their ears and several points of yellow illumination could be seen bobbing down towards them. He didn't need the lamplight to know the identity of the slaver who stepped up to his cage. The excitement radiating off the man was practically tangible. The grin on Rahzon's shadowed face made Issai's hands involuntarily twitch as if they too longed to claw themselves into that face in the absence of the knives they usually held.

"It's time."

18

Issai glared at the slaver lord, damned if he would show anything other than contempt.

"Still nothing to say, even now." Rahzon squatted down until they were eye to eye. "No, maybe fear has already struck you mute. I'm told you already know what comes next."

A loud, derisive snort behind him caused the slaver to stiffen and whirl his head around to glare at the men that had accompanied him.

"He just doesn't think you're worth the effort," Hahri mocked, breaking through the sudden tension. "Even an idiot like you should've figured *that* out by now."

Issai wanted to laugh, the feeling was already tickling his throat, but he just couldn't bring himself to do it because he clearly understood what Hahri was doing. Hiding, always hiding his true thoughts and emotions behind loud words. These bastards would never see the fear; they would only hear the mockery, the hate.

A chuckle. "Looks like this is going to be more fun than I imagined. Most brats are usually catatonic after a night down here, but I keep forgetting that you're not really children, perhaps not even *human*. It's a shame the ritual must be done in such haste. I would've loved to hear that smart mouth of yours begging all day for mercy. I guess I'll just have to settle for having the Violet-eyed Old Soul watch as I feast on your entrails." He turned back to Issai and gave him a nasty grin. "I wonder if you'll find your voice then?"

Rahzon gestured to his men, and they split off to both cages, removing their metal bindings and drawing them from their prison. Just as Issai had been brought down, they were each carried by two men to the surface, Hahri in front.

However, about halfway up the stairs, the men carrying Hahri suddenly stopped, and for a moment, Issai thought the other boy had done something in a last ditch effort to escape. Then he heard the click of a latch followed by the grinding of metal on stone and looked to the side in enough time to see Hahri and the slavers disappear into an opening in the cavern wall. He had not noticed the door on his descent.

Issai was taken through the door as well, into a narrow, short corridor that was so brightly illuminated at the end in contrast to the previous blackness that it stung his dark-adjusted eyes. The corridor opened up into another cavern, this one much smaller. It was about the diameter of a lord's house from end to end, though the ceiling rose in an indeterminable height that faded into pure darkness.

The light was flickering erratically, casting shadows that looked like people moving all around the room. Torches, Issai realized as his eyes adjusted a bit, placed within sconces along the cavern walls. Then his eyes froze when he caught a glimpse of gray stone in the center that was different than the earth tones of the cavern. It was a stone rectangle at least three arm-lengths in height and twice that in length.

An altar.

The two slavers carrying Hahri were already heading for the stone, even as Issai was being moved to a point off to the side. At that moment, violet eyes met blue briefly, and a familiar pain squeezed the air from his lungs, one Issai had involuntarily felt only one other time. One he thought he would never feel again.

Then without warning, Issai felt the hands holding his back and feet leave him, and he was falling. His back slammed into the stone floor, dropped as if he was merely a piece of meat while several men around him laughed. Pain shot up his back when his own bound hands jabbed brutally into his lower spine, but he clenched his jaw against the grunt of pain wanting to tear out of his throat.

"*Shi* or slavers, you people have no imagination when it comes to your absurd rituals," he heard Hahri quip through the taunting laughter around him. "I mean, a stone slab? Torches? Come *on*—what era are you from? At least the last idiots had inscribed runes of 'Ancient' on the thing..."

Issai lifted his head and saw four slavers struggling to hold a thrashing Hahri down onto the surface of the stone altar while another two tried to shove his recently released hands into iron manacles attached to the stone above his head. His shirt and tunic had already been removed, discarded in an untidy pile at the foot of the altar.

Issai winced when he felt one of the slavers slap Hahri hard against his left cheek, but this went unnoticed as the group of slavers guarding him were too busy jabbing him roughly in the side and face with their boots.

"Ow! I guess I hit a nerve," Hahri continued, and Issai could physically feel the ancient boy's grin within his entire being, encasing the fear like a soft blanket. "Not to mention, what kind of sicko enjoys eating guts? What part of *that* could possibly make a man immortal? Whoever told you it could must be laughing his ass off right about now with the thought that someone was actually stupid enough to believe something so obviously a *lie*."

Although Issai was too far away to see Rahzon's face

clearly, he could tell the man was as rigid as a marble column as insult after insult continued to spill from Hahri's lips.

"I knew you'd start begging for your life once we got you bound here," the slaver lord said, voice tight with barely controlled anger. "Your lies are useless. Nothing you say can save your life. Besides, I don't think you have any right to complain, having already lived longer than a hundred men combined. It's time that immortality was passed on to me."

"Well then, I hope my guts are tasty since all you're going to get is a full belly," Hahri added condescendingly. "I guess there's just no reasoning with madmen."

Issai bit back a cry as one of the slavers suddenly grabbed him by his hair and yanked him up until he teetered precariously on his knees, the position forcing the rope binding his thighs together to cut more deeply. A circle of slavers now surrounded the stone altar, blocking most of Hahri's body from view, but he had a clear view of the auburn-haired boy's face, probably because Rahzon wanted him to see Hahri scream.

Issai could see the slaver lord facing him on the other side of the large stone, in position to make the cut to Hahri's abdomen. The flickering shadows moving over the whole scene made it seem surreal, as though he were witnessing a nightmare that he couldn't wake up from. This was the first time he had viewed this horrific scene from the *Shi*'s perspective.

His attention was abruptly drawn from that ghastly scene to the cold metal moving softly across his neck.

"Look familiar?" a voice sneered as a knife was dangled from between two fingers directly in front of his face.

Issai caught a glimpse of a plain black, leather-wrapped handle and instantly saw red. The bastard dared to hold his own knife against his neck! Then, almost in the same thought, he saw a possibility. All he had to do was bring his chin down and slide his head sharply to the side, and it would be over in moments.

As if sensing his intentions, the slaver suddenly withdrew the blade and took a step back, though he continued to twirl both blades in his hands. "Wish I could gut you myself with these." He smirked. "I like the irony of it, but I guess I'll just have to settle for watching the boss eat you and your friend alive."

"You sick bastards!" Issai couldn't help snarling as he strained against the hands gripping a handful of his hair and both shoulders.

He tried to wiggle his wrists again in an effort to loosen the rope, but they might as well have still been confined within the iron stocks for all he could even move them.

Rahzon was currently making a big show of holding his slaver's dagger, sheath and all, with fully outstretched arms over Hahri's midsection as if he was offering it up in worship to the gods. The slaver lord was speaking, but his words were too low for Issai to make out. Based on the rhythm, he was more than likely chanting some inane ritualistic nonsense.

Then, on some unseen signal, all the men except Rahzon stepped back a couple of paces, and Issai suddenly had a clear view of everything. Hahri was still straining against his bindings, but it was evident that only divine intervention could free him now.

"I hope you choke on them!" Hahri spat out, and Issai felt a sudden surge of fear through the Bond.

Unfazed, Rahzon unsheathed his dagger and tossed the sheath behind him to one of the men. Then he held the tip of the blade only a breath away from the skin of Hahri's belly. Hahri turned his head, and Issai felt the full brunt of the doomed boy's fear that distance and masks prevented him from seeing.

All Issai's anguished mind could think was, *I don't want to see this!*

Yet, he couldn't close his eyes, couldn't cut that connection between them.

I can't see this!

He trembled within his bindings and wondered if this encompassing agony was what it felt like when your soul was dying.

Stop!

White hot rage filled him, pushed away all the combined fear smothering his being until all that was left was his pain and fury and the sight of the dagger rising to gain momentum for the final plunge.

No!

Issai lunged forward, tearing out of the grip of his tormenters as the rope he had been steadily trying to wiggle his hands out of broke like blades of grass against the preternatural force of his anguished rage. He snatched one of his knives in mid-twirl from the slaver's hand, and before the man could get over his astonishment to react, Issai drew the knife to his own neck and viciously slashed a short line of cold fire into the damp flesh.

The slaver dropped the second knife and screamed in horror as a gush of hot blood splashed across his face and chest as Issai threw himself at him, stabbing the man just under his sternum. His momentum and weight carried the small blade all the way down to the man's groin, and Issai fell to the ground amidst a nightmarish mess of the slaver's own blood and guts, the putrid smell of the man's perforated bowels hitting him like a punch to the face. Gagging, Issai used the hand still gripping his knife to push himself back away from the contorting body and back onto his knees while his other hastily covered his neck wound in an effort to staunch the flow of blood.

He then swung the blood-covered knife in an arc towards his earlier tormenters. As flecks of blood flew, several screams of terror echoed across the cavern, intermingled with the slap of fleeing feet against the stone floor, but Issai only cared about one particular sound that easily overtook that sudden cacophony. He raised his eyes in enough time to see Rahzon fall screaming to his knees as though he was the one being gutted, his hand smearing blood across his skin and into his hair as he frantically scrubbed at his face.

The slavers that had circled the stone block were already racing past him towards the exit until only the slaver lord and the man Issai had killed remained of the enemy.

Blood painted Hahri's neck and dotted his bare chest in various-sized blots. He stared across the distance at Issai, eyes widened with the look of a deer caught in the jaws of a wolf.

Feeling the warmth sliding down his neck, Issai quickly sawed through the ropes binding his legs and jumped to his feet. A wash of weakness and dizziness immediately assaulted his body, and legs already numb from hours of immobility threatened to collapse out from under him. Issai cursed and pressed his hand more firmly against the wound in his neck and stumbled over to the stone altar where Rahzon was still screaming, apparently so lost in his fear to realize that Hahri's blood had done nothing other than stain his skin and hair red.

Issai slammed his knee into the back of the man's neck, and only the echoes of his terror remained as the slaver toppled over onto his face like a felled tree. Satisfied the bastard would be out for a while, Issai turned to the sacrificial altar and was met with eyes still wide with shock.

Hahri's mouth moved silently as if wanting to speak but either afraid or unable to. Blood continued to ooze out of the wound, sluggish as if it was already beginning to scab over, but in reality was just mirroring the pressure that Issai's fingers applied to his own wound.

"I'm sorry for that," Issai felt the need to say and winced when the slice in his neck seemed to open wider with each word. He hastily brought his finger to his lips when it looked as if Hahri was about to reply.

He dropped his knife on the stone beside Hahri and set about loosening the bolts that tightened the manacles around the other boy's wrists until he was able to pull them free. As Issai moved towards Hahri's shackled legs, the room abruptly began to spin, and he found himself slumping onto the stone for support. Damn, he was almost out of time.

Hahri had automatically raised a hand to the slash on his neck. Issai grabbed it, blood and all, and sank to his knees. "If I pass out," he whispered carefully, "the rest is up to you. Find out how that piece of scum knew where to find us."

Then without waiting for a reply, Issai closed his eyes and concentrated on healing the gruesome wound.

"Wait!" Hahri hissed, squeezing his hand urgently.

Issai ignored him. If he didn't attempt the healing

now, he was afraid the blood loss would affect his ability to concentrate properly. He would be damned if he had saved them only for them to bleed to death anyway.

He was vaguely aware of the clammy hand that covered their joined hands a few moments later. Then he suddenly found himself looking at a dual image within his mind. One was the wound he was currently tracing, and the other was of his own face, eyes closed and forehead wrinkled in concentration as blood slowly dripped from between the fingers that pressed against his neck. With a start, Issai realized that he was seeing himself through Hahri's eyes, and he was so surprised, he almost lost the detailed image he was supposed to be building.

Cursing mentally, he did his best to ignore this unexpected variable and finished tracing the wound. Then he quickly issued his mental command to heal before anything else could happen. Issai could feel a sharp sting as the edges of the split skin began to merge back together within an explosion of warmth inside his entire neck. Although he could feel the usual drain on his strength, another wave of extra energy followed closely in its wake to replenish it, and he knew he wouldn't pass out this time either.

When he could no longer feel any pain, Issai opened his eyes, expecting to be met with the other's smile of relief. What he got was a glare that could boil water.

"Thanks *so* much for that pleasant memory," Hahri

snapped. "Couldn't you have picked a less horrible way to make us bleed onto these bastards?"

Issai shook his head. "Nothing sprays blood like a throat wound," he said. "I've cut countless throats over the centuries. Even panicked, don't you think I would know exactly where and how deep to slash my throat that would both yield the best results and not be immediately fatal?"

Hahri shuddered. "Quit saying things like that so seriously! It's creepy."

"Just be glad you're only wearing your blood instead of some lunatic sucking it off your guts," Issai grumbled. "I already apologized. What more do you want?"

"For starters, my legs out of these damn shackles. I'll get back to you on the rest later."

Issai didn't know whether to roll his eyes, laugh, or just smack the other hard in the back of his head. He settled for shaking his head; he'd had enough things bashing into his head lately.

Once freed, Hahri immediately jumped down from the stone block and made a beeline for the unconscious slaver lord, kicking him soundly in the side before Issai could even react.

"You idiot, don't wake him!" Issai hissed. "We still need to bind him, and I'd rather he not be conscious when we do it."

The ancient boy shrugged. "I'll just hit him again if he stirs."

Hahri used a corner of the man's robe to wipe most of the blood from his neck and chest. Rahzon didn't even twitch. Issai watched him mutely, noting the way the other's hands were trembling. As the silence stretched on between them, he shifted uncomfortably. He knew he should say something, but as usual, the words just wouldn't come. It was probably best to just pretend he hadn't noticed.

Issai picked up Hahri's shirt and tunic from the foot of the altar and handed them to the other boy.

"Thanks."

While Hahri dressed, Issai also used a section of the slaver's dark robe to wipe the blood from his own neck. Only when he tried to wipe the blood from his hands and wrists did he realize that some of the blood on his wrists was from several rope abrasions, probably when he had finally broken through the bindings. He hadn't even felt the dull pain until now and was surprised his companion hadn't brought it up yet. Perhaps Hahri thought the wounds were the result of his own struggles, and after all the howling the cerulean-eyed boy had done earlier because of the throat slashing, Issai wasn't about to claim responsibility if he didn't have to.

"That was too close."

Issai paused in his inspection of his wrists and looked up at his companion. There was no hint of the joker in the eyes that met his gaze, but he was relieved to see the emotion that was there, even if he didn't quite know how to deal with it.

Issai closed his eyes and nodded. It was all he could offer.

He moved over to lift Rahzon's legs. "Help me with him."

"Onto the stone block?" Hahri asked, the strange look in his eyes melting away as his lips stretched into a wicked grin.

Issai couldn't help but smirk as well. Maybe there was something he could do after all.

"The bastard wanted to be one of us. Why not give him at least a taste."

19

Korin waited all night until the faint murmurs of a dozen distant voices broke the silent stillness of the room he had reserved for the appointed "ritual cleansing" and he was certain morning had finally arrived. They had not come, and although he had half-expected that outcome, the ancient monk couldn't stop the panic beginning to squeeze the breath from his lungs.

Had Senn even found Kye? Had he, the gods forbid, been captured as well? Korin had no way of finding out either without drawing some potentially dangerous eyes to himself at a time when his relationship with the girl was so fragile that a single word could irrevocably shatter it.

His only consolation was that he had not felt any

significant fluctuations in the strength of his shared vibrations with the girl, so he was at least confident that she had not left the city, even if he was not so sure she had not left the temple.

Korin sighed wearily. He supposed he had waited all he could. Soon, someone would come to check on him, and he was in no shape to properly handle their questions. The sword wounds stung abominably, and he couldn't remember the last time he had gotten a decent night's sleep. He was pretty sure he had dozed off a couple of times during the night despite his best efforts to stay alert. He was honestly surprised he was still conscious, even considering that his stamina and body constitution was a bit better than a normal man's.

He dreaded going back to the temple. That was no little girl he had left there. He wasn't sure when, but sometime last night, Korin had finally stopped thinking of her as such. After talking with her so long, he had clearly seen that there had been nothing even remotely childish about her.

What would the girl say when he returned alone? Would he even be able to convince her to stay another day? Worse yet, what if he opened the door to her room and found it empty?

He wished he had at least learned her name. Without a name to tie to her face, the distance between them seemed as insurmountable as the time when he had first lost her. Without a name, she was still not real.

It was slow going, but Korin managed to leave the bathhouse and navigate the city with minimal contact; he outright succeeded in avoiding the Guard.

An hour later, exhausted, in pain, and his legs a step away from collapsing, the ancient monk stood before the girl's closed door. None of the monks had stopped him with any complaints of trouble once he had entered the temple, so he was still hopeful that she had indeed heeded his warning and had decided to accept his offer of Sanctuary.

He knocked sharply. "It's Korin. I am coming in."

Receiving no answer, his heart sank in dread even as he pushed the door open—and gasped in shock.

———

THEY STOOD on either side of the sacrificial altar, watching the motionless face still painted with Hahri's drying blood stir to life. Issai's eyes met Hahri's, and his partner nodded. Hahri lowered the lit torch in his hand closer to Rahzon's face until his eyes flew open, and the man tried to sit up in a blind panic. He instantly fell back with a cry when the iron surrounding his wrists prevented him from moving very far.

"Morning!" Hahri said cheerfully, the malicious grin on his face belying his tone.

The slaver lord froze, and his eyes widened. "What the—how..."

"Now that's the question isn't it," Issai said, and the man's head whipped towards him so fast that his neck audibly cracked. The look of absolute terror that instantly transformed Rahzon's face brought a matching grin to Issai's lips.

"But, but I saw—" His eyes turned back to Hahri. "Something cut your throat! Your blood...!"

Rahzon's entire body abruptly started thrashing. "Get it off!" he screamed, straining his hands against the manacles futilely. "The blood! Get it off my face!"

"A bit late for that," Hahri said calmly. "You're definitely cursed, right? Horrible death and all that. Isn't that what you bastards are always going on and on about? If I were you, I would worry more about being shackled and at the complete mercy of the two people you were just about to torture to death."

Issai slashed a knife across the slaver lord's cheek. As he belatedly gasped in shock, the resulting thin crimson line began to slowly bead with blood.

"Start talking," Issai growled. "How did you know we were going to Kairash?"

Rahzon spat towards Issai's face, but he was anticipating something like that and easily jerked out of the way. He calmly slashed the slaver's same cheek in retaliation, just below the first cut. Rahzon cried out and once again began to strain his arms against the manacles.

"Damn brats! You won't get a damn word out of me! I'll die first!"

"That's the idea," Hahri quipped in a pleasant voice, but his whole demeanor was that of the ancient Hahri. Even Issai felt a chill go down his spine when confronted with such a contradiction. "Right now, it isn't your life that's in question. It's how long you want to remain stubborn about not answering. We'll get what we want out of you in the end, so you might as well do yourself a favor and tell us what we want to know."

Rahzon bared his teeth like a trapped animal then pressed his lips tightly together in continued defiance. Issai was a bit surprised. As much as the man had screamed and carried on earlier in regards to the blood, Issai thought he'd spill his guts with only a bit of bullying, no problem. Now it seemed he may have to spill the bastard's guts literally before all was said and done.

He scowled irritably. Although he had not sensed any significant movement other than their own for a while now, the fact remained that they were still deep within enemy territory without a clue as to what the slavers were doing or might decide to do once they were thinking lucidly again. They just didn't have time for this crap.

Issai grabbed Rahzon's left hand and forcibly stretched out the pinky finger. The man only had enough time to widen his eyes in beginning horror before Issai cut it off.

"How did you know we were going to Kairash?" Issai repeated while the slaver lord screeched in agony.

When he didn't immediately answer, Issai grabbed another finger and sliced it off just as quickly.

"*Shit*! I didn't know! I didn't know!" the slaver lord screamed, his whole body thrashing. Issai steadied the bleeding hand and nodded to the other boy again. Hahri lowered the torch to the two stubs, and the slaver lord's screams doubled in volume.

Once satisfied that the hand was no longer bleeding, Issai grabbed another finger. "Wrong answer," he said and raised his knife.

Rahzon wailed as if he were slowly being cut in half and tried to tear his hand out of Issai's grip. "I swear I didn't know!" he pleaded.

Hahri held up his hand, and Issai paused. "Then why did your men know exactly who to attack if someone didn't tell them what we looked like?" Hahri asked.

It was as though a dam had suddenly broken open. Rahzon couldn't get the words out fast enough. "I've had men on the lookout for the Violet-eyed Old Soul for years, in as many cities and towns as I could manage. That you were captured in Kairash was just pure coincidence. I swear it!"

Though it seemed impossible, Hahri's eyes became colder. "But it was me, not your old nemesis, who was attacked. My identity as an Old Soul was only revealed in the last few days, so let's try this again."

He looked over at Issai and nodded.

Issai gripped their captive's middle finger more firmly and sliced it off. Rahzon screamed and cursed them for a long moment after that wound too had been cauterized before Hahri was able to continue the interrogation.

"How did you find out about me? We've been traveling together for only a couple of tendays. Someone had to have fed you information about us relatively recently for your men to have been up-to-date enough to know they were hunting *two* Old Souls and particularly, what the newest Old Soul looked like."

"Gossip!" Rahzon hissed through clenched teeth, his eyes flickering fearfully to the knife hovering within his view. "Any new information about Old Souls was immediately sent back to me. My hunting parties made sure of it. I heard bits and pieces from different subordinates, no matter if they thought it rumor or truth."

"You know," Hahri said softly, nearly emotionless eyes boring down at the terrified man, "I don't think you're telling us the whole truth. What have you left out?"

Rahzon's eyes flashed panic. "Nothing! I swear it! Nothing!"

Issai reached for the slaver's thumb, and the man screamed and thrashed violently against his bonds as though he were having an uncontrollable fit. Tears streamed from eyes that had gone bloodshot and crazed with fear and pain. He was useless to them in such a state.

Deciding to change tactics, Issai grabbed the man's chin and forced him to turn his head. He contracted his fingers until this newest discomfort refocused his captive's attention enough to meet his violet glare.

"You know too much about us and the *Shi*'s rituals for it to have been gleaned from mere gossip and legend. *Shi* are just too greedy and secretive to go blabbing those kinds of details for anyone with ears to hear. You are either working under a *Shi* Lord and decided to steal the chance for immortality from him, or you bought the knowledge from someone. Which is it? Deny it again, and I'll start splitting your belly open. It's still up to you how you choose to die."

Issai released his chin and raised a knife above his exposed abdomen for emphasis. When Rahzon didn't immediately answer, he stabbed the knife shallowly into the far side of the man's belly and began to slowly draw it across the damp flesh towards him.

"Soujin!" practically exploded from their captive's mouth. "The bastard's name is Soujin! He taught me everything there is to know about you abominations!"

His hand stilled. For the first time since they began the whole thing, Issai felt his pulse speed up in anticipation. "Who is he?"

"No one really knows who the bastard is! He was the one who approached me, said he'd heard I was digging for information about the Violet-eyed Old Soul. Never said why he was willing to teach me about Old Souls. He never asked for gold or anything. I've only met him that one time, and no amount of digging I did gave me even a hint to his identity. Some of my men even infiltrated other groups hunting you monsters, but they knew no more about this Soujin than I did. Probably isn't even his real name."

"Was he the one who tipped you off that we were heading to Kairash?" Hahri asked.

Rahzon tried to flinch away from the knife still piercing his skin as if already expecting punishment before he even spoke. "I told you before that was just a coincidence!" he said desperately. "That meeting with Soujin was years ago!"

"Why is it that I still don't believe you?" Hahri said. "That still doesn't explain why your men in Kairash knew my identity so quickly. Not to mention the fact that I was traveling with the very Old Soul you sought, and you understood just how to use me as bait."

"My men heard the information from other hunting parties! I'm not the only one they would have passed it on to, nor am I always the first to hear it. I've known about you two traveling together for over a tenday now! I had more than enough time to set my various traps!"

Issai locked eyes with Hahri, and the slightly startled flash in those cerulean eyes let Issai know the other was probably thinking the same thing. How in the world had that piece of scum known they were together so soon? Their trouble at Nisei had only happened about a tenday ago, and that was really the first time anyone had seen them together. They had killed all their attackers in the hallway of the inn. Were they not ordinary guardsmen nursing a grudge after all, or had someone else been watching them in the forest when they had fought each other?

However, even if that were the case, it still should have taken longer for truth and rumor to spread so far across the kingdom. Taken together, everything the slaver lord told them just wasn't fitting together into a coherent whole. Either Rahzon was still lying even with all the torture, or their captive didn't have the entire picture to begin with. Either way, they still hadn't made very much progress in understanding the forces that had started to stir around them.

"This Soujin, what did he look like?" Issai demanded.

"He—" Rahzon paused.

A strange look overtook the suffering in his eyes for a brief moment, as if he was confused, before a look of pure terror replaced it. It was so intense that Issai almost glanced over his shoulder to see what manner of man or creature could make the slaver look a breath away from soiling himself.

"I can't...!"

Issai raised an eyebrow. "You 'can't'?" He couldn't believe the man was still resisting. Was this Soujin *that* terrible? If Rahzon feared his benefactor more than the thought of having his belly sliced open, then they had to pry the information out of their captive at any cost.

Even if the cost is the last bit of humanity left in me.

"You know, I was once skinned alive by one of you bastards," Issai said quietly, looking down at the slaver lord with as much hate as he could muster. He felt a jolt of jumbled emotions from Hahri that caused his lungs to constrict so sharply that he could not breathe for a few beats. He could also sense that the other wanted to speak, but the only sound was the heavy breathing of their panicked captive.

However, Issai's expression didn't acknowledge any of that as he continued, "The pain is indescribable. Turns out that you can live quite a while before your body dies of shock, longer if you're an Old Soul. I wonder how long ordinary scum like you will last?"

Rahzon made a sound like he was choking as Issai roughly jerked his knife from the slaver's stomach and dug it shallowly into the base of the man's neck, dragging the blade slowly down towards his sternum as if he were skinning a pig.

Rahzon's scream certainly mimicked said animal, but this time, there were tears in his voice as he shouted, "I can't remember! *Please!* I can't *remember!*" Issai paused. "I know that he was at least a head taller than me, that he wore the silk robes of a lord. I can even tell you that the silk was a deep blue! But his face, his hair—there's nothing! I can't even remember if he was fat or muscled! Young or old! Or the timbre of his voice! Just that silk and what it looked like as he towered over me! I can't tell you what I don't know! I'm begging you! Please believe me!"

"And yet you recognized me immediately even though the last time you saw me was in a dark alley when I was a boy," Issai scoffed.

"Don't you think I've learned by now exactly what kind of demons you are! What unspeakable tortures you still can do to me!" he cried desperately. The slaver lord wasn't even trying to stop the tears from flowing anymore. "But Soujin is a man who has consumed a thousand Old Souls! A man who has become a *god!* If I can't remember his face, then it's because he doesn't want me to!"

Issai and Hahri shared a long look while the slaver lord continued to sob. A bit of Hahri's emotions trickled over through the link—slight bewilderment, but also skepticism.

"A thousand Old Souls, a god..." Hahri echoed. "That's quite the claim. If you expect us to believe that piece of drivel, then you're really as stupid as you look.

It's no wonder you believed all that Old Soul ritual nonsense." His eyes narrowed. "Either that or you're still spinning lies in an attempt to save your own sorry ass."

The slaver was shaking his head frantically. "He showed me proof! Soujin created an immortal without the ritual! I saw it with my own eyes! He gathered with his bare hands what looked like dust made of pure light out of the very air and showered a girl with it until her body had absorbed it. Unlike you, she doesn't age! I saw her recently. It's been almost eight years, and she still looks like the same girl of sixteen that I saw then. Soujin told me that after I consumed enough Old Souls, then I could do the same, that I could become more than just an immortal!"

"And that's why you wanted to eat both of us," Issai said slowly. He didn't know what to think. Although a few more things concerning the slaver lord's motives were starting to make a bit more sense, with regards to the man named Soujin, everything was a jumbled mess. There was still so much of the man's story that just didn't sit well with him.

"If he wields such a power, then why not just make *you* immortal?" Issai demanded. "Why send you out after Old Souls in the first place? For that matter, why help you at all? You said so yourself; he asked for nothing in return. What could possibly be in it for him?"

"I told you I *don't know!*" Rahzon screamed, his hands straining sharply against the manacles as if he meant to strike out with fists. "Who am I to question a god?"

Issai caught Hahri's eye and raised an eyebrow questionably. The ancient boy shrugged, then looked down at the struggling man again, his lips pressed into a thin line. Then he looked back up at him and shrugged again. A feeling like acceptance washed over him from his partner, and Issai nodded in tentative agreement. No matter how strange the explanation, there was no way the man was *that* creative.

Issai pushed his knife down a little deeper to draw Rahzon's attention back to him. "One last thing," he said as the man cursed him. "Where is the boy you sent to stall me while the others were transporting my partner to Yuzu? And don't plead ignorance. You know damn well who I'm talking about."

Either something in Issai's eyes or his tone set the man to thrashing frantically against his restraints again so that he managed to cut himself more deeply with the knife still embedded in his skin before Issai could move it away.

"You *demon* bastards! Tormenting me with lies now! You know damn good and well that slavers trade in brats, not employ them! I've told you everything that I know, may the gods damn you!"

At this point, Rahzon truly did look as though he was one scream away from permanently breaking. Whether he was still trying to protect a few more secrets or not, they had probably gotten everything they were going to get out of the bastard. There was only one thing left to do; he needed to correct a mistake.

Issai wiped his blade clean on the man's pants and sheathed it. He nodded towards Hahri and stepped away. Quick and painless—it was better than the scum deserved.

Afterward, they removed him from the altar and laid him next to it. If anyone dared venture down to this sacrificial chamber ever again, then perhaps they would think the Old Soul blood did him in. Issai seriously doubted any soul would set foot in the chamber again anytime this century. They would probably be telling this horror story for even longer.

The only problem remaining was whether or not they could leave without anyone seeing them.

"Those bastards took my armbands while I was out cold," Hahri growled. "My knife, too. Do you think we could look for—"

"Forget it," Issai cut him off flatly. "I'm not about to go poking around a slaver compound. We need to get the hell out of here!"

"So says the guy who is always losing his knives and making me look for them. Those bands aren't exactly easily replaced, you know."

"And who's the one always making me lose them? Just forget about them; they probably tossed them out along some random street back in Kairash."

"Fine then. Let's go," Hahri huffed. "If we hurry, then maybe we won't have to chase Korin all over creation. Let's hope those slavers forgot to close the door on their way out or else we may just have to go cave exploring. In the dark."

Issai cursed. He had forgotten all about that thick, iron door.

20

Korin's first instinct was to *run*.

Four sword points flooded his vision as he stood frozen at the threshold of his room. He had been prepared for an angry girl, even an empty room. This was the last thing the ancient monk had expected to see behind the door, and his exhausted mind could not make sense of what he was seeing for a long, terrifying moment.

Then a flash of black beyond the swords caught his attention, and abruptly understanding, he slowly exhaled in an effort to still his racing heart. In his rush to return to the temple, Korin had completely forgotten about the very likely visit from the Guard. Unfortunately, none of the four guardsmen were familiar.

"Can I help you?" he said as calmly as he could through the panic that still constricted his throat.

His eyes briefly darted over the shoulders of the men, but the cot was empty, the girl nowhere to be seen. Had they already arrested her? Had she not claimed Sanctuary? And where was the Prior? The Guard were never allowed to roam freely within Temple walls without a proper escort.

To his relief, all four men lowered their swords, but he tensed again when they did not sheath them.

"Brother Korin," one of the middle two guardsmen acknowledged. "Our apologies. We thought that maybe you'd have the child in question with you."

"What child?" he asked just to be sure.

The guardsman frowned. "We were told by several witnesses that you were attacked by a boy of about ten near the Merchant District yesterday. They said you had the boy brought to the temple, and the Prior confirmed he was being held in this room. However, the room was empty when we arrived."

Alarm bells went off in Korin's head. Under no circumstances would the Prior have directed them here without talking to him first. Were these men truly of the Guard? This couldn't have happened at a worse time. He was so exhausted he could barely think straight.

Korin forced a smile. "Let us adjourn to the Prior's study. I just only returned from a night of performing a Soul Purification, and it appears much has happened while I was away."

The man who had spoken nodded to the man on his

right, and that guardsman stepped towards Korin, then reached around him to close the door.

"We can talk just fine here," the guardsman said firmly. "The Prior assured us of your cooperation. Please sit down."

Korin nodded, struggling to keep a neutral expression on his face as he took a seat at a desk cluttered with several books and parchments. They had been neatly stacked when he had left the room last night. He was pretty confident it had not been the girl who had gotten curious. Korin was also now fairly certain these "guardsmen" had never spoken to the Prior.

The man settled in the chair beside the right edge of the desk and leaned an elbow casually onto the surface as if they were old friends about to have a chat. The other three guardsmen positioned themselves in a semi-circle behind Korin's chair as if he were a prisoner being interrogated.

"There has been a bit of a misunderstanding, I am afraid, ah..." Korin said before the man could speak. "... I am sorry; I am being rude. I have not asked your name."

"Captain Sahnti," the guardsman replied, "but more importantly, what do you mean 'misunderstanding'?"

"I was attacked by the boy in question, yes, but the blame lies entirely with me. I startled him, and he merely acted in self-defense. As such, I have no desire to file any grievance against him."

"You might not, but we've been chasing him for a long time because of several prior crimes."

"But this child has only been in this city for a couple of days at the most. You must be mistaking him for another."

"Maybe," Sahnti allowed, "though we can find out easily enough by bringing the kid here."

"Well, it's true that he was in this room last night. Considering how upset everyone was about what had happened, I thought it best to grant him Sanctuary until I had the opportunity to visit the guard station about the matter. He was understandably scared. If the boy was not here when you arrived and the Prior did not know of his absence, then chances are he decided to leave. We cannot force anyone to stay."

The captain's eyes bored into him for a long moment before he asked, "You said you were performing ritual Purifications last night. Could the boy have gone looking for you there?"

Korin shook his head. "He did not know I was going there. I bade him goodnight and promised him we would talk more in the morning."

"Do you usually take such an interest in delinquents? From what I hear, the kid sliced you up like a roasted pig. You'd think you wouldn't have been able to get out of your sickbed, much less have the strength to perform your duties all night. The rumors of Korin the Watcher must be true."

The captain was staring at him so intently that it was all Korin could do to keep from fidgeting nervously. This man was definitely fishing for information, though whether he was trying to imply something about Korin, himself, or simply making a comment to gauge his reaction, the ancient monk wasn't sure. The question of whether or not these men were truly guardsmen of the Kairashian City Guard no longer mattered. What did matter was whether or not these men were slavers or the Old Soul hunters Kye had spoken of. How quickly things were spiraling out of control.

"My work for the Temple mainly involves children," Korin replied earnestly. "Street children and orphans mostly. Whether I was hurt or not is of no consequence. Besides, my wounds were very shallow and probably looked much more serious than what was actually true. I think the poor child was trying to swat me away, and I simply stepped too close."

"Several people witnessed you chasing him through the marketplace," Sahnti pressed.

This time, Korin didn't have to force the small smile that touched his lips. "Children do not always like to talk to adults. Especially to monks—more so if that monk is Korin the Watcher and like you, have heard some of the more colorful rumors. This boy was so terrified of me it took several people to subdue him after the incident. I had thought I had tempered some of that fear yesterday, but if he has left...." Korin shook his head in sadness that was not altogether feigned. "Tell me, what crimes have the child you seek committed?"

"Assaults, thefts," Sahnti said offhandedly. "He's quite the vicious brat. We've had so many complaints that I'd like to jail him today if at all possible and be done with the whole mess."

"What makes you believe they are the same boy?" Korin asked.

The captain's answering smile never reached his eyes. "I hear that your boy has eyes as red as fresh blood."

Korin flinched before he could stop himself. "A coincidence perhaps. Rare to be sure, but that said, I personally know about three others in this city alone. As I mentioned before, the boy is not originally from Kairash."

"And as *I* have said before, the matter can be easily settled by handing the kid over to us."

"Then I suggest you finish up here quickly and start your search. I left him alone in this room hours ago. He could be halfway to the eastern border of the kingdom for all we know or simply wandering around the marketplace again."

Korin stood, pointedly ignoring the guardsmen behind him. "I must speak to the Prior about the boy's disappearance," he said, looking gravely down at Captain Sahnti, who was still seated.

The man jerked back as if Korin had taken an unexpected swing at him, nearly tipping his chair over sideways. He quickly jumped to his feet as well and backed away from the ancient monk, the expression on his face unable to completely mask what looked like fear.

"Of course," Sahnti said probably more roughly than he had intended. "If the boy comes back here, we ask that you report it to the guard station right away."

Korin nodded politely. "I can escort you to the Prior's study if you wish to ask any further questions."

"That's not necessary," he said. "We know our way out."

And no doubt your own special way in as well, Korin thought with a mental frown as the men piled out the door.

Only when he could no longer hear their footsteps did he relax his tense stance. He felt as though he could just collapse right where he stood and sleep for a whole tenday, but sleep had just become a luxury he could no longer afford. Things were about as worse as they could possibly get. Now, instead of one lost "child," there were three. Not to mention the countless unfriendly eyes that would probably be watching his every move from now on.

He needed to chase after the girl, to find Senn and Kye, but his body also screamed for sleep. He also needed to talk to the Prior before doing any of those things. Korin moved towards the door, but only managed a couple of steps before the room violently tilted. He stumbled and fell heavily to his knees. He managed only a small gasp as the pain was awakened once again in his wounds before his vision darkened, and he felt himself teetering over to the side.

It seemed fate had taken the choice from him.

AT LEAST WE *have a little light,* Issai thought grudgingly as he carefully followed a torch-bearing Hahri up seemingly endless stairs to what was probably going to turn out to be a colossal waste of time. Then again, only moments before, he had thought he wouldn't be leaving this underground hell on his own two feet, so he supposed anything was possible. Not likely, but possible.

"I thrashed the whole way down," Hahri spoke suddenly. "Even with the torch, looking down over the side, I can't see the bottom. I was lucky they never dropped me. I was so focused on trying to escape that I never realized just how deep this prison ran. I know I said we may have to find another way out, but seeing how deep underground we really are..."

Issai felt a flash of panic wash over him, but he decided not to acknowledge it. Entombed within a dark cave until they either starved or killed themselves was not high on his list of ways he preferred to die. He sensed voicing what they were both thinking would just stoke the flames of Hahri's rising panic.

"Stop looking down, and keep walking," Issai commanded sharply. "With my luck, you'll trip, and only *I* would end up falling over the ledge."

The panic all but disappeared as his companion huffed in annoyance, and Issai couldn't help but smirk at the other's back. It seemed he was getting better at dealing with the other boy.

"Finally!" Hahri exclaimed, interrupting his thoughts as he looked around Hahri at the large iron door. Because of the darkness, they both knew it would be closed, but they had hoped the panicked slavers had not paused to lock it.

Issai stepped up next to Hahri and placed both hands onto the door. Hahri did the same. As one, they pushed with all their strength and the door lurched forward almost immediately, screeching with the sound of metal on stone. A thin line of light opened up along the right edge, but any elation they may have felt was instantly halted along with the door that stubbornly refused to open any farther.

"Dammit!" Hahri snarled, hitting his shoulder against the iron and in the process nearly sending himself backward down the stairs if Issai had not hastily caught his arm to steady him. "It swung open just fine when those bastards brought me down here. Do you think they might have barricaded it?"

"Well, something is definitely blocking it. Move back, and I'll try to take a look."

Issai edged over to the crack they had managed to make and knelt down in order to peer through it. The corridor beyond the door was moderately dim with only torchlight to illuminate it, but it was enough for his dark-adjusted eyes to see only the far wall of the corridor with nothing that looked as if it could be blocking the door.

"I can't see anything," Issai said. "Maybe it's just stuck on the stones. I think the floor may have been cobbled instead of smooth. Let's try pushing it again."

However, their second attempt didn't move the door at all, and this time it was Issai who kicked the door in frustration.

"I can almost hear the gods laughing at us," Issai spat as he slumped angrily against the door. "Now what?"

For some ungodly reason, Hahri was grinning widely at him. "Well, we can try to pull the door closed. If something other than the cobblestones is jamming it, then maybe it will pull it loose enough for us to push it out of the way with the door on the next try."

Issai straightened once again and scowled. "If you don't wipe that smile off your face *right now*, I swear you won't have any teeth left to smile with."

"Then *you* stop sulking like a little boy angry with his parents, and maybe I won't feel so amused," Hahri shot back, folding his arms against his chest as if in challenge.

"I'm not—" Issai began defensively. "No, never mind. I keep forgetting that arguing with you only gives me a headache. Let's just do this."

The door pulled closed with only a minor resistance, but once they shoved it forward again, it still stalled almost at the same point.

"Something is definitely jamming it," Hahri said. "I heard the door hit something right before it stopped moving. Can't you stick a knife in the crack beneath it and try to push it out?"

"The door is too thick. We would need a sword, and unfortunately, I don't think any of our hosts carried anything longer than their daggers. We'll just have to keep pulling and pushing the door until it gives."

"I'm surprised nobody has come running with all the noise we're making."

Issai snorted. "I got the impression that although not everyone bought into the Old Soul myths, all of Rahzon's slavers were aware of us and what that bastard wanted to do with us. Having a handful of men run screaming from this pit sans their lord probably had them rethinking their beliefs. It may be the thickness of the rock separating me from the house beyond, but the only significant movement I'm sensing right now is from you and a few sources of water within the cave, itself. I seriously doubt anyone will dare even set foot anywhere near this door again."

"All the better for us then," Hahri said. "If we ever

get this damn door open, perhaps the rest of our escape won't be such a pain."

Issai didn't know how long they pushed and pulled the door, but after a while, when his muscles in his arms and back had gone well past the "burn" threshold into the realm of true pain, it felt as if both had been laboring for days. They had managed to widen the gap between the edge of the door and the stone frame significantly, but it still had not been wide enough for either of them to squeeze their heads through the last time they had tried.

Panting, Issai paused in his pushing and said, "Try it again."

Without a word, Hahri moved over to the gap, a testament to how tired the other boy was if he was no longer bothering to speak between pauses. Issai slumped against the door and watched him as he squeezed his body sideways through the opening and began to pull his head through the gap. Hahri hissed with the strain, but he didn't stop. Issai grimaced at the phantom pain on the sides of his head that echoed the other's. It seemed Hahri was trying extra hard this time.

Issai was about to tell him to stop when the other's head abruptly slipped through, and Hahri yelped in surprise as the momentum carried him to the ground.

His weariness instantly vanished in a surge of adrenalin as Issai rushed over to the gap. "Finally!"

"Yeah, but I think I left the top layer of my skin on

that rock," Hahri complained as he picked himself off the ground. Both temples were bleeding a little from multiple scrapes, but really, a wound not even worth noting.

"So what's jamming the door?" Issai asked.

Hahri turned his head, and his eyes narrowed. "Those damn bastards. Nobody probably had the keys, so they crammed a couple of their daggers between the floor and the bottom of the door to jam it." He moved out of Issai's line-of-sight, and moments later, he heard a couple of cracks that sounded like joints popping. "Pull the door from your side just a bit, and I'll see if I can pull them out. We warped them pretty good."

Maybe the gods finally took pity on them or had gotten bored with this little entertainment, but Hahri managed to pull the daggers free on the first try, and Issai was finally free of the prison, too.

Hahri stuffed both warped blades behind his belt. Issai looked at him pointedly, and he shrugged.

"They both had emeralds in the hilts, and I suddenly find myself in need of a new pair of armbands," he said.

Then, inexplicably, Hahri grinned widely and dropped to his knees. For a long moment, Issai stared down at him in utter confusion before the other stretched out his arms before him and lowered himself facedown onto the stones in an over-exaggerated show of prostration.

Only then did Issai remember the other's offhand

words about worship. "You idiot! I swear if you don't get up *right* now, I'll kick you so hard you'll feel it for your next ten lives!"

Hahri lifted his head, his eyes practically laughing. "Just keeping my promise. You know we never should have survived that."

Issai grabbed his arm and jerked him to his feet. "And we *still* might die. I can't believe you're cracking jokes when we're still inside this slaver lord's effing compound!"

"That's why I'm doing it," Hahri said with a gentle smile before easily tugging his arm out of Issai's suddenly lax grip. "Are there any slavers nearby?"

"No," Issai replied sharply, a bit discomfited because he didn't understand the other boy's sudden change of expression. He began walking down the hall. "I do, however, feel some movement all around us. It's distant enough that it can just be people moving about the city, but at the same time close enough that it could be those that live within this compound. I was inside a sack when I was brought in, so I have no idea where within the city this place lies or if we're even still within the city wall."

"This is Southwestern Yuzu, on the outer edge of the Merchant District if that helps you any," Hahri said. "When I realized that nothing short of a blade was going to get me out of my bindings, I pretended to be unconscious up until they brought me to that bastard slaver lord. It's still within the city walls, but just barely. The wall makes up the back portion of their property wall. Short of climbing the walls, the northern gate I was brought through was the only entrance I could see. There are probably drainage tunnels, but without knowing exactly where they are..."

Issai paused and ran a hand frustratingly through his hair, glaring down the dim corridor. "Then you lead. I don't even know how big this place is."

His partner sighed. "Unfortunately huge. This is just one of about a half-dozen buildings I could see as I was brought in. The head of the Mahze clan must be a pretty important figure in this kingdom. However, I've never been in this city so I couldn't tell you their true family name."

"That's why I don't like the larger cities," Issai spat. "Too much scum, and I'm not just talking about on the streets."

Although both boys were ready to collapse, they cautiously moved through the seemingly endless corridors of the building. There were very few rooms, looking more like an enclosed maze than a building meant for habitation. If this was the only place they stored their captives, then the layout made perfect sense. Luckily, Hahri seemed to know exactly where he was going, even though most of the corridors looked identical.

Issai was more alarmed than relieved that they hadn't run into so much as a servant as Hahri turned a final corner that led into a small atrium that was as empty as the many corridors at their backs. The wooden door stood slightly ajar, adding credence to the theory that everyone from the building had fled in fear after all.

Issai stood back and eyed the door suspiciously as Hahri cautiously approached the opened edge. He unconsciously gripped the knives in his hands more tightly and shifted to a more battle-ready stance. The sensation of movement tickled his skin, but Issai still couldn't tell if they were about to walk into an ambush. He watched as Hahri squinted into the crack without touching the door.

Then without warning, a flash of white light illuminated the crack in the door, and Hahri fell back with a surprised cry half a beat before a boom resounded all around them, nearly causing Issai to jump out of his skin, though he did lose his grip on one of his knives.

Cursing, Issai bent to retrieve it, and then looked up sharply to glare at his companion who was laughing. "Yeah, we'll see if you're still laughing later when you're soaked to the bone and half-frozen."

"Heh—now there's a thought. I wonder if we'll feel twice as cold?"

Issai frowned. He hadn't considered that. However, rain or no rain, they couldn't stay there.

Another ear-splitting boom seemed to shake the very walls. They were running out of time. Though he couldn't sense any rain falling yet, judging from the frequency of the thunder, it could be any moment now.

He hated rain. Not only did it make his skin crawl annoyingly, it pretty much rendered his ability to sense people around him useless. It made him feel vulnerable, something that was almost as alien to him as laughter. He looked at Hahri speculatively. His ability to sense the people around him had dramatically increased the last time they had touched souls. Did they dare chance it?

"That first lightning struck somewhere within the compound," Hahri said, interrupting his thoughts. "It might be more dangerous to go outside than to stay here."

Isssai shook his head. *What am I thinking—of course we can't.* "Screw the lightning. I'm not staying here a moment longer than I have to. Did you see anyone nearby?"

"Not a soul, but it's not like I could see much from such a thin opening. This door faces north, and there are two buildings about a hundred strides across an open lawn. They both look like they could either be barns or stables rather than anything residential, but on the downside, they make the perfect hiding place. We can only presume that they think their lord is dead. I mean, the bastard screamed like my blood was melting his face off so I wouldn't be surprised if they decided to kill rather than capture."

"Which means potential archers," Issai added,

nodding grimly. "Where is this building within the compound? Anywhere near one of the perimeter walls?"

"Yes, near the western wall. I see what you're thinking, but it won't work. The compound walls are a little over half the height of the city wall. There's no way we could get over before somebody saw us and picked us off. I don't remember any trees near enough to them to offer any cover either. We'll have to go out the front gate or creep around looking for any drainage tunnels large enough for us to squeeze through. Can't say I'm crazy about either choice, but I think our best bet is the gate."

Issai wanted to yell in frustration. Why did everything always have to be so hard? "Is there any cover at *all* in this damn place?"

"I was brought in rather quickly, so I didn't have all that long to look around, but I did see a lot of trees around the northern buildings. We'll just have to make a run for it."

"Then let's get on with it," Issai growled. "The longer we stay here, the longer we'll have to be out in the rain. We should probably go around the far side of the right building; the other is too close to the western wall, and I don't want to get penned in."

He positioned himself behind Hahri. "On the count of three..."

The moment the two Old Souls burst from the door was the very moment the clouds decided to unleash their torrents on the earth. They shot towards the right building at top speed, reaching it without incident.

Brushing his rain-soaked bangs from his eyes, Issai peered around the corner, but the grounds still appeared empty.

"Nothing on this end," Hahri abruptly said loudly into his ear, startling him a bit. He hadn't even felt the smaller boy lean in. Gods, he *hated* rain.

"Same here," Issai replied without looking at him. "However, I just can't believe that everyone abandoned the compound completely." As his eyes continued to sweep the area before him, he added, "There's a small copse of trees a few strides from the other side of this building. There's a stone pathway leading to it from the north and east, so it might be a pleasure garden or even better, a grotto. Maybe the trees will give us enough cover to pause long enough to figure out the best route to the gate—"

Suddenly, he was roughly pushed forward by the full weight of Hahri's body slamming into him, and Issai was barely able to swing his arms forward to catch himself before getting a face full of mud. He heard it as they both landed heavily onto the ground, a slight whistling within the hiss of rain.

Before he could even draw his next breath, Issai felt the heavy weight disappear from his back. As he pulled himself to his knees, Hahri's hand was already gripping his arm and jerking him back on his feet.

"Where—" Issai tried to ask, but his partner was pulling him towards the aforementioned trees. Another whistle sounded extremely close to his right, and an arrow embedded itself a couple of steps in front of Hahri. He cursed loudly as several more arrows flew past them from the front.

Where were they firing from? He still couldn't see anyone on the grounds.

Issai jerked his arm loose from Hahri's grip and plastered himself behind the first tree he reached. Out of the corner of his eye, he saw Hahri do the same a couple of trees down. He couldn't believe that neither of them had been hit. Maybe rain wasn't so bad after all...

He thought he could hear a few arrows hitting the trees, but it was difficult to hear anything definitively over the roar of the rain and thunder.

"I can see some of them!" Hahri shouted. "Look to the north. There's about twenty coming at us with staffs. I still can't see any archers. We need to go now before we're surrounded!"

It's already too late, Issai thought grimly as he caught movement to the west at the edge of the trees. Their only option now was to fight their way through or—his lip curled in distaste when his mind completed the thought. Still...

Cursing under his breath, Issai dashed towards Hahri as the boy stepped from behind his tree and leaped onto his back before the other could even turn around. Hahri instinctively grabbed his legs under the knees as he staggered a bit before sputtering, "What the hell are you doing?"

Issai tightened his arms against the other's neck warningly. "Just shut up and *run!*"

21

His eyes snapped open, and for a long, terrifying moment, Korin thought he had been taken prisoner. There was almost no light, a faint illumination in the far distance the only source. A dozen, man-shaped shadows circled him in the darkness, converging on him as he strained against the cold iron encasing his wrists. Then the vision dissipated, replaced by the familiar wooden rafters high above his temple room.

He could suddenly move his limbs freely again, and he sat up sharply, something damp sliding down his face and onto his lap. It drew his eyes as if they were connected to it. It was a white handkerchief outlined in a deep blue thread, wet and folded to a small rectangle.

Korin stared at it for a long, confused moment, his heart still hammering away at his chest as if he were fleeing from something. It was not one of his, nor did he recognize the pattern.

He could feel the cold, stone floor beneath him sapping the little warmth remaining from his body as his eyes slowly took in his surroundings. Yes, this was the room the Prior had recently given him. The darkness, the shadows, the bindings—it had all been just a dream.

What am I doing sleeping on the floor? Korin thought in bewilderment, his mind still a bit hazy with sleep and lingering panic.

His gaze traveled across the room and settled on his cot, a thick, woolen blanket lying crumpled and half-falling off the side. His eyes widened. The girl! Where was she? Even as he glanced around the room frantically, a torrent of memories suddenly pushed out the last traces of sleep from his mind. He recalled coming here only to find unwelcomed visitors instead of the one he had expected, enduring their not-so-thinly-veiled threats. Then he...

Korin pressed a hand to his forehead and groaned. He had passed out; that's what happened. One of the most important times of his existence and his body had chosen that moment to fail him. Were the gods testing him?

The ancient monk started to get up and felt the folded up handkerchief fall from his lap. He frowned down at it. He had forgotten all about it. Who had placed it on his forehead? If it had been one of his Brothers, then he couldn't imagine them leaving him sprawled out on the floor, much less alone.

His heart briefly sped up. Had the girl come back? Did he dare hope? Maybe she was still somewhere within the temple, hiding from not only the monks but the guardsmen beyond the walls.

Korin bent down and retrieved the damp cloth, clenching it tightly. The humming within his soul was steady and strong. The only thing that told him was that she wasn't moving away from the city. She could be anywhere in the temple, in the city.

How long had he been out anyway? His room had no windows so it was impossible to know if it was day or night, though he couldn't imagine it being longer than a few hours. He had been seen entering the temple by many of his Brothers. Had it been days, someone definitely would have found him unconscious here.

Korin set out for the Prior's chambers. At the very least, he could warn him about his unexpected guests before he set out to search again.

The Prior was not in his chambers, and after a few inquiries, he was told that the Prior was taking Audience at the moment. Audience was usually held right after the midday hour up until the evening sermon, so unless he had been unconscious for over a day, things were not as bad as he first thought.

He headed towards the large room where the citizens who sought Audience with the Prior waited. The room was crowded, the low murmur of a hundred or so voices washed over him as Korin edged around them along the walls, trying not to draw too much attention to himself. Because of the incident in the streets with the girl, he was pretty sure that word of his return had already gotten out. He didn't want to add fuel to the fire by revealing himself here, so he kept the hood of his cloak up and his head down as he made his way over to the group of three monks standing next to the door where the Prior received the people in turn.

"Brother...!" One of them began to exclaim loudly once he had neared, but Korin hurriedly shook his head and raised a finger to his lips to indicate silence. Luckily the monk took the hint and broke off before he could get Korin's name out. Korin cringed inwardly as he felt a hundred eyes suddenly bore into his back, but thankfully, no one approached them. Now that the attention of the whole room was on them, he didn't have much time.

He bent nearer to his Brothers and murmured, "I must speak with the Prior once he is finished with this one. It cannot wait until Audience is over."

"Has something happened?" the oldest of the three whispered anxiously.

"Perhaps," Korin hedged. "Once I speak to the Prior, he can tell you about it at his discretion. Here is not the best place to speak of it..."

Korin jumped as the door suddenly swung open in front of him, and he barely turned his face away from the emerging person in time. The monk who had almost given him away earlier stepped forward and hurriedly ushered the person away as the remaining two monks pushed him through the door.

The Prior stood as the door shut behind Korin, his expression registering both surprise and worry. Korin lowered his hood and bowed his head respectfully before gesturing for the Prior to retake his seat while he sank into the opposite chair.

"I am sorry to interrupt, but this cannot wait. I need to leave now, perhaps even leave the city, and I am not sure if I shall be able to return to this temple anytime soon. I could not leave without telling you about the men I found waiting for me in my room this morning when I returned from my all-night Soul Purification."

The Prior frowned. "I gave no one permission to visit your personal room."

Korin nodded. "I thought as much. There were four of them, dressed in the uniform of the City Guard. They claimed that you had given them permission to interrogate me."

The Prior snorted. "Apparently they have no knowledge of the Guard or the Temple to have disregarded such a basic law between us. What did they want?"

Korin sighed. "The little girl I was protecting."

Understanding flashed in the elder's eyes. "Slavers,"

he stated in disgust. "You did mention that she had unusual eyes. Children with unusual or rare features always have fetched an ungodly price in the underground markets. That they showed up here claiming to represent the Guard means they must have learned of that unfortunate incident yesterday. Did they take the girl?"

"No. Thankfully, she disappeared before they arrived. I played along with their interrogation, but I do not think they believed me when I said I had no idea where she had run off to. I cannot be certain they even left the temple. If none of the monks encountered them at any of the entrances or in the halls, then it is safe to say they have ways to infiltrate the temple unseen. That being the case, those who have sought Sanctuary here are no longer safe."

"I will have the monks make a thorough sweep of the temple immediately. If they are here, then we will find them. Is this why you are leaving this temple?"

Korin nodded. "My presence and the problems I bring with me are endangering everyone here. I have no doubt that these slavers and any associated with them will be watching not only me but the temple carefully. Even I am not certain the girl is not still hiding somewhere within the temple.

"The two boys that accompanied me from Rihott are in as much danger as the child. Now that I have lost contact with all three, it is imperative that I find them as soon as possible. If any of them turn up here looking for me, implore them to stay and send one of my Brothers to find me in the city. I shall not leave the city without sending word to you of my plans with one of our Brothers."

The Prior sighed, his smile a touch sad. "Always, you try to carry all the burdens yourself. I wish you would accept more of our help, but I suppose you would not be Korin the Watcher if you did otherwise. Just promise me you'll be careful, Brother. I don't want to see you being carried in here covered in blood ever again."

The ancient monk grimaced. "It was not the homecoming I envisioned either. I cannot promise that it will never happen again, but I can promise I shall do everything in my power to prevent it."

Korin left the room through the Prior's entrance and managed to leave the temple without incident even though he half-expected to be attacked once beyond temple grounds. The courtyard sundial marked the hour at two lines past the midday line. He had several hours yet before he needed to return to the bathhouse to wait for Senn and Kye.

He decided to just walk the streets of the city and concentrate on the humming within his soul. Perhaps if he paid enough attention, he might be able to discern enough fluctuations in the strength of the vibrations to determine if he was closer to her. It was a bit better than wandering around with no guidance at all.

However, within a half-hour of his search, a wrench appeared in his plans in the form of three men that seemed to appear in the crowd no matter what path he decided to follow. As they had not attempted to approach him once, it seemed his earlier paranoia was justified. He couldn't allow them to use him to bait the others, but at the same time, he couldn't just give up his search.

The answer to his problem came as he entered the marketplace and saw a dozen of his Brothers at one of the fruit stalls, their arms already burdened with sacks and baskets of various goods. He hoped this group was about to distribute charity to the poor and sick rather than just restocking the temple kitchens.

Although he didn't like it, Korin was about to do something he had been trying to avoid since he had returned to the city. He waited until they moved on from the stall back into the flow of people before lowering his hood and approaching them openly.

"Good day, Brothers," Korin greeted once he had caught their attention. "Need another pair of hands?"

As they greeted him enthusiastically with hugs and words of welcome, his face was the very picture of carefree happiness even as his heart was being squeezed painfully by the hands of guilt. He needed to find the girl; he needed to make sure the bathhouse remained a safe place for them to meet without fear of ambush.

Korin knew he could no longer do any of those

things alone. The Prior had been right to chide him. Now he would have to rely on his notoriety and the good will of his Brothers and the people of the city to shield them all should trouble decide to strike. He only prayed that it would be a decision he would not come to regret later.

"GET DOWN! I get what you're thinking, but right now it's impossible!"

Issai slipped back down onto his feet immediately. "Are you that tired?"

Hahri hastily pulled them behind a thick tree as another volley of arrows zipped passed them. "That's not it. It's not open enough here. I can't just instantly run at top speed. I have to have the time and space to build up the momentum. We'll have to get beyond this compound first."

Issai cursed. "Then we're screwed. Slavers are coming at us from the west, too. There's no way we can make the gates without taking some major hits!"

Hahri's reply was completely drowned out by an ear-splitting boom that was so close it seemed to shatter the air and trees around them. Even his bones seemed to vibrate with its intensity as he instinctually threw his arms over his head. His skin felt as if millions of ants were chaotically crawling all over him in a frantic dance.

A loud cracking sounded to his right, and Issai immediately whipped his head in that direction, his chest tightening with panic when he realized what he was hearing.

A large tree several paces over had been split in half, both sides in the process of falling in opposite directions to the ground—neither one in their direction. But that wasn't what had him grabbing Hahri's arm in sudden excitement. That small break in the dense tree line opened up a perfect view of the compound's eastern outer wall in the distance and more importantly, the thin, rectangular stone structure situated against it.

"Look there!" Issai shouted over the hiss of the rain and his still ringing ears, pointing towards the structure.

The smaller boy followed his hand, squinting against the haze of the rain for a moment before his eyes suddenly widened. "Is that..."

"...a watchtower," Issai finished with a rare grin.

The swarm of arrows flying around them had abruptly ceased after the lightning strike. They had perhaps only beats before their attackers gathered their wits enough to resume. Though several hundred strides of dense woods separated them from the tower, it was a better chance than they could've ever expected.

Violet met cerulean. It was now or never.

They shot out from the cover of their tree, running in erratic patterns between the trees even though no arrows had appeared. The watchtower would no doubt be staffed and had the advantage of the higher ground, so Issai watched for possible arrow strikes from the front. Any other time, it would have been suicide to try such a frontal assault, but they were simply out of options.

Issai was mildly surprised that there were still no arrows or visible men coming at them from behind, but rather than feel relief at that seemingly good fortune, it only made him more paranoid. Were they just overestimating the competence of the slavers' fighting abilities, or were they actually running straight into a trap again?

He was actually relieved when the first arrow landed near his left foot the moment they both broke through the cover of the trees and into a completely open lawn. Here was something he had expected.

The watchtower was still about a couple of hundred strides away. There was nothing to do but run towards the base of it with everything they had in them, zigzagging to make themselves as hard a target as they could as a rain of arrows and water fell down on them, and spider webs of lightning zipped across the sky.

Issai nearly stumbled as a line of fire abruptly erupted across his right cheek followed by a loud curse from Hahri who was several steps ahead of him. One of them had been hit, and for a few breaths, he didn't know which until a flow of liquid warmth began making its way down his rain-chilled skin.

Great. Now he would never hear the end of it later unless—

It was his turn to curse loudly as what felt like a red hot poker stabbed through his left forearm. He didn't even spare it a glance as several shadows emerged from the torrents, and he immediately flicked his knives into his hands, wincing as the movement aggravated his newest injury.

As Issai raised his left hand to swipe at the nearest body, he totally expected to see an arrow shaft sticking out of it, but there was nothing. Either the arrow had gone completely through his arm, or Hahri had taken the wound. He couldn't decide which prospect was worse. He would suffer for it either way, he was sure.

He took down several men with his knives before he caught sight of Hahri just as the other boy kicked the watchtower door in, the door crashing into at least two more men as Issai followed him into the gloom beyond. After Hahri did something to the fallen men that he couldn't see, Issai was almost shocked when no one else came out of the darkness or down the stone steps to challenge them. Nor did anyone come pouring in through the broken door behind them. The only sounds were the hiss of the rain and the relentless booms of thunder.

Issai stepped up to Hahri just as he was breaking off the tip of the arrow shaft that was sticking out of his forearm.

"You see?" Hahri griped, showing the wound to him. "This would've never happened if I had my armbands! Now I have to run around with the rest of this *damn thing* still rammed through my arm so I don't bleed to death!"

Issai couldn't help rolling his eyes. "You won't bleed to death just from a hole in your arm, idiot. Now quit howling and let's *go*! No one's here now, but I'd be willing to bet both our eternal lives that there'll be slavers waiting for us at the top of those stairs and the gods know how many more coming at us from the grotto! Just so you know, if we get caught again, I'm going to cut our throats again..."

Hahri muttered that ancient curse word once again, hitting Issai like a knife to the gut. Why was it that Hahri always had to remind him of it when it was impossible for him to question him about it? It was maddening!

The staircase wound along the walls of the tower in a spiral, which unfortunately gave the archer at the top ample opportunities to shoot down at them. They had no choice but to race up the stairs at full speed and hope they didn't stumble and fall over the railing-less edge.

Once Issai came within striking range of the archer, he threw one of his knives straight at the man's neck, hitting him directly in the throat. The man was already falling when Hahri reached him and brutally slammed into his chest without slowing down, knocking the dying archer backward onto the small landing at the top. Issai was just glad Hahri hadn't swatted the man over the edge as he passed. He wanted that knife back.

Issai paused long enough to pull his knife from the dead man's neck, but he needn't have hurried since the scene that greeted him as he stepped out onto the roof of the tower into the hard rain was Hahri standing in the center of three more fallen bodies. A quick glance around confirmed that there was no one left to challenge them.

Issai walked over to the edge and cautiously peered down. The watchtower stood a couple of arm-lengths above the compound wall it had been built against. They could easily jump down onto the top of the wall and then jump down into Yuzu, or they could make their way across the top of the compound wall to where it intersected the city wall. Both walls were certainly wide enough not to be much of a problem even adding the rain and wind to the mix. It was the lightning and arrows they had to worry about. It would be just possible to boost each other up to the taller city wall and exit Yuzu altogether.

The sensible thing would be to jump down into the city, lay low in someone's root cellar for a day or so, and then try to sneak out in a farmer's wagon or the like. It would still give them enough time to meet up with Korin as planned. However...

"I don't want to spend another breath more than we

have to in this damn city," Issai growled as Hahri joined him at the edge.

His companion nodded. "If you're prepared to deal with the City Guard when they start shooting arrows at us for scaling their precious wall, then I'm game."

"Will you be okay with that?" Issai nodded towards the wound in the other's arm. Only an echo of pain remained in his own arm.

"Yeah, as long as you scale the city wall first and pull me up. I should still be able to run us the hell out of here once we're on the other side."

Both ancient boys carefully jumped down onto the top of the rain-slicked compound wall and moved towards the city wall as quickly as they dared. They only made it halfway before arrows started to slice through the air around them. They were coming from somewhere within the compound below.

Issai paused and chanced a glance behind them, but he couldn't see anyone attempting to follow them on the wall or any movement on the watchtower roof. He had expected those who had been chasing them on foot through the grove to have reached the tower by now. It seemed the slavers had decided to make this purely a long distance assault.

He quickly moved on when he felt a shaft brush the back of his hair. The wind was currently blowing the stinging rain directly into his face making it extremely difficult to keep his eyes open, even with his head down and his hand shielding over his brow. The occasional sudden wind gust also wreaked havoc with his balance, nearly sending him over the edge more than once. Luckily for them, the wind was also wreaking havoc with the slavers' arrows, sending most of them careening way wide of their intended marks.

Hahri suddenly swore behind him, but Issai couldn't spare him a glance. He knew the other boy hadn't been hit because he felt no new pain.

The city wall loomed a few paces ahead. Once there, they couldn't waste a single moment if they hoped to continue without resembling a pincushion. He only hoped that neither one of them would get hit in the legs. Only a chest or head shot would be worse.

Another couple of steps and Issai turned and shouted, "Loop your hands together, and boost me up now!"

He stepped into Hahri's hands and prepared to grab the lip of the city wall as he was abruptly heaved upward. Hahri had thrown him with enough force that he was able to fling half his torso over the edge before his fingers tried to find purchase in the natural crevices of the granite blocks. The stones were slicker than he expected, and for a terrifying moment, Issai started to slip backward. He dug his fingers into the rock as hard as possible and hung on seemingly by sheer will.

He pulled himself a bit farther over the edge with his forearms and swung his legs up and over the side once he was certain he would not slip back down. An arrow embedded itself in the mortar right where his body had been hanging only moments earlier.

"Hurry the *hell* up!" Hahri screamed from below. "That last batch almost brained me!"

He was sure there were a thousand different ways he could have retorted. Too bad he couldn't think of any of them as he turned towards the edge and scooted as much of his body as he dared over it, extending his right arm down as far as he could while his other hand gripped the edge of the wall. The next volley of arrows was likely only a couple of breaths away.

"Jump!" Issai shouted.

As soon as he grasped Hahri's wrist and felt him do the same, Issai heaved upwards as hard as he could before gravity could pull them both back over. He was able to pull Hahri up just enough that the other was able to grab the lip of the wall with his free hand. From there, it was just a matter of grabbing him under his armpits and pulling him the rest of the way up. They both flattened themselves onto their stomachs just as several arrows flew over them.

Angry voices floated up with the wind, but the hiss of the rain and the thunder made deciphering the words impossible. Issai also couldn't tell if they came from the slaver compound or beyond the city wall.

Still on their stomachs, they wormed their way to the opposite edge and peered down. Issai half-expected a guard battalion with arrows nocked and aimed waiting for them below, but as far as he could tell, there wasn't a soul in sight. Now their only problem would be the three-story jump down.

"Let's go before we get skewered or cooked up here!" Hahri shouted.

Then the smaller boy swung himself over the edge without waiting for his reply. Issai cursed and looked down in enough time to see the other rolling in the mud below.

Thank the gods the idiot didn't break anything, he thought as he positioned himself half over the edge, arms stretched down, before letting himself fall forward into a dive. He immediately tucked into a couple of summersaults and sprang forward into a roll the instant his feet touched the ground, rolling across the muddy ground as Hahri did until his momentum was naturally spent.

Issai was infinitely grateful that he ended up on his back when he finally stopped rolling and not facedown choking on a mouthful of mud. He sat up stiffly and started looking for Hahri. The other was already hurrying over to him. The rain had already washed a good bit of the mud from his body. He was cradling his injured arm against his chest. Issai was a bit surprised that his own arm was not echoing the pain that Hahri was surely feeling. It was something else about the Bond they would have to consider later.

"What a showoff," Hahri said with a grin as he offered his good hand to Issai.

He merely shook his head in exasperation as he was hoisted up. In the next breath, Issai violently jerked forward with a gasp as something slammed into the back of his right shoulder. He staggered for a moment, reaching out a hand to steady himself on the equally unsteady body before him. The look of horror on Hahri's face instantly drew his eyes to what the other was staring at. His teeth clenched in anger when he saw the bloody tip of an arrow sticking out about a hands-length from his own shoulder.

Literally beats away from escaping Yuzu and *now* he had to get shot!

Issai pushed away from Hahri and grabbed the wooden shaft, breaking the head off before reaching behind him and pulling it out with a single, angry yank.

Hahri hissed in pain before suddenly grabbing Issai's arm and jerking him sideways as a couple more arrows whistled through the air. Cerulean eyes darted briefly over his shoulder and narrowed.

"Never mind that! The Guard is here! Get on my back *now!*"

Issai jumped onto Hahri before the smaller boy had even turned completely around. He nearly sent them both to the ground when he inadvertently grabbed onto the newly appeared arrow wound on Hahri's shoulder, causing him to stumble forward with the unexpected pain. That stumble had the unintentional consequence of causing the next arrow to miss embedding itself into the side of Hahri's head by a thread, passing close enough over his head to ruffle his hair.

Cursing worse than Issai has ever heard him, Hahri managed to regain his balance, and then promptly spit out a new string of expletives as he was forced to support one of Issai's legs with his injured arm.

"Quit grabbing onto my shoulder, dammit!" he screeched. "You're gonna make me pass out! And don't choke me either!"

Before Issai could even try to rearrange his hold, Hahri shot off to the northwest, and he quickly lost the ability to move at all as he was pressed painfully tight against the other's back. Unfortunately, his head was frozen in the perfect position for most of his face to get pummeled by what felt like a million tiny stones.

As if that wasn't enough, his shoulder screamed with pain, but all Issai could do was close his eyes, grit his teeth, and pray that this run would not end in a brutal tumble like the last time.

22

The first indication Issai had that they were slowing down was that he no longer felt as if he was trying to breathe through a thick sheet of linen pressing down hard over his face. The second was that he could suddenly move his head a little. They couldn't have been running for more than a tenth of an hour, but it had felt like an eternity within the agony of what he could have sworn was a hot poker relentlessly stabbing and twisting into his shoulder. Thankfully, the pummeling of his face had stopped within the first hundred beats or so.

He struggled to open his eyes a bit against the air pressure but immediately closed them when even just a glimpse of the speeding landscape made his stomach jolt unpleasantly. How Hahri was able to see where he was going while running at this speed was anyone's guess.

At this point, he supposed it really didn't matter where they were. If he was hurting this much, then Hahri, with his extra wound and bearing the weight of two people, had to be near collapse.

"You've run enough," he breathed into Hahri's ear the moment he was able.

The change was almost instantaneous. Between one breath and another, they were no longer moving forward, but falling to the ground. Issai only just managed to keep from collapsing onto Hahri's back. Fortunately, he managed to fall over onto his uninjured side.

The jolt to sudden stillness made him want to hurl. He was glad his stomach was too empty to comply. For the next few breaths, Issai kept his eyes shut and concentrated on not moving at all.

"First chance I get," Hahri wheezed, "I'm gonna go back and raze that damn compound to the ground!"

Issai opened his eyes and was greeted by the blurry image of Hahri sitting within a sea of white, his forehead resting on his raised knees, and his good arm awkwardly cradling the other. His entire right side and the lower half of his left sleeve were drenched in bright red.

As everything came back into focus, Issai realized

that what was tickling his face were not weeds but stalks of white flowers.

He slowly sat up, wincing when even that careful movement caused the fire in his shoulder to intensify. His face both throbbed and felt strangely tight and numb in places.

"So we made it to Kairash," Issai said, eyes scanning his surroundings.

He thought he saw some movement in the distance to the west. The southern road, perhaps?

Hahri lifted his head and nodded. "Two or three spans away, I would guess."

Issai stared. He couldn't help it.

Hahri's face and what skin was visible on his neck were entirely covered with angry, red welts, a few broken and oozing blood. Issai imagined his face looked just as awful, if the gods-awful way his skin was beginning to burn and sting were any indications.

"No wonder I feel like you towed me facedown through a gravel pit."

"Yeah, well that's just too bad," Hahri snipped, though he too was staring with a kind of horrified fascination at Issai's face. "I may be fast, but even *I* can't run between raindrops!"

He carefully swung his body towards Issai and scooted a bit closer. "So are you gonna heal us now or sit there smelling the flowers all day?"

Issai paused in his inspection of his equally-stinging

hands and frowned thoughtfully. "If I can. It's only been about a couple of hours or so since I last healed us. Plus, you just exerted a huge amount of energy to get us here. Don't be surprised if it doesn't work or I pass out. Hell, we could both pass out this time."

"Either way, we can't go into Kairash looking like we're dying of some gruesome disease. Never mind any stray *Shi* or slavers that may still be in the city, we'll be killed on sight by the City Guard."

The ancient boy held out his hands expectantly, and Issai took them without another word, wincing when Hahri squeezed the welts on his hands too tightly. Out in the open as they were, they had to do this as quickly as possible before someone accidentally stumbled onto them.

He closed his eyes and quickly traced out every hurt he could find in his body, conscious of the increasing warmth of Hahri's hands as he did so. He had not noticed that happening before. Of course, they had been close to death during the last two healings, and he may have just been too distracted.

Almost from the moment Issai released his mental command to heal, his body began to feel strangely light, as though he was suddenly floating in a still lake. Then an image of himself appeared in his mind's eye, sitting cross-legged in the white blossoms as he was right now. His eyes were closed, and a frown of concentration touched his lips and creased his brow. His face really did look awful, but not as beat up as Hahri's. He could see his reddened hands stretched out and clasping Hahri's hands tightly, though Hahri, himself, was not visible past his forearms.

A wash of fascination filled him as Issai watched the welts on his skin slowly go down and the angry red fade back to his skin's normal hue until only the small blots and streaks of drying blood remained. He felt himself blink, something that wasn't mirrored by his face, and that's when it finally hit him. His eyes were closed; he shouldn't be blinking at all, much less feel it. This wasn't a vision he was seeing—this was what *Hahri* was actually seeing! The fascination was what Hahri was feeling!

Issai tore his hands from the other's grip and scrambled backward on his hands and feet, panic squeezing the breath from him so that he couldn't even cry out in distress. He had just enough time to see Hahri double over as if he had suddenly been punched hard in the gut before all the warmth and strength seemed to drain out of him, and Issai collapsed heavily onto his back.

"Issai! W-What—!" Hahri stuttered as he stiffly scooted on his knees into Issai's field of vision.

"No! Don't touch me!" Issai gasped frantically as Hahri reached a hand out to him, trying futilely to calm the waves of panic that threatened to drown him.

The auburn-haired boy immediately backed away, now looking more scared than concerned. "What happened? What can I do to help you?" Hahri demanded, his voice going almost shrill as he, too, began to panic. His hands clenched and unclenched in helpless agitation.

Issai shook his head, forcing himself to take slow, deep breaths. "Just—stay there for now," he instructed.

He was finally beginning to calm down. The heaviness and weakness that had completely negated that initial adrenaline rush, bad as they were, were familiar ground for him. It was how he had usually felt right after a healing before Hahri had entered his life—right before he passed out.

Issai waited for the darkness to start creeping into his vision, but as one tense moment led to another and another and he did not lose consciousness, it became apparent that it wasn't going to happen.

"Issai, can you please tell me what happened?" Hahri said quietly after a few more moments of silence between them.

The gods are playing with us, that's what...

"I have no idea," he finally admitted after another awkward stretch of silence.

Issai tried to sit up, but quickly gave it up as a lost cause when he could barely manage to lift his head. He noticed that his shoulder and face no longer hurt.

He turned his head back to the other boy. "Are we healed?"

"All but my forearm, yes," Hahri replied. Then tentatively, "Did it hurt or something this time?"

"No."

"What then?" Hahri pressed a bit impatiently. "I can't help you if you won't talk."

"I..." Issai closed his eyes and growled in frustration.

How could he explain when he had no idea what happened? How could he even begin to put into words how unsettled the whole creepy incident had left him? Could it happen again? Would there be any adverse effects to him if it did? He looked over at Hahri who was sitting on his haunches about an arms-length away. There was only one way to be sure.

Issai stretched out his hand before he could change his mind. "Give me your hand."

"Okay..." Hahri did as he asked with the air of a guy who expected blood in his near future.

Issai was grateful that the ancient boy didn't demand an explanation first. He clasped the other's hand tightly.

"Just keep still for a moment," he said.

Then he closed his eyes and waited. About a quarter-hour passed with nothing but darkness and, more importantly, his own thoughts in his mind before Issai decided that it wasn't going to happen again. He had vaguely felt a tinge of impatience and bewilderment that he was sure had come from Hahri, but only towards the end. It wasn't anything he hadn't experienced before.

Just touching Hahri for a prolonged period didn't seem as though it was going to trigger that unexpected phenomenon. It had to be because of the healing, perhaps because of something that either he or Hahri had done differently this time. Had he concentrated too hard on their connection? Had Hahri?

"Issai, you're *killing* me! Just tell me what's going on already!" Hahri suddenly whined, breaking him out of his thoughts.

Issai opened his eyes and tugged on their still-joined hands. "Help me sit up first. I still feel like I've been running for two tendays straight."

"So—what? Being in contact with me didn't help you at all this time with the healing?" Hahri asked as he pulled him up. "But I could've sworn I had started to feel a little more tired right before you tore our hands apart, so I just assumed—"

"What!" Issai exclaimed, then cursed when his head started to spin violently.

He grabbed his head with his free hand and bent closer to his knees. He was glad that Hahri had not yet let go of his hand or else he would have toppled over again.

"Dammit—"

"Maybe you should lie back down," Hahri said worriedly.

"No—I need to—*we* need to figure this out." Issai cautiously lifted his head, determined to see his companion's reactions. "You said you were beginning to feel more tired. Did that not happen back in the slaver cave?"

Hahri frowned. "I'm not sure. I mean, I was really freaked out about you cutting our throats at the time, so it wasn't like I was really aware of anything else. Is that it? Were you feeling so weak that you thought the healing was going to take too much out of us, that we might die because of it?"

"No—it's probably my fault that I feel so drained right now. I broke contact with you before the healing was fully complete. My strength didn't leave me until we were no longer touching. This is something I figured would happen if a healing were ever interrupted."

Feeling a little more balanced and less dizzy, Issai let go of Hahri's hand, watching the ancient teen closely for any signs of the pain he had exhibited the last time.

Hairi looked at his hand pensively then back to him. "So you felt it, too?" he asked, apparently thinking along the same lines. "It really hurt when you pulled away during the healing. It was similar to the proximity pain I imagine I would feel after sitting on your lap for hours, only magnified a thousand times. It only lasted for a few moments, but I don't think the effects have completely disappeared. Even now, being this close to you hurts more than it should, and in a slightly different way. Along with the feeling of being smothered, my whole body stings like a bit of salt sprinkled on a raw wound. I've never hurt like this before, not even back in Rihott."

Issai's chest tightened with guilt, then a bit of alarm, when the familiarity of Hahri's last words sank in. His companion's description of pain was very similar to what he, himself, had felt back at the Rihottan temple after their attempt to divine the whereabouts of Korin's missing girl. *Like a skinned knee...*

"No, it didn't hurt for me," he replied, troubled, "and I have no idea why. Had I been thinking straight—no—had I been thinking at *all*, I never would've dared let go of your hands."

"And so we finally come back to it," Hahri said, his eyes keen and serious. "What could have startled you so much that you completely lost your head?"

There was nothing accusative in his tone, just simple curiosity. It made Issai feel even worse. Had their roles been reversed, he knew he would've been mad as hell.

"I—panicked," he admitted, "because for a few moments, it was like I had suddenly become—you."

"Huh?" The stupid look on Hahri's face pretty much summed up his own confusion about the whole incident better than words ever could.

"I saw myself as clearly as I see you now," Issai continued, "saw our hands clasped before me, saw the wounds on my face beginning to fade, but it was completely from your point of view. It wasn't anything like the visions I saw when we were looking for Korin's missing girl. I could feel myself blink even though my eyes were shut! It was *you* blinking!"

He held up his hand when Hahri opened his mouth to speak. "You were watching me closely the whole time, weren't you? You were fascinated by it. I could feel nothing else but that fascination until I let go of your hands."

"Yeah, I was," Hahri confirmed slowly. "But—ever since we connected in the forest, we've both been able to feel a trickle of each other's emotions on occasion, right? For me, my ability to sense your emotions has gotten stronger over the last couple of days. Couldn't you have just taken it to the next level and accidentally connected our minds for a moment? Like mind-reading or something?"

"That doesn't seem like something you accidentally do," Issai retorted. "I really don't think I did anything differently while I was healing us, but..." He shrugged.

Hahri sighed. "Let me guess—you think this is my fault, don't you?"

Cerulean eyes widened in surprise when Issai shook his head. "If anything, it was probably something we *both* did. Maybe I was concentrating too hard on the wounds. Maybe you were too, and thinking so strongly about the same thing caused it to happen. What do we really know about the true capabilities of Old Souls? We may think we touched souls back in the forest, the inn, and in Korin's temple, but how can we be sure that's what we're really doing? After all the strange stuff that's happened since we've met, I'm starting to think we were only kidding ourselves thinking we knew anything at all. Doing everything so half-assed without giving the consequences more consideration may have been more dangerous than we realized."

Hahri abruptly stood. "Well then, if you think you can walk, let's go find Korin the Watcher and try to figure some of that out together. About that Soujin bastard, too. With any luck, the monk's already found the girl, and it'll be some epic Old Soul reunion. I'll even suck it up and let you heal the hole in my arm later. Luckily, it looks like the arrow didn't tear anything important. It's not bleeding much anymore, anyway, so I should be fine until we reach the bathhouse."

"It's not my wound, so don't be so certain I can," Issai warned. "I never have been able to heal anyone other than myself. Like for instance the knot on your head from when that *Shi* brained you back in Kairash. You still have it, don't you?"

"But you haven't *tried* to heal it, have you?" Hahri argued. "I'm guessing you have to consciously account for every wound first before you do whatever you do, or do you just think 'heal' and your body complies? You never have explained the process to me."

Issai sighed. "If only it were that simple. We can try once we both have eaten and rested, but don't be too disappointed if it doesn't work. We don't even know why, much less how, my wounds manifest on your body. Or better yet, why I can heal at all."

Issai shakily climbed to his feet, pleased that his dizziness did not return. His legs, however, felt as weak and uncertain as a newborn foal's. He took a few cautious steps towards Hahri and was relieved when his legs held.

"I think I'm okay to walk," he said, "but running is definitely out of the question."

"I could carry you," Hahri offered.

Issai scowled. "Absolutely not! Between your injured arm and whatever damage I did to you by breaking the healing, you shouldn't be coming near me at all!"

"Okay, okay."

Hahri turned and squinted into the distance. "I think that might be the southern road out of Kairash," he said. "It's still pretty early in the morning, so the road should still have a scattering of the more outlying peddlers. If we're careful, we should be able to jump onto one of their wagons. We'll attract too much attention marching back into the city with clothes this bloody and torn."

He had a point. Although their dash from Yuzu had squeezed most of the water from their clothes and hair, they were both still a bit damp. Hahri's shirt was now more red-brown than white.

Then Issai remembered. "I left my pack under a couple of big stones about a span out of Kairash near the southern road," he said. "If it's still there, then I have a couple of spare shirts the monks gave me we can change into and some traveler's rations. Never mind entering the city, we can't very well roam around the streets covered in blood, either."

Hahri grinned. "I just assumed the slavers took it from you. Hopefully, the wildlife hasn't gotten to it either because I'm *starving!*"

Shaking his head at the other boy's unbridled enthusiasm, Issai slowly began walking towards the road and his pack, Hahri falling into step beside him. For millennia, he had existed alone within a pseudo-life filled with pain and an incomprehensible compulsion to *act* in pursuit of some unknown purpose. That such a dismal existence had changed to something more promising with just the meeting of the boy beside him was something he had never expected.

The gods only knew what awaited them within the city, the answers to be found, if any, but now that he was no longer alone, he could look to the future with a sense of anticipation again. For the first time in a long time, Issai felt more than a sliver of hope that they might actually succeed in finding them.

THE TIES THAT BIND THE SOUL (BOOK TWO)

The search for answers continues...

Barely escaping the Mahze clan compound with their lives, Issai and Hahri sneak back into Kairash, hoping to meet Korin as planned and to also delve deeper into the strange and sometimes frightening true nature of an Old Soul. However, they soon learn that the *Shi* and slavers aren't the only ones that have been hunting them, and that they may not be the only Old Souls being hunted...

NOW AVAILABLE

ABOUT THE AUTHOR

C.G. Garcia lives in a small West Texas town whose claim to fame is having the world's largest Rattlesnake Round-Up. She has a degree in computer science, but due to life's twisted sense of humor, ended up working in a pharmacy. A lifelong lover of all things fantasy and science fiction, she is also the author of the *Fractured Multiverse* Urban Science-Fantasy series and *The Golden Mage* Epic Fantasy series.

For more information visit:
www.cggarciaauthor.com

www.ingramcontent.com/pod-product-compliance
Lightning Source LLC
Chambersburg PA
CBHW031418240626
47154CB00001B/88